ON-SIGHT RECRUITMENT

Howard caught a glimpse of sudden motion. Looking out over the crisscross of slender trees, he saw figures moving stealthily through a small sandy area separated from the clearing. He saw complicated silver weapons being handed out as silent orders traveled along the line of warriors from an exceptionally tall Attercack. Looking down at the Breakneck Boys, whose backs were to the newcomers, Howard realized that he was witnessing the launch of a massacre.

With a turn of his Key, Howard appeared in front of the leader of the Rain of Blood. "Care to rethink this move?" he asked. "My team has some excellent entry-level positions, and we're willing to match your current benefit package."

By Geary Gravel
Published by Ballantine Books:

THE ALCHEMISTS

THE PATHFINDERS

THE FADING WORLDS:

RETURN OF THE BREAKNECK BOYS

Book Two of
The Fading Worlds

Geary Gravel

A Del Rey Book
BALLANTINE BOOKS • NEW YORK

This book is dedicated with love
to my sisters,

Dixie Calvert Price & Kathleen Mary Gravel,

two unique and intricate individuals,
who by their very natures
have always encouraged their brother's
appreciation of the fantastic in life . . .

Special thanks to Ellen Harris
for the Key role she played
in transporting the Breakneck Boys
to the printed page

A Del Rey Book
Published by Ballantine Books

Library of Congress Catalog Card Number: 90-93466

ISBN 0-345-36947-5

Manufactured in the United States of America

First Edition: March 1991

Cover Art by Romas

Contents

CHAPTER I

Back To the Head

HOWARD BELL WAS IN LUCK.

As he began his third swooping pass above the vast sprawl of the deserted city, something about one of the dark spires clustered below him sent up flags of recognition in his mind.

His eyes narrowed and he dipped lower, the great wings above his back cupping the wind like sails. The tower he was searching for had octagonal windows cut into its black stone and a band of golden metal sct several feet below its sharply pointed top. Ordinarily Howard would have had no trouble retracing his path. The last time he had seen this particular edifice, however, his feet had been firmly planted on the pavement several hundred feet below. Then a strong gust of wind had seized him just after he had lifted off on his exploratory mission and whirled him high into the air.

By the time he regained control of his flying suit, he was hopelessly lost, flapping dejectedly above the bristle of slender structures that rose into the lavender sky like a crown of dark needles above the domes and vaulted rooftops of the city's center. His fingers moved deftly among the control rods, quickening the flying suit's descent as he craned his neck to scan the latest likely candidate among the hundreds of similar towers, each with its own unique combination of identifying marks at base and top.

"All right!" Howard laughed with relief as an eight-sided opening came slowly into view below a thin strip of gold. A glimpse of the intricate mosaic of colored gems set just beneath the window's edge confirmed his hopes. He dropped through

1

the cool air, threading his way like a swallow among the maze of spires.

A trio of octagonal openings about three feet in diameter were equally spaced around the tower at this height. Howard glanced at his battered Timex as he approached the nearest one. He was only a few minutes late for his rendezvous; with luck his companion, who was ascending by way of the tower's interior, had reached the top and was waiting for him.

He hovered a few yards from the window, hands tight on the control rods. Wild winds buffeted him from all sides, and it was difficult to hold his position as he peered into the shadowed chamber for signs of occupation. He thought he saw a hint of movement and coaxed the flying machine closer to the opening.

Transferring the control rods to one hand, he cupped the other next to his mouth and bellowed through the noisy wind. "Yo the tower! Anybody home?"

There was an answering flurry of motion among the shadows in the middle of the room, then short fingers, backed with dove-gray fur, appeared over the sill of dark stone. Finally a pair of shiny black eyes rose into the light, blinking under heavy lashes.

Howard thought of a stuffed animal or a cartoon sheep as he hung several feet from the rounded muzzle framed by ringlets of tightly curled wool.

"You know, you really shouldn't show yourself at the door without checking to see who it is first," Howard shouted in a conversational tone. "For all you know, I could have been a Jehovah's Witness or the dog officer or something."

"Ow-er-bel, you come lately—whoop!" The pale sheep-like face dropped suddenly out of view. Small hands scrabbled at the rim of the window, and the blunt muzzle resurfaced laboriously. "Too high for Trilbit in here!" the little creature shrilled. "Feet too far from floor, belly too heavy for hands—" The explanation turned into a strangled squeal as the stubby fingers of the left hand lost their grip. The woolly head swung out of view once more, and only the three fingers and thumb of the right hand remained on the sill.

"Don't strain yourself," Howard called. "Just back away from the window, and I'll join you inside."

A bobbing crest of gray wool signaled frantic assent; then the remaining hand fell out of sight.

With difficulty, Howard brought himself closer to the small opening. Wind pushed and tugged at him as he tried to maneuver his legs onto the window ledge. At last he squatted precariously on the stone sill. Then, wedging his elbows against the rough sides, he carefully reached back with one hand to finger the small buttons set on the ceramic housing that rode near the base of his neck. He gripped the rim of the window while the great wings jerked and shuddered, fighting the wind as they folded in upon themselves against his back.

When the humming in the housing had ceased completely, Howard eased himself forward, dangling his legs into the dark room. He made out his friend's slight figure some five yards away against the opposite wall. The drop to the floor looked to be about four feet. Hunching forward to prevent damage to the flying machine, he pushed himself away from the ledge.

When his feet hit the stone, he heard a strange snapping sound, and Howard wondered for an irrational instant if he had broken his ankles. Then there was a low grinding noise as the floor beneath him divided itself into a dozen independent sections, each one tilting steeply in a different direction. A squeak of surprise came from the other side of the room. Howard fell heavily to his knees, then slammed onto his backside on the rolling, rocking surface.

"Yam! Are you all right?" He tried to locate his friend among the shadows and crazy motion. He remembered an old silent-film version of "Uncle Tom's Cabin" in which swiveling blocks of wood attached to great handcranks had been used to simulate the flight across an ice-choked river. He had wondered at the time how the actors had managed to get through the scene without throwing up.

He heard a muffled response from Yam, proving that the diminutive warrior was conscious. There came a series of sliding noises, and then something incredibly heavy dropped on him from the darkness above, flattening him down onto his back against the pitching section of floor.

Cold, hard metal bruised his cheek. He struggled to lift his head. His body was pinned under a giant net constructed of metal links as thick and ponderous as tire chains. One leg was folded beneath him; the compacted mass of the fragile flying suit gouged his back in several places. The room clanged with noise, and dust clouded the air as the floor plates heaved and fell. Straining upward with his neck and shoulders, he found enough strength for a few quick glimpses into the chaotic darkness before the weight forced his head down against the struts and angles of the suit again. Each bucking segment of floor had been similarly covered. Howard winced at the thought of little Yam pinioned under the crushing mass of metal.

He squirmed beneath his bonds with little result. The edges of the netting hung over the sides of the floor section, and the constant movement prevented him from concentrating his strength long enough to try to raise a portion and work himself free.

Then another noise was added to the general din. It was a faint hiss, originating from above. Howard sniffed the air cautiously, then tucked his nose and mouth down against his chest in panic as acrid fumes stung his eyes.

With great effort, he dragged one arm up onto his body and worked it underneath his loose vest. His head swam, and he was beginning to cough. His fingers closed on a leather thong about his neck and followed it to the hard, smooth object fastened to its end. Fumbling the thong from his shirt, he forced the object toward the other side of his body. When the slender metal shaft was securely anchored in the fingers of his left hand, he grasped the handle with his right and gave the device a frantic turn.

There was a sharp double click and a moment of freezing cold.

The crushing weight was gone.

Howard took a deep, shuddering breath, gasping at the pain that knifed through his chest. He tried to sit up and discovered that his hands were caught somehow, pulled out at right angles from his body and held together above him in the darkness.

It was a different sort of darkness now. A pale reddish glow came from somewhere, and the air, though odd-smelling, was clear, free of the choking dust and the sharp taste of the gas. Howard hauled himself to a sitting position, realizing that the object that he still gripped so tightly with both hands was fastened to something in the wall at his left side. Gingerly he released one hand, running his fingers over his bruised face as the echoes of the grinding, clanging din faded gradually from his ears. He turned his head, squinting in the red dimness.

He was near one end of a long, straight corridor. The floor gleamed like polished marble at the edges of the wide strip of cushioned fabric that covered most of it. The Key that he still held in his left hand was imprisoned in a hole or crack level with the top of his head. Unwilling to release it completely, he ran his other hand lightly along the smooth surface, feeling a suggestion of wood grain beneath his fingertips.

He caught sight of something shiny a few feet above his head.

It looked like a small, rectangular plate of metal set flush with the wooden surface. Howard peered at it as his eyes slowly adjusted to the dimness. Marshaling his battered muscles, he pried himself up from the floor with a stifled groan and looked around, keeping his hand on the Key.

The reddish light came from a tiny box on the ceiling at the far end of the corridor. Something tugged insistently at Howard's memory, and a strange sensation began to prickle in his stomach. He brought his face to the metal plaque and stared in wonderment. Two words had been carved in flowing script into the shiny surface:

Executive Washroom

"Oh, my God . . ." Howard touched the cold metal, then lowered his eyes to where the Key protruded from the gold lock plate just below a knob of faceted crystal. He shook his head dazedly. "Wait'll I tell—"

His head snapped back. "Whoa! Yam!" He released the Key with his left hand and grasped it immediately with his right, muttering under his breath as he closed his eyes and tried to form a picture of the tower room as he had left it. He focused on the chaotic, snapshot-like image he had glimpsed of his small companion lying motionless beneath the heavy metal bands.

There was a noise at the far end of the hallway. Howard heard the sound of muffled footsteps and felt rather than saw a beam of light play upon his face. Taking a deep breath, he gave the Key a savage twist. Someone cried out.

The world erupted in a fury of sound and motion. The room swam with clouds of dust and greenish gas, and Howard was thrown forward onto a bucking mound of hard ridges. Holding his breath, he reached out, straddling the heaving mass with his knees as he pulled the edge of the netting upward with all his strength. Yam lay curled in a loose ball against the pitching floor, eyes shut.

Thick metal cables rose from the netting into the dark ceiling. Keeping a hand on one for balance, Howard scooped up his small friend with his other arm, turned and gauged his chances of making it to the nearest window. Two segments of net-covered floor rose and fell pistonlike between Howard and his destination. He allowed himself a small breath as he started out and immediately began to cough as a sharp taste gathered at the back of his throat.

Think mechanical ice floes, he told himself as he leaped onto the first moving plate, steadying himself with another of the vertical cables. Think Simon Legree on our tails and a studio exec who won't allow a second take. He lurched, swaying, from one side of the plate to the other, poising himself for his next jump. Think happy ending . . .

He felt as if he were moving in slow motion as he stepped drunkenly onto the final plate, then realized that the motion of the room itself seemed to be slowing.

He pulled himself up to sit cross-legged on the window ledge, cradling Yam's limp body against his chest as he turned to draw a deep breath of fresh air from outside.

His cheek flattened against something smooth and hard.

A thick transparent plate now covered the outer rim of the octagonal window. Coughing furiously, he scanned the perimeter of the room, noting the telltale glassy gleam in both the other windows.

Concentration was needed for the Key to function properly. Howard plucked it from where it dangled above his stomach and closed his eyes, wearily framing an image in his thoughts.

There was a snap like a metal wire breaking, then aching cold.

Howard lifted his eyes to a pale green sky as warm sunlight poured over his skin. High above, something broad and flat that was probably not a bird glided under wisps of lemon yellow cloud, a tail of long, multicolored streamers fluttering in its wake.

He lowered his head, coughing convulsively. In front of him lay a rippling desert of red-orange sand, an orderly alternation of flattened hills and shallow valleys that stretched from horizon to horizon. Here and there a reddish mound topped with ocher vegetation reared against the sky. The air was dry and smelled of cinnamon.

He felt a slight movement and looked down to see Yam stretching groggily in his lap. Large dark eyes fluttered open as Howard scratched the top of his friend's head and tweaked a downy gray ear.

"Rise and shine, Little Eva," he said. "We made it."

"What did we make?" Yam attempted to straighten up, winced in pain, then settled back against Howard's stomach. "And why did we make it so hot and sore?"

"We made a narrow escape," Howard said. "The windows sealed up when those nets came down so the only way out was to use the Key again. Not that there was much hope of using my flying suit, even if we could've gotten past the glass . . ." He prodded with a tentative finger at the tangled mass still strapped to his shoulders and sighed unhappily. "I'm afraid this baby's going to be in the shop for a while."

"Whose baby?" Yam's eyes had drifted shut again. Now he opened them and surveyed the green sky with its small bright sun. "Where have you brought us with your Key?" He craned his short neck with effort. "Ah!" he squeaked. "Kansas!"

Howard shook his head. "I don't know why you guys insist on calling it that. It was an old joke, and I don't think the real Kansans would appreciate it. Anyway, I had to go somewhere before the gas got to me. The red desert just popped into my mind when I tried to think of a safe place. I mean, it's hot and it's dry, but except for those shy little crablike things that try to bite your feet if you stand near the rocks, I don't remember any dangerous native inhabitants. It's also the first place I appeared on the Fading Worlds—months ago—and I haven't been back since. Are you okay, by the way?"

Yam eased himself from his comrade's lap to the accompaniment of groans from both of them, and propped himself in a sitting position against Howard's arm. "Lucky we Trilbits are made small and tough like pebblenut shells. I will ache for a Round, but my bones are whole."

"Yeah, I'm not too sure about my own status—bone-wise, that is." Howard felt gingerly along his sides. "I'll have to get a checkup once we get back to the camp. Maybe somebody's packing a solar-powered, miniature X-ray machine on their belt . . ."

"Ow-er-bel, do you know what happened up in that tower? I was peacefully waiting by myself for several minutes. Then when you came in through window, whole room went mad."

"Well, this is my theory." Howard unsnapped a flexible flask from the black mesh belt about his waist and pried off the stopper. "Drink? It's bigtassle tea from your own recipe."

He waited while Yam took a healthy swig, then drank himself and wiped his mouth on the back of his arm. "That's better. Anyway, it seems to me that the snare must've been activated in one of two ways: by entry through the window, which I did and you didn't, or by a certain amount of weight, which I had and you hadn't." He shrugged. "Either way, it's a nifty trap. I'd have been a goner if it wasn't for the Key."

"And I, also," Yam said soberly. "I brought no new air into my body after I heard gas released, but I cannot postpone breathing for more than ten minutes without strong discomfort.''

"Yeah, me either," Howard said. "Good thing its effects don't seem too serious—somehow I don't think you and I would have an easy time of mouth-to-mouth."

"One thing I still do not understand is why you have brought us here to Red Desert World." The Trilbit smoothed the sand at his side and idly inspected his fingers. "Why not use your Key to return us directly to our camp?"

"Because I haven't figured out how to make it work that way," Howard confessed. "It just doesn't seem designed to make local stops. I was fooling around with it again a few days ago. When I turn the Key while I'm visualizing another place on the same world it just makes me nauseous and I don't go anywhere at all."

"Peculiar," Yam said.

"Yeah. So that means I've got to pop in and out of another world just to cross the street with this thing." Howard lifted the thong and twirled the ornate golden Key with his forefinger. "Major detour . . ."

"That means you had to come here twice, correct?" Yam watched sunlight flash on the slowly revolving shaft of metal. "Once now, and once before, when you crossed that chamber to rescue me."

"That's the funny thing," Howard said softly, his eyes narrowing with a faraway look. "I didn't think about this place then. With everything that was going on, I wasn't conscious of thinking at all. I just turned the Key."

"And where did you find yourself?" Yam asked.

"The last place I ever expected," Howard said, lowering the Key to lie against his vest. "I found myself back on Earth."

CHAPTER II

Sand Castles

YAM-YA-MOSH, CHOSEN WARRIOR OF THE TRILBIT Holding and stalwart of the illegal battle-gang known as the Breakneck Boys, slept peacefully, his velveteen muzzle cradled on his folded hands.

At his side, Howard Bell undid the straps that bound the flying suit to his back and carefully removed the mangled device. He gave it a cursory inspection before he set it aside, clucking his tongue ruefully. Then he clasped his fingers behind his head and lay back onto the warm sand next to Yam, pondering the latest events in what he was coming to recognize as a rather singular life.

Howard had grown up in a small town in western Massachusetts, raised with his younger sister by an elderly aunt. After college he had worked at a variety of odd jobs, never quite comfortable with the decisions he had made for himself. He had a quick mind and a talent for repairing things that others gave up on, and a heightened sense of pattern recognition that enabled him to retrace his steps through the most confusing of labyrinths or accurately predict the number of jellybeans in containers of various sizes and shapes. After his aunt's death, he had taken his small inheritance and moved to Boston, there to draw inspiration from the pulse and whirl of a big city—and to make a last-ditch effort to finish the sprawling novel he had been laboring over for the previous five years. To support himself, he had taken evening work with a small repair company.

It was under the aegis of Foster's Fix-It Ltd. that Howard had found himself on the sixtieth floor of the newly constructed Matrix Building in downtown Boston, late one night in the early fall. While searching for a much-needed restroom, he had dared to swipe an ornate key from the ring of a snoring custodian. Fitting the key in the lock of the door to the Executive Washroom, Howard had given it a triumphant turn and found himself in another world.

This world.

Howard shook his head, recalling his solitary march across the orange-red desert and what he had found at the end of that march. He remembered the ally he had made atop one of the red-trunked bed-mounds that dotted the desert—and the shock he had felt when both mound and world had faded out from under them in the midst of their first conversation.

In the months that followed, Howard's life had undergone a series of bizarre and often life-threatening alterations. In rapid succession he went from desert nomad to brutalized prisoner of the battle-gang known as the Meticulous Victors, then from prisoner to fugitive, and finally to nominal leader of his own recently formed battle-gang. His followers were a strange collection of human and nonhuman warriors culled from a score of worlds, united only in their desire to throw off the yoke of the Keyholders, hidden tyrants at whose command the warriors were forced to battle one another in a great game played out against the ever-changing backdrops of the Fading Worlds.

Howard himself was an enigma—neither he nor his newfound allies could explain why he was able to use one of the mysterious Keys to travel between worlds, a feat once thought reserved solely for the unseen Keyholders. In the end his unusual accomplishments had earned him the title of Nonesuch, and the rebel warriors whose cause he championed had chosen him as leader of their fledgling band.

Howard grimaced and batted a small flying insect away from his nose. Lying in the sand was not going to solve any of life's mysteries, but at that moment he felt like doing little else. It had been late in a cool afternoon when he and Yam made their escape from the tower room in a deserted city on the world called Field of Flowers. Judging by the position of the sun, it was midmorning in the red desert. Howard shaded his eyes and peered thoughtfully at the tiny orb, recalling how swiftly it had raced across the sky during his previous sojourn on this world.

Yam snorted suddenly at his side, then rolled over and sat up, his small pink tongue protruding from his lips.

"I think I may have swallowed a large sand fly," the warrior announced sourly.

"No one's going to begrudge you a snack," Howard said, "even if you didn't think to share." He gave a prodigious yawn. "You mind if we catch some rays here for a little while before heading back?" He got to his feet and dusted orange sand from his thigh-length shorts. They were black with silver piping, part of the uniform they both wore.

"Fine idea." Yam wrinkled his muzzle, testing the air with sensitive nostrils. "Smells of this place are always pleasant."

"Good. I'm really exhausted for some reason." Howard illustrated his observation with another protracted yawn. "It might be because I turned the Key so many times in such a short period. I have this feeling it's decided to use me as a battery, since I didn't give it time to recharge. Or I could be completely off the mark." He shrugged, a weary grin on his face. "Who knows?"

"If there is any expert in Keylore on this world, it is sure to be yourself, Ow-er-bel," his small companion said. "It had long been accepted that only our hated masters could use Keys to journey from world to world. Stories say those warriors who dared to try traveled quickly to their own deaths." Yam gave an almost human shrug. "But in these few Rounds since our first meeting, I have watched you coax all manner of impossible things into being."

"Yeah, well, they don't call me Nonesuch for nothing." Howard lifted his arms from his sides and stood on tiptoe, grunting as pain snarled in his ribs and lower back. "Shall we head for one of those bed-mounds? I wouldn't mind stretching out on something other than sand for a little while."

"Fine idea. Mosstop may also provide a better viewing point for our surroundings."

"You mean there's actually something to see here besides sand and rocks and bed-mounds?" Howard slung the flying suit over his shoulder. "You sure couldn't prove it by my last excursion. Maybe it's time for a new travel agent."

They walked slowly down into the nearest pocket valley, making their way toward the tall red mound that crowned a hill about half a mile away.

"So, what're the odds of us running into a battle-gang out here?" Howard asked as they slogged through drifts of fine sand.

"Small, I think," the Trilbit replied. "We never came here very often when I fought for Stillpoint. And these Fading Worlds are many. It would be narrow chance if this one happened to be in play on the same day you chose to visit."

"Let's hope so. I'm not exactly up for an encounter with the Redoubtable Hoopsters or the Black-eyed Susans or somebody." Howard scanned the almost featureless desert as they walked. "I wonder if this is anywhere near where I first appeared. Of course, how could I ever tell? I should've carved my initials into a couple of bed-mounds. Do you know if the whole planet's like this?" He outlined a dimpled sphere in the air. "Just one big sand-covered golf ball?"

"I believe so, though I cannot speak from my personal knowledge," Yam said. "Battle-gang combat always commenced within a certain distance from Stillpoint. Never enough time between Fades to travel far or make much exploration on any one world."

From what Howard had been able to learn in his short time on the Fading Worlds, the great city known as Stillpoint existed in many places at once, to varying degrees of reality. When a world was put into play, Stillpoint moved closer to it through the dimensions, discharged the battle-gangs slated for combat, and slowly withdrew into misty intangibility. Howard had never been inside the city, though he had gotten a single tantalizing glimpse of soaring structures and ethereal gardens through its massive Gate.

"Interesting," Howard said. "Maybe it all takes place inside a big studio, with dozens of these separate little stages—only everybody gets Faded to the next scene before they've had the chance to walk over there under their own steam."

"All things are possible, Ow-er-bel." The Trilbit shrugged again. "But these worlds feel real to me, and I do not believe we will find much steam on this one." He eyed the far horizon, where thin yellow clouds lay low against a sky of rich jade. "You must have had a large surprise when first you turned your Key and fell into another world, correct?"

Howard snorted. "Imagine how you'd feel if you went off looking for the nearest men's room and found yourself on the set of 'Lawrence of Arabia.' " He pointed to the western sky, where a pair of airborne manta rays trailed their streamers. "Only with those guys flapping around overhead."

"Difficult for me to imagine," Yam said. "I was born and raised to fight on these Fading Worlds. No large surprises for me until I meet Ow-er-bel the Nonesuch and learn it is possible to defy Keyholders." A wicked grin split the Trilbit's innocent face as his eyes narrowed in remembered pleasure. "Now life is less predictable, but more filled with hope—thanks to my friend."

"That's us, two hopeful but unpredictable guys," Howard said absently, his eyes on the top of the low hill they had begun to climb. "Jeez, I'm starting to remember how monotonous this place was: up and down, up and down. They need a good trolley line here, or at least a couple hundred escalators."

He peered at their destination from the top of the hill, frowned, and shaded his eyes. "That's weird. Take a look over there, would you?" He stooped and grasped Yam under the arms, then stood and lifted the Trilbit into the air above his head. "Does that look funny to you?"

"As if land runs away," his friend confirmed. "Maybe there is an end to this desert, after all."

"We'll have to check this out from the bed-mound. What say we jog through the last dip?" Settling Yam onto his shoulders, Howard trotted down the slope.

The bed-mound that crowned the next hill was of medium size. It appeared to be made of compacted earth or rock, and its reddish trunk stood just over seven feet tall from gold-fringed bottom to ocher-nested top. Howard circled the base cautiously, noting that the long fronds ringing it were flushed with a delicate rose-pink.

"Look—it's fed recently." He prodded gingerly with his sandal at an area where many of the fronds overlapped, curling protectively around a small object. None of the tendrils adhered to the sandal, confirming that they were in a state of recent satiation. At his touch a few of them fell away, revealing the cleaned bones of an animal about the size of a large house cat.

"I wondered what these guys found to eat out here." Howard squatted down to inspect the skeleton. "What do you think it was—some kind of lizard?"

"Large rodents live in burrows in pocket valleys during the day," Yam said, looking over the top of Howard's head. "Come out after dark to mate and gather colored stones. You can find their hiding places by markers they set into the sand, like upside-down trees with sticky threads. These they use to catch fat insects for their own meals. The Victors hunted them a few times when we were here—for sport rather than food." He grimaced. "A most uncivilized battle-gang."

"Tell me about it." Howard recalled his own brutal treatment at the hands and claws of the Meticulous Victors. "Well, it looks like this little fellow wasn't too lucky in his search for companionship or colored rocks, but at least it means the mound is safe for us to use." He lifted Yam from his shoulders and boosted the small warrior onto the moss-covered surface of the mound.

"All clear?" he called. "No mites, no snakes, no crawly things?"

"You think I would admit to vermin's presence after you have tossed me up here to do your investigations for you?" Yam's gray muzzle appeared at the edge. "All is clear."

"Great." Howard grabbed handfuls of the wiry moss and heaved himself up and over the rim.

The mound was topped by a spongy ocher mat, and the moss was noticeably softer near the depressed center than at the edge. Howard settled himself at the lowest point, his back and legs supported by the sloping sides of the nest.

"Ah, that feels nice." He grinned at Yam, who still crouched near the edge. "Like the finest Barcalounger. All I need now is a couple of good videos and a TV tray for my chips. Speaking of Kansas—you'd love 'The Wizard of Oz,' you know. It had more people of your height in it than most movies."

"Perhaps when you have rested, you will allow me use of your own towering height," the Trilbit remarked, gazing off into the distance. "You have made me curious to take a better look at land beyond this desert."

"Oh, right." Howard clambered to his feet. "At your service." He hoisted Yam onto his shoulders with a grunt. "Arr, matey—back in the crow's nest ye go. Can ye spot the Jolly Roger?"

"Land is surely lower there, and has a flatter look." Yam leaned forward, his small legs clasping Howard's neck. "There is something else, too. Hard to see, as it has same color as the sand . . ." He looked thoughtful as Howard lowered him to the moss. "Perhaps it is just a formation of rock carved by wind, but it had seeming of a large structure of some sort. Have we time to approach it?"

"Hmm." Howard checked his watch, then shrugged. "Actually, the others aren't expecting us home from the city for another day at the earliest. We can relax here for a while, mosey on over to whatever-it-is, and still be ahead of the game." He sat back down on the bed-mound, closed his eyes, and squirmed his back against the springy moss with a sigh. "Besides, it's bound to be more hospitable than those towers of doom back on Field of Flowers."

* * *

He came to with a start. According to his watch, he had been asleep for less than an hour. Looking at the sky, he realized that midmorning had become midafternoon while he dozed, and that they would soon be losing the light of the world's rapid day. He roused Yam and they set out at a brisk pace, the Trilbit once more riding on his friend's shoulders.

"I am seeing more examples of the whatever-it-is in the distance now," Yam reported as they paused on the crest of a hill several minutes later. "Very large, they seem."

Howard nodded, squinting into the distance. "I wonder how we get down to that flat area," he said. "It looks like a pretty big drop from this level. Maybe it used to be a lake or something."

Howard was forced to expand his conjectured lake to a small sea as they mounted the last of the sandy hills and looked out over the great, flat expanse. No opposite shore was visible from their vantage point.

The sand of the desert ran down onto the flat area in great peninsular ramps. The material that floored the lowland also appeared to be sand, though a paler shade of orange-red. The nearest of the strange formations rose from the level plain about a mile from where they stood.

"How tall would you say that is?" Howard tilted his head to one side. "A couple hundred feet?"

"Hard to judge," Yam replied. "But see marks on this side— surely those are carvings."

"Only one way to find out. Buckle up for safety." Reaching up to anchor Yam's legs with his hands, Howard started slowly down the nearest incline, sand sloughing away from his boots in miniature mountainslides as he descended. His pace quickened rapidly as he moved forward, struggling to maintain his balance on the dissolving surface. Soon they were plunging down the slope.

"Pardon me, Ow-er-bel, but have you given any consideration to question of braking?" Yam called as they raced toward the bottom of the incline.

"Actually, I've thought of little else for the last thirty seconds or so—" Howard gasped in reply. "Any suggestions you care to offer would be most welcome."

"Nothing comes immediately to mind," the small warrior admitted, his fingers clutching his friend's ears as a patch of sand suddenly gave way beneath Howard's right foot, necessitating a series of frantic course corrections.

The last few yards of the incline were substantially steeper than they had appeared from above. Their speed increased dramatically as the sand rose toward them like an orange wall.

"We're going to die," Howard announced.

The lowland sand was of a much finer grain and apparently ran considerably deeper than its upland counterpart. Howard churned up clouds of orange dust as he pounded into the yielding material, his legs working like pistons. The sand was up to his thighs in a matter of moments. He came to an abrupt halt several seconds later and pitched forward, Yam sailing a good three yards beyond to raise his own small dust cloud.

After a few moments of disorientation, the little warrior righted himself and began to sneeze uncontrollably. He covered his nose with his palms and half ran, half crawled back to where Howard lay with his face in a small impact crater of its own devising.

"Ow-er-bel, are you all right?" Small hands trembling with anxiety, Yam tugged gently at his companion's shoulder.

Howard knuckled the dust from his eyes and gave his head a violent shake. "Well," he said, pausing to spit orange sand, "that didn't go so badly, after all."

With Yam's assistance, Howard extricated himself. After a few moments spent catching their breath, they started off toward the nearest formation. Yam had an easier time of walking on the fine-grained material, his lighter weight allowing him to stay near the surface while Howard sank to his boot tops with every step.

"I think you were right about the markings," Howard said as they approached the towering structure. "It definitely looks like some sort of deliberate carving."

The whorls and curves outlined sweeping, elaborate shapes that neither Howard nor Yam could identify. The designs were composed of double parallel lines that had been cut several inches into the sandy surface. Wading through the orange powder to within a few yards of the structure, Howard cocked his head to one side and regarded the fantastic edifice. "It looks like a giant sand castle."

"Is truly made of sand." Yam stood at the base of the nearest wall. "Look." He ran his palm lightly along the orange surface. When he removed his hand, a light coating of sand came with it. "Something sticks it together."

"Pretty impressive." Howard joined him at the wall and tilted his head back. "It's as big as an airplane hangar—I wonder if it's hollow. Let's look for a way inside."

The structure thrust up from the desert floor like an African anthill, the walls fairly irregular in outline, the turrets and battlements that topped them only vaguely indicated, as if they had indeed been executed by an amateur builder. Halfway around the base they found a single opening, a low archway that curved about three feet above the ground. Howard paused at the dark entrance, frowning at the sky over his shoulders.

"Something is wrong?"

"I guess not." Howard shrugged. "Except this opening looks like it might've been made by a great big hand pushing inward. Suppose this *is* a giant sand castle—I'm just wondering if the giant kid who built it is coming back today."

"Perhaps she has lost interest in it," Yam said. "Young children often have some difficulty in attending to a single task for long periods of time. Or perhaps her family has summoned her home for their evening meal. Or—"

"Okay, okay," Howard said, raising his hand. "If you're willing to go in there, I am, too. Can you see anything?"

"These outer walls appear quite thick," the Trilbit said. "But there is some small light coming down several yards inside. Perhaps a ventilation shaft."

Howard squatted at Yam's side. "Mmm. This is definitely a Trilbit-size tunnel, rather than a human-size one. I have a choice of crawling on my hands and knees or walking this way—like a duck." Howard took a few duck steps forward, his shoulders hunched and his palms resting on his knees. "Are you coming?"

"I am allowing you to lead the way, O Nonesuch," Yam said from behind. "It is a remarkable spectacle from this vantage point. Indeed, I was unaware that your body folded in this fashion."

"Yeah, well, I don't think it's meant to. This is the sort of unusual treatment they always exclude from the warranty—" Howard teetered backward and sat down heavily. "It's too uncomfortable. I'm going to crawl the rest of the way. There's not much sense in trying to salvage any dignity at this point."

"Here is hole." Yam padded past him, entering a circle of filtered sunlight after a few paces. "It is a vertical tunnel with something obscuring the end of it, perhaps four yards above."

"Looks like a cloudy window," Howard said, kneeling at his

friend's side to squint up into the orifice. "I wonder if I can straighten up in here." Drawing his shoulders in, Howard got to his feet with difficulty, the edge of the hole catching him at the base of his spine as his body slowly disappeared to just below his waist.

"How is it for you in there?" Yam asked.

"Pretty uncomfortable," came the muffled reply. "And a lot more claustrophobic than I'd expected. Learn something new about yourself every day . . ."

"Can you climb this shaft?"

"Hmm. What a thought." There was a faint scrabbling noise, followed by a shower of dust. "It won't be easy, but I think I can gouge some handholds in the sides and pull myself up by my elbows. At this point it'd probably make more sense than trying to ooze back out the other way."

More noise followed, and then Howard's boots left the ground. Yam tented his hands over his muzzle and backed away as sand and dust poured from the opening. Howard's legs rose jerkily into the shaft, accompanied by indecipherable muttering from above. Several minutes passed, and finally the movement subsided. After waiting for the worst of the dust clouds to settle, Yam moved cautiously back to peer up into the opening. Howard peered back down at him.

"Guess what? There was a single layer of stuck-together sand over the hole, sealing it like a wafer-thin window. I broke through it with the top of my head."

"A creative use of available tools," Yam said. "Shall I come up now?"

"Yeah, if you think you can make it all right. Want me to—"

Three seconds later, the Trilbit pulled his dust-smeared body from the hole and plopped down next to his friend.

"My people are fairly nimble climbers," he said, blinking blandly at Howard's expression of annoyance. "What is this place, Ow-er-bel?"

"I haven't really nosed around, but it seems to be a central chamber of some sort." The room was shaped like a squashed sphere some sixty feet in diameter. The shaft they had climbed was off to one side, near the chamber's curving walls.

There was about a foot of clearance for Howard's head as he got to his feet. More shafts had been cut at various angles into the vaulted ceiling; pale light streamed from several of them. The perimeter of the room was scalloped with broad, low archways like the one through which they had originally entered the sand castle.

"Twelve of these," Yam counted, revolving slowly in the dimness at the room's center. "All very dark."

"It might be time to break out the firejelly." Howard drew a small bundle of twigs from the pocket of his shorts. He opened one of several small pouches attached to his belt and twirled a dab of bluish gel onto the end of a stick, then raised it to his face and spat onto it. A three-inch flame sprang from the gel.

"Openings seem identical," Yam said, crossing the room to inspect one of the archways.

"I think they lead to different levels," Howard commented, down on his knees again between two of the low openings. "Look, they alternate—half of them slope upward and half downward."

"You are leader, Ow-er-bel. Which shall we explore first?"

"My vote's for up," Howard said. "Unless you have some strong desire to descend in near-darkness through a narrow passageway into the bowels of an unknown world."

"Up is a fine idea," Yam said.

They had gone about twenty feet into one of the ascending tunnels, Howard crawling in the lead with his tiny torch while Yam brought up the rear, when Howard abruptly halted his climb. He was lifting the lighted twig as Yam bumped into his legs.

"Why do we stop?"

"Shhhh, wait a minute. Didn't you hear that? It was like a wet clicking sound."

Yam drew closer in the darkness.

"Heard nothing," he whispered in Howard's ear. "My mind was dreaming and my ears asleep. Did it come from up ahead?"

"I'm not sure," Howard looked back over his shoulder. "It almost seemed to be coming from right—"

At that moment something large snatched the little torch from his hand, and the tunnel was plunged into darkness.

Howard cleared his throat. "Uh-oh," he said.

CHAPTER III

Down and Out

HOWARD DOUBTED AT FIRST THAT HE HAD OPENED his eyes. He brought his fingers to his cheeks and carefully pried apart his lids.

Absolute blackness.

He was lying on his back. Was he still in the tunnel? He lifted his hands to feel for the ceiling, but found nothing. His chest ached when he moved. He pushed up with his elbows and felt sand beneath his bare arms. Could he be outside? It might be nighttime, overcast. It was cold enough to make him shiver, and he hunched his shoulders and crossed his arms, finding goose bumps where there should have been cloth.

"Oh, swell," he said under his breath, running his hands along the rest of his body. He turned over onto his knees and felt along the sandy floor. Nothing.

He got slowly to his feet, his head throbbing.

His fingers found a lump on his forehead, and another tender spot behind his right ear. As he lowered his arm, he saw something move in the nearby darkness. His heart thudded in his chest as he stood motionless, a spot of pale green glowing in the air in front of his face like a ghostly eye. Then he chuckled in comprehension and lifted his right hand to cover his other wrist. The dimly illuminated dial of his Timex winked at him in the darkness.

Raising his arms till they were perpendicular to his body, he made a slow circle in the cold sand. His fingers found only air. It was difficult to keep his balance in the total absence of light, and staring at the watch face only added to his disorientation. He shut his eyes and frowned at the faint afterimage.

Something about the glowing dial . . . had it been a dream? He searched his memory, but found little that he could rely on after the torch had gone out.

He chose a direction at random and shuffled blindly forward until his arm met a sandy wall. He sighed in relief as the cool surface helped him regain some of his equilibrium. With the fingers of his left hand grazing the wall, he moved quickly through the darkness, soon establishing that he was in a chamber with curving walls. After a few yards, he paused to gouge a narrow vertical strip into the wall, estimating the diameter of the room at approximately twenty feet when his fingers encountered the depression again less than a minute later.

He stood still for several moments, contemplating his surroundings. The air had an odd, sweetish smell to it, but it did not seem stale; Howard reasoned that there must be at least one opening to be found. He walked the perimeter of the room again, this time more slowly, his senses alert for the slightest hint of an incoming breeze. As his fingers scraped idly along one section of wall, he noted a slight change in the sound they produced. He paused, then stepped backward a few paces and moved forward again, this time applying more pressure with his hand. An area about a foot wide buckled slightly under his palm. Remembering the thin, windowlike layer at the top of the vertical shaft, Howard gradually increased the pressure of his hand until he felt a portion of the wall crumble and give way. Suddenly realizing that the chamber could be some distance underground, he stepped back slightly from the small opening. Tearing down the walls might not be his wisest course of action.

When nothing happened after several seconds, he reached forth again and pushed gingerly at the lower edges of the hole, quickly enlarging it to a size that he could step through to the other side.

Ducking his head, he squeezed carefully through the opening. The darkness on the other side of the hole was the same, but the air seemed slightly fresher. Howard moved away from the opening, keeping one hand on the gritty wall.

He froze when he heard a soft rustling sound. After a few seconds it came again, and he was able to pinpoint its direction. Trying to hold his breath, Howard left the wall and walked slowly toward the center of the chamber.

His left foot brushed against something soft. He stepped back quickly and stood still. After a moment he sank cautiously to one knee. He extended his hand, halting instantly when his palm encountered something wet and cold.

There was a high-pitched squeak. Howard snatched his hand back.

"Hey." He reached out again, found curls of wool. "Yam?"

"Ow-er-bel, it is you! I heard sounds, then something landed on my nose."

"Yam, where are we? How did we get here?"

Howard felt warm breath on his knee as the Trilbit changed position. "You were before me in tunnel. Torch went out and I heard cracking sounds. Then something lifted me up. I was confined very tightly around my chest, as if they used tongs of wood or metal to handle me. I could take in no breath while they carried me, and after a time I lost consciousness. Just now I woke up to find myself here in darkness."

"Hm. The cracking sound was probably my head." Howard lowered himself, wincing, onto the cold sand at Yam's side. "They must've taken us to one of the descending tunnels. That might explain the temperature. Hey, do you have any clothes on?"

The darkness rustled. "No, they have taken everything. From you also?"

"Everything but my watch. My wrist is kind of sore, though, like they tried to get that, too. Maybe they couldn't figure out how to undo the strap." He raised his hand to the long hair brushing his shoulders. "They even swiped the cord Alaiya gave me for my ponytail!"

"Your Key?"

"Gone," Howard said bitterly. "I should've figured out a better place to keep it—like under my tongue or something."

"We will locate it, Ow-er-bel." Small fingers patted his leg. "Our situation could be worse."

"True," Howard agreed. "I mean, we're naked in the dark in somebody's freezing root cellar, but it's not as if we don't have the correct time." He raised his wrist to his eyes and squinted. "Looks like quarter to three—thank God for illuminated dials."

"Is that what causes that little green blur? I thought my eyes were pretending."

"Yeah, I forgot about it myself. It has to be pretty dark before it shows up. But we were walking under bright sunlight for a while, and I must've been holding the torch right above my watch as we went through the tunnel, so it's full of juice."

"It reminds me of something," Yam said. "I cannot think what."

"I had the same feeling."

They sat in silence for a few moments.

"So, did you get any kind of look at them?" Howard asked. "Were they carrying a light?"

"Hard for me to know what I am seeing," Yam answered after a pause. "They carried me upside down, facing away from them, I believe."

"Yeah, I didn't see anything either."

"Opportunity to explore this room before you found my nose? Is there an exit from this place?"

Howard explained what he had learned of their surroundings. Together they shuffled slowly around the pitch-black chamber, finding it to be about the same size as the one in which Howard had awakened.

"So. No doors, no windows, nothing. Just a little cell for each of us. I guess we're lucky we got adjoining cages." Shivering, Howard squatted on the cold sand floor. "There has to be a way out. They stuck us in here somehow."

"Perhaps through ceiling?" Yam's voice came from nearby. "Another vertical shaft?"

"Good idea." Howard clambered to his feet and raised his arms above his head, swaying in the darkness. "I can't feel anything. Maybe if you . . ."

Howard held Yam at the end of his outstretched arms and they moved slowly around the room, finally encountering the ceiling's sandy surface when they neared the wall.

"I can touch it only here by the edge," Yam reported, wobbling in Howard's grasp as he strained upward. "This ceiling must curve in a dome, as in first room, and this is where it lies lowest."

"We came up at the edge of the room through the shaft the first time," Howard said. "Let's look for an opening."

Half a minute later, Yam reported cool air blowing on his face from somewhere. Then he gave a small squeak of triumph.

"A hole lies right above us! Stand still now . . . Oh." The enthusiasm died from his voice. "It is very small, Ow-er-bel, room enough for my arm only."

"Okay, it's a start. Let's see if we can find a bigger one."

Though they circled the perimeter of the room several times, their search failed to yield another opening.

CHAPTER IV

Illuminations

AN HOUR LATER THEY WERE LYING ON THE SANDY floor at the center of Yam's cell. The little Trilbit had been dozing quietly at Howard's side for some time. Suddenly he sat up.

"What is this noise?" he whispered urgently. "Ow-er-bel, are you experiencing difficulty breathing?"

"No—I'm doing sit-ups—trying to keep warm," Howard said, panting. "My stomach's going to feel like hell—but I figured it would help—cover up the hunger pangs—when they start."

"Understand. I thought to hear another sound, as well, but that must—" Yam broke off in midsentence, his small hand clutching Howard's arm. "Sssp! Stop—it sounds again!"

"What is it?" Howard tried to control his heavy breathing. "Your ears are sharper than mine."

"It came from over there," the Trilbit said softly after a few moments. "I think it must be in other room."

"Let's check it out," Howard whispered. "Stay close." He got quietly to his feet and made his way toward the wall, following one of the shallow grooves he had made in the sand with his heel while he and Yam were completing their investigations. He had become increasingly oriented to the round chamber, despite the darkness. In a few seconds, he stood by the opening.

"I'm going in," he breathed over his shoulder, then stooped and eased his body through the narrow hole. He heard a soft crunch as Yam came through.

"Hear nothing," the Trilbit whispered, close to his side.

They moved into the chamber, Howard in the lead with his arms outstretched before him. Moments later, his left toe made forceful contact with an object that had not been in the room an hour earlier.

"What is it?" Yam asked, as Howard bit his lip and fought the urge to hop on one leg.

"I stubbed my big toe—ow—ow—" he said softly through clenched teeth. "Something on the ground. I hate being naked outside my own home! There are too many cold, hard, sharp things in the world."

"Is round." Yam made scraping sounds at floor level. "Also made of sand, but tight-fused." There was a pause. "Is more than one!"

Howard knelt at his friend's side and felt the rough surfaces of the bowl-like objects as Yam guided his hands.

"There's something wet in this one." He brought his hand to his face and sniffed cautiously at his knuckles. "Hmm." He touched the tip of his tongue to the moisture. "It's water, I think—with something sweet added to it. What about the other ones?"

"Two more. Nothing in this one. Wait a moment . . . Oh!" Yam bumped against Howard's side. "Something moving in the third one—insect grubs?" Howard heard a hushed smacking sound. "Tasty."

"Oh, gross! Yam, you haven't eaten a bug in all the time I've known you—unless you swallowed that sand fly on purpose."

"None available of proper quality before now," Yam retorted. "Sand fly too salty. Wish to avoid hunger pains? Time to broaden tastes. You Averoy are omnivores like Trilbits, correct?"

"Yuck." Howard shook his head in the darkness. "I'm holding out for the dinner menu." He explored the empty inner surface of the second bowl with his fingers. "So what've we got here? Water and food—sort of—do you suppose this other container is their idea of a rest room?"

"Seems sensible." Yam was chewing on something that crunched.

"From the executive washroom to a homemade chamber pot," Howard mused sadly. "How are the mighty fallen."

"You think hidden captors leave door open this time?" the Trilbit asked.

Yam clutched the bowl of grubs and the two moved carefully around the curved wall, testing for more weak spots and finding none. When they were a few feet from the passage into Yam's chamber, Howard caught a glimmer of pale blue light. He reached behind him and grabbed Yam's shoulder, then silently guided the little warrior to a position at his side. The two stared into the other room as the light faded, replaced almost instantly by a rose-colored flicker from another direction.

Howard brought his lips down to Yam's twitching ear.

"We're pretty dumb to've fallen for this one—they waited till we were out of the room to make their deliveries." He edged closer to the opening. "Let's go in quietly. If they take off, try to see where the exits are."

They slipped through the irregular doorway. Near the center of the chamber, bursts of pale, flickering light outlined two large shapes. It looked as if a pair of circular shields, each about seven feet in diameter, had been propped upright in the sand and angled slightly toward one another. The wavering colors emanated from the inner surfaces, which faced away from Howard and Yam, and as the two crept up behind the shield-shapes the room was filled with a soft, many-hued flicker.

As they approached, Howard was able to see that each of the objects was composed of two flat shells, fitted together at the rims like a pocket watch. They were about six feet from the strange shapes when Howard felt something dig into his side with tiny pincers. He yelped and swatted at it with his palm. "Damn!"

"What is it, Ow-er-bel?"

"Shh! One of your damn snacks got loose." Howard peered tensely toward the glimmering objects, which remained motionless. "I don't think these things are alive. At any rate, they don't react to noise. Maybe they're machines of some sort, and whoever left them is already gone."

"You notice where grub fell?" Yam's small fingers were searching near his feet.

"For God's sake, forget about the bugs! I'll buy you a whole ant farm if we get out of here alive."

"Hungry," Yam insisted. "Not my fault they did not supply your favorite food."

"Look, let's split up and circle around the things. Try to stay in the shadows."

Howard was close enough to touch the nearer object when there was a soft rasping sound and the farther one abruptly swiveled in the sand to face him. Colored light detonated like flashbulbs on the thing's inner surface, sending Howard reeling toward the wall in temporary blindness. He ducked instinctively as the creature lunged after him, feeling cool air stir his scalp as a long, flat object passed within inches of his head.

"Yam—head for the hole!" His hands groping at the wall behind him, Howard stumbled toward the opening to the other chamber. "I think they're too big to fit through!"

The Trilbit was there before him, one small hand reaching back to help pull him through the narrow portal. They were backing away from the opening when Howard's heel came down on the lip of the water bowl and he flipped heavily onto his side in the cold sand.

"Look, Ow-er-bel!" Yam pawed at his shoulder, pointing toward the hole, where lights flashed and strobed angrily. "They come!"

Howard watched through a haze of multicolored afterimages as one of the shield-covered objects pressed itself against the portal. Patterns bloomed and faded like silent fireworks among the winking lights of the broad surface. Then the creature lowered the front rim of its shell and proceeded to slice silently through the wall surrounding the hole. Howard had the impression of dozens of waving tendrils all around the curving rim. He sat on the sand, his hands tight on the heavy bowl cradled in his lap, as first one and then the other giant shape slid noiselessly into the chamber. The first shield-shape raised its shell to stand erect on a pair of short, bowed legs. The second paused for a few moments at the opening, cilia rippling furiously.

"Look—it closes door!" Yam squinted through the barrage of lights. "Like many fingers working to repair." As the creature sidled away from the wall to join its fellow, they saw that behind it the opening had been completely sealed.

"So that's how they do it." Howard drew his arms back cautiously, getting ready to hurl the bowl if the shield-shapes charged. "You might want to stand behind me, Yam."

The Trilbit stood his ground. "If things attack, fall to left. I will run between them, maybe causing loss of balance. Door place must be weak—one of us can push through it, then other follows."

"And then what? Back and forth between the two rooms till somebody dies of exhaustion?" Howard set the bowl down on the sand and pushed to his feet. "There's got to be a better solution than that." He raised both hands palm outward toward the creatures. "What do you say, guys? Can we talk before this turns ugly?" He rotated his wrists slowly to show that he carried no weapons.

The effect on the two creatures was instantaneous. The fringe of fingerlike tendrils withdrew between the front and rear shells, and the dazzling light show dimmed immediately to a muted pulsation of vivid green. As they watched, the light faded further, dividing into a dozen round spots of color equally spaced around the outer rim of each front carapace.

"I've seen this before . . ." Howard frowned in bewilderment, then smacked his forehead with his right hand. "Of course!" He slowly rotated his left wrist. The creatures quivered like excited children as the tiny dial of the Timex came into view. Howard undid the strap and slipped the wristwatch carefully from his arm, suspending it in the air in front of him. "Look at that," he said to Yam. "Just look at that!"

A vertical bar of pale green light had appeared on each shell, pointing upward from the center of the carapace; from its base, a shorter bar glowed down at an angle toward the right.

"Four o'clock on the dot," Howard breathed. "Look, they're even starting to get the second hand!" A fainter streak of green was sweeping with measured slowness around the perimeter of each circle.

"I wonder . . ." Howard placed a finger over half the dial. At once, the right sides of both shells went dark. "This is fantastic. I bet we could learn to talk to them."

"If it is sentience we are witnessing, and not mere mimicry," Yam said doubtfully. "Perhaps they possess no generative skills."

"Oh, right, Professor—and I suppose you think all those chimps are just studying to be street mimes. Wait a minute—what's going on now?" The shield-shape on the left had moved slightly forward, its carapace darkening, while its companion continued to mirror the face of Howard's watch. Abruptly, brightly colored lines and shapes began to scroll from right to left across the front shield-shape's curving surface. "Looks like a news bulletin coming in." Howard raised his arm to shield his eyes. The colors dimmed instantly.

"Thanks," he murmured. "I wonder what they're trying to tell us. You know, those patterns resemble the carvings on the outside of the mound." He glanced around the near-empty room in frustration. "I wish I knew how to respond."

"I wish you knew how to ask for more sweet-water," Yam said at his side. "You have stepped in our first allotment."

"That's an idea." Howard sank down and reached behind him, still holding his watch up to the shield-shapes. He hefted the heavy bowl in his left hand, and tilted it forward to show that it was empty. Neither creature reacted.

"Perhaps their eyes are only for your timepiece," Yam suggested.

"I don't know. They seem to have plenty to spare." Howard had noticed small clusters of knob-tipped stalks situated at roughly two, four, eight, and ten o'clock on the edge of each carapace. "Maybe it's a matter of directing their attention." He gradually lowered the watch until it sat within the bowl, raised it slightly, and drew it slowly around the circular rim. "See? Dry as a bone."

Both shells went blank for a few seconds. When they came to life again, it was in a flurry of agitated flashing.

"Good grief . . ." Howard stood open-mouthed as chaotic rainbows melted into sophisticated animated renderings: detailed three-dimensional images of the sand bowl appeared on both surfaces, rotating through several perspectives like computer simulations.

"Yeah, I'd say they're starting to get the picture." Howard pointed to the right-hand shield, where a depiction of the bowl had suddenly divided into two images, one of them remaining orange while the other slowly filled with what appeared to be bluish liquid. Curving, double-lined symbols marched above and beneath the representation.

"Yes, yes!" Howard nodded vigorously. "Bring us some water!" He bobbed the watch up and down, then twirled it in his fingers. "God, I hope I'm not telling them to drop dead or something. I wish I had a flashlight and my old Etch-a-Sketch."

The creature on the left swung forward on its stubby legs, a third jointed limb tipped with a long, flat claw appearing from within its shell to angle toward Howard. He extended the bowl hopefully. There was a gurgling sound and cool droplets sprayed his hand. "Here, let's hope he got our order right." Howard passed the full bowl to Yam. "You're the thirsty one. You go first."

The Trilbit sniffed the sparkling liquid, then dabbed at it cautiously with his tongue. "Is sweet-water," he confirmed after a moment. "Delicious!"

"In that case, give me a swig, will you?" Howard smacked his lips. "Not bad. Thanks, guys!" On a sudden impulse, he stepped forward and placed the watch faceup on the packed sand in the center of the room, pointed at it several times, then returned to his place at Yam's side. The nearer shield-shape moved closer, eyestalks alert. The fingerlike cilia reappeared, writhing at the rim of its carapace. There was a glint of metal as something small and gold emerged from between the eye-clusters at the top of the shell, and the object was carried downward, passed with rapid dexterity from tendril to tendril as the creature ambled forward on its stubby legs. It leaned at an alarming angle, lowering itself until it was almost horizontal above the glowing dial. Right-hand tendrils grasped the watch at the same moment left-hand tendrils deposited the golden object a few feet away in the sand. Then the shell-shape folded back to its upright position and sidled away to rejoin its comrade.

"I think we have a decision to make, Yam." Howard began to edge forward under the multiple gaze. "Either we can choose to remain here and undertake a lengthy, and no doubt rewarding, linguistic and cultural exchange with our newfound friends . . ." His hand closed over the cold metal shaft and he backed away. "Or you can grab hold of my arm and we can try to get our naked selves back to what passes for civilization on Field of Flowers."

"Rare opportunity, to wander the trails of a totally foreign way of life," Yam observed. "Unfortunate to forgo such an exhilarating experience." His small fingers grasped Howard's elbow. "Even more unfortunate if this novel way of life happens to include slaughter and ingestion of mammalian bipeds."

"I agree," Howard said with a sigh. "A difficult choice. But someone must bear the burden of decision, and as your elected representative—" He bowed low to the motionless shield-shapes. "Gentlemen or ladies, we trust you will understand our desire for a speedy departure. Please keep an eye or two out for those other personal belongings we seem to have mislaid during our all-too-brief stay at your establishment. It wouldn't say too much for you as hosts if they should turn up in a yard sale in the near future."

One of the creatures took three steps toward them on its bowed legs, an elaborate sequence of maroon and orange shapes flashing on its carapace.

"Whoa," said Howard, and turned the Key.

CHAPTER V

All Is Revealed

THE BREEZE WAS GENTLE, LACED WITH WARM CUR- rents and laden with familiar spices. A white sun hung above like a pearl at the center of a dome of rich amethyst, while silver rain clouds massed on the far horizon. Beneath Howard and Yam's feet, a plain of smooth lavender stone, a shade or two lighter than the sky, stretched toward a vast sea of multicolored flowers.

They were standing several yards from a curving wall of gray and purple trees. About half a mile away along the forest's rim was a circle of crude dwellings: patched and sagging tents alternated with huts fashioned of local wood and topped with a thatch of long silver needles. Smoke rose in thin trails from cookfires scattered among the buildings.

"Ah, lovely sky, with smells so sweet!" Yam expanded his small chest around a deep breath, plucked the last pale grub from the sand bowl he still carried, and popped it into his mouth. He sighed happily and looked around. "You have brought us to a place some short distance from camp to avoid startling our friends with our sudden appearance—correct, Ow-er-bel?"

"Something like that." Howard shifted his weight from one foot to the other on the sun-warmed stone, his arms crossed stiffly on his chest.

"We will rejoin them now?" Yam took a few steps toward the encampment, looked back over his shoulder, and paused.

"Sure thing," Howard said, making no move to follow. "Sounds good."

"You are troubled, Ow-er-bel?" Lines furrowed the Trilbit's

forehead. "Perhaps there is a thing you wish to do before we enter camp?"

Howard expelled a breath through pursed lips, then scratched his chin self-consciously.

"See, I don't have any *clothes* on, Yam." He raised the golden Key and flicked it with his forefinger. "I can't even wear this—they took the cord off."

"Yes, I am also bereft of coverings." Yam blinked down at his furry torso. "Pleasant, in this sweet warm breath of wind."

"It's not the same for you," Howard sighed. "No offense or anything, but you look more dressed now than when you had clothes on."

The Trilbit nodded. "And I mean no insult when I observe that your own fur covering is patchy at best. Is this a source of shame for you? I tell you honestly, Ow-er-bel, you look no worse than any other Averoy I have seen undraped."

Howard laughed. "Thanks, pal, I appreciate that. It's not that I'm ashamed of how I look. It's just . . ."

Yam regarded Howard thoughtfully. "A matter of some cultural complexity, yes? Among battle-gangs, age-old customs and beliefs of our many races have long been suppressed by Key-holders. For a warrior, clothing has two functions: to protect its body, and to indicate team affiliation. Perhaps you are feeling a loss of identity without uniform of Breakneck Boys. Or is it that your own world attaches another significance to absence of garments?"

"Bingo," Howard said.

"Ah, Alaiya has spoken of this deity of yours." The Trilbit nodded wisely. "So it is a religious boundary you fear to overstep."

"No, not exactly." Howard grimaced and shook his head. "Look, this is no big deal. It really shouldn't bother me—especially knowing that it means nothing to anybody else. Most of the folks on the team aren't even my own species, for God's sake." He clapped Yam on the shoulder and turned resolutely toward the encampment. "How about we just march in there with pride in our eyes and a song in our hearts." He started forward, but after half a dozen steps his bold stride faltered. He looked back at his small companion, face scarlet.

"Look, Yam, would you consider me an awful coward if I asked you to run on ahead and do me a favor?"

"Never, Ow-er-bel." The Trilbit was indignant. "You are

the Nonesuch! I am happy to provide this favor to ease your discomfort.''

"Great. Then go into the camp and hunt down Alaiya. Catch her alone, if you can. Tell her I'm out here with no clothes on and I'd appreciate a little thoughtful assistance before I come on in.''

"Easily accomplished. Anything additional?''

Howard shook his head. "Alaiya knows me pretty well by now. I know she'll be able to handle this without thinking I'm too crazy.''

The Trilbit bowed smartly. "Message will be conveyed.'' He turned and began to trot briskly in the direction of the encampment.

"Thanks a lot! See you soon,'' Howard called after him. He shook his head and lowered himself awkwardly to the stone. "I hope she remembers my shoe size.''

The warm sun felt good on his bare skin. He sat with his back to the camp, arms clasped loosely around his knees, and gazed out at the far sweep of brilliantly colored blossoms.

Howard found himself eager to see Alaiya again, though they had only been separated for a few days. As battlechief of the Breakneck Boys, she had decided to stay behind while he and Yam explored the deserted city. Howard knew that she was already planning the team's first true assault on the Keyholders. With their camp on Field of Flowers firmly established, and time at last to concentrate on more than basic survival, Alaiya was looking forward to gathering strategic information from the members of the newly formed battle-gang. For his part, Howard freely admitted to having no head for warfare, and was more than happy to confine his leadership to nonmilitary concerns.

He lay back in the sunlight and grinned, anticipating the friendly teasing Alaiya would give him when she delivered his clothes. Though they had known each other only a few months, he found himself completely comfortable in her presence, and had begun to suspect that she knew him better than anyone else ever had. He began to organize the events of the past few days in his mind, so that he would be ready to recount them to Alaiya on their walk back to the encampment.

The breeze brought him the scent of fresh mint from the distant flowers, mixed with a hint of approaching rain. He had slipped into a half dream when he became aware of a rhythmic sound. He concentrated, but could not be sure he was actually hearing something other than his own heartbeat, or feeling vibrations through the rock beneath him. He sat up and frowned in the direction of the camp.

A feeling like cold electricity passed through his body.

Making its way toward him across the plain was what appeared to be the entire population of the encampment, some thirty-odd warriors representing a dozen alien races. And striding at the head of the marching, gliding, darting band came Alaiya the Redborn, her long, red-gold hair fluttering like a banner in the breeze.

Alaiya's red-gold hair was about the only thing fluttering in the breeze. As the battle-gang approached, Howard was able to see clearly that none of the warriors had on a stitch of clothing.

It was too late to run into the forest. Howard conquered the urge to remain seated with his back toward the group and got slowly to his feet. He tossed the Key back and forth in his palms while he tried to decide what to do with his hands once the others arrived.

Then he found himself looking into Alaiya's dark gray eyes as she halted the strange band several yards from him and came forward by herself to take his hand. "Greetings, Nonesuch," she said formally, her English slightly accented. "Your battle-gang is overjoyed at your safe return and waits eagerly to hear of your adventures." More quietly, she added, "I knew what I must do when Yam brought me your message. Of course it would not be proper for the Nonesuch to come unbelted among his people unless they also discarded their garments. I am honored that you felt you could trust me with this decision, and hope we did not keep you lingering on the plain past your patience."

"Oh, no," Howard said. "I've just been sitting around waiting for the rest of the volleyball team to show up."

He allowed himself to be led to where the others waited. Interspersed among the several alien species that comprised the Breakneck Boys stood five human warriors—members of Alaiya's race, the Averoy, which the Keyholders mockingly called the Sunset People. Arpenwole, a tall, fair-skinned Averoy with silver hair cropped close to her scalp, watched Howard with undisguised amusement as he self-consciously joined the milling group. "You see, it is as Alaiya said," he heard her remark loudly in the Averant language to another warrior. "He does change color rather alarmingly from time to time."

He exchanged greetings with half a dozen well-wishers, suggesting as soon he could manage without seeming impolite that they return to the encampment. Alaiya placed herself on his right side and Yam skipped at his left, beaming in satisfaction. Finding himself at the center of the crowd as they headed across the lavender plain, he tried to focus his attention on counting heads, his eyes skipping quickly from face to face. In addition to the Averoy, there were two Attercacks, tall, six-limbed lizard-folk with crests of dyed quills flexing in the breeze atop their narrow skulls; three Ga'Prenny, flat-bodied, lightweight creatures that reminded Howard most of upright flounders; five Domenai, basically humanoid, whose damp hides were chocolate brown, and who walked with a strange, stop-motion glide that Howard found difficult to watch.

He lost his tally when he noticed that one member of the battle-gang had not come out with the group. He turned to question Alaiya concerning the whereabouts of their missing comrade and found her grinning at him.

"What are you so pleased about?" he asked grumpily.

"Oh, it is just that you are handling things so well. I knew you would be equal to the situation if it was thrust upon you. Now you have proven me correct."

"Thrust upon me . . ." He looked at her for a long moment before his jaw dropped. "Are you telling me you organized this sunshine frolic on purpose, just to get me comfortable with walking around in my birthday suit like the rest of you?"

She raised a finger to her lips. "You may wish to keep your voice down, O Nonesuch. Some of our teammates are progressing quite rapidly in their study of English." She laughed playfully and reached out to smooth his unbound hair back from his face. "After all, it is a wise ruler who recognizes his limitations, an even wiser one who knows when to forsake his own comfort for the greater good."

"I can't believe it," Howard said. "What was all that stuff about being honored to be trusted with this big decision?"

"Ahwerd, you surprise me." Alaiya shook her head in mock despair. "Where is the sense of ready humor that you have told me is so necessary for survival?"

"Humor—this is your idea of humor? I suppose you pull the wings off flies when you want a real knee-slapper."

"Ahwerd, your body is perfectly presentable." Alaiya looked him up and down frankly as they walked. "You should feel no qualms about exhibiting it."

"Fine. Thank you." Howard felt his face grow hot again. "I'd just like to be involved in scheduling the shows from now on, okay?"

Further discussion was precluded by a shower of cold rain that quickly attained gale proportions, scattering the battle-gang and sending Howard racing to his tent, feet sliding on the slickened stone and teeth chattering.

Alaiya's head poked through the front flap a few moments later, her ivory face jeweled with droplets and framed by lank strands of dark red. "Am I allowed to enter, or is your anger so great it fills all the empty space?"

Howard made room on the layer of evergray boughs that floored the tent. "You might as well come in," he said. "God knows what hideous pranks you'd plan if I made you stay outside."

"My thanks." She had picked up a roll of thick cloth from somewhere. Shaking it out in the small space, she began to towel herself dry. When she was done she turned to Howard. "Shall I take the water from your skin as well, or do you wish to cover your nakedness with garments as soon as possible?" She folded a length of the cloth around her hand and drew it slowly down Howard's chest. Howard made a small noise in his throat.

"It was most difficult to convince the Intzwam to discard their garments," she said as she worked. "The Po'Ellika, on the other hand, fairly spun out of their uniforms."

"The Intzwam?" Howard arched his back and sighed under Alaiya's thorough ministrations. "All they ever wear besides their belts are those little headbands."

Alaiya gave an Averoy hand-shrug. "Apparently, the region so concealed is the cause of much emotional fervor among the Intzwam. They were vigorous in their protests."

"I know how they feel," Howard said. "You should have excused them from the assignment."

"But it is important for the Breakneck Boys to start thinking like a unified battle-gang. One way to accomplish that is to insist on compliance with rules by all members—regardless of individual or racial quirks. It is a technique that has worked most effectively for the Keyholders. Oh—" She drew back. "Are you sore in that area?"

"Yeah, a little bit. Don't stop—it feels great." Howard was silent for a moment. "I'm not so sure I'm comfortable using the Keyholders' tactics on our own people," he said. "I mean, isn't that what we're fighting against?"

"You are the leader, man from another place." This time her shrug was of the American variety. "But I do not think we will have much success against our enemies if we abandon all discipline.'' Alaiya set down the towel and sat back on the carpet of soft needles.

Howard rolled over onto his side to avoid a new leak in the worn canvas above him. ''Sounds like a monsoon out there,'' he remarked.

Alaiya moved to peer through the tent flap. ''It is a large storm. It may be some time before the rain stops.''

''So, do you want to hear all about what Yam and I have been up to for the past couple of days—or should we use the time to work out a compromise on this philosophical disagreement of ours?''

''Are these our only options for passing the hours?'' Alaiya remained kneeling at the opening, her eyes on the storm.

Howard put his hand on her shoulder and drew it slowly down her arm, ending with his fingers twined in hers. ''Are you kidding?'' he asked.

Alaiya fastened the tent flap, then turned and pressed her palm against his chest, pushing him gently backward onto the boughs. ''There is still so much you have to learn about my sense of humor,'' she murmured.

CHAPTER VI

A Snack By the Pool

HOWARD WOKE SOMETIME IN THE MIDDLE OF THE night. Moving quietly, so as not to rouse Alaiya, he pulled on a pair of shorts and slipped from the tent. The stars were out, the air cool and rain-washed. One of the moons shone high in the sky, while the other sat like a silver coin on the dark curve of the flower sea.

The sentry, a rotund marsupial known as a Sarsi, lowered its humorous face and bobbed its spear respectfully as the Nonesuch slipped into the forest past an ancient, double-trunked tree. Howard's memory supplied him with the turnings of the path he followed, and an occasional sliver of moonlight stole through the close-set trees to light his way. Small, gray-furred treehangers clung by their tails alongside complicated nests of sticks in some of the lower branches. The smallest member of one family group uncurled slightly to blink a sleepy black eye at Howard as he passed by.

He walked some distance from the camp, making his way to one of the deep, circular pools that dotted the woods. The air was still as he leaned against a tall trunk, the whole world wrapped in perfect silence. He tilted his head back and looked down past his nose, watching moonlight paint arcs of silver on the small rush of waves that lapped softly at the edge of the pool.

Waves? Howard straightened with a frown as the ripples increased in size. Holding onto the tree trunk with one arm, he leaned out over the pool, squinting toward the source of the disturbance. There was something large under the water, pale

38

in the scattered shafts of moonlight. Was it rising or falling? He craned his neck.

Something erupted from the water in front of his face. Mounting high into the air, it fell back onto the surface of the pool with a tremendous wallop that drenched Howard with cold water from head to toe.

He stumbled back from the pool's edge, shivering and spluttering as he knuckled the water from his eyes.

"Hawa, you have returned!" boomed a rich voice from the direction of the pool. "What a pleasant way to end my reverie."

"Great cannonball, Awp." Howard shook his head like a terrier and hunched his shoulders against the cold. "This is the second time you've managed to surprise me by this pool."

"Yes, it is becoming quite a ritual between us." A bulky shape climbed slowly from the dark waters, chalk white skin shimmering in the moonlight. "Had I known you were waiting here, I would have surfaced in a more decorous manner."

"Don't worry about it—I already got nailed by a rainstorm this afternoon. I wasn't exactly waiting for you, though. When Alaiya told me you'd gone into the woods to do some thinking, it didn't occur to me that it might be at the bottom of a well."

"Yes, I've lately found that mulling things over underwater frees me from many distractions," Awp said, opening its massive arms to enfold Howard in a chill embrace.

"So, are all Hants amphibious—or just you grownups?" Howard patted the being's damp shoulders as his feet left the ground. "Whoa—careful of the ribs, there. I've put some mileage on them since the last time you picked me up."

"You have suffered an injury during your exploration of the city?" The Hant returned Howard carefully to the wet clay at the edge of the pool. "Is Ya-mosh well?"

"Yeah, we're both doing fine. We've had an interesting time, though. I should probably still be resting, but I felt like a walk." Howard leaned back against a tree trunk and patted his flat stomach. "I feel like something to eat, too. I don't suppose you've got anything other than Hant foodstuff on you?" He tipped his chin hopefully at the broad belt crowded with pouches that was clasped above the Hant's black shorts.

"As a matter of fact, I spied some intriguing rootbulbs near the bottom of the pool when I descended yesterday. Wait a moment—"

Before Howard could open his mouth, Awp turned and

dropped like a boulder into the pool. Two minutes later, it emerged with a cluster of dark objects in its many-fingered hand.

"You have become wet again, Hawa," the Hant observed as it left the water. "Was this my doing?"

"No problem. My aunt said it was tough to keep me dry when I was an infant, too." He took one of the proffered bulbs and examined it dubiously under a moonbeam before returning it to Awp. "You sure these are edible? Remember, my metabolism's not as forgiving as yours when it comes to lethal poison."

"I will make certain of it. If you will excuse me for a moment—" The Hant turned its back for a few seconds. "There. You have my assurance the item is now completely harmless to your human system."

"What did you do to it?" Howard brought the moist root to his nose and sniffed at it suspiciously.

"I effected a simple chemical adjustment to safeguard against any toxins, Hawa. I was fairly certain you would not wish to witness the procedure involved—however, I will describe it to you if you think—"

"Don't say another word if you expect me to put this in my mouth," Howard warned. He curled his lips back from his teeth and took a delicate bite of the firm flesh. He chewed for a moment, considering, and swallowed. "Not bad," he admitted. "Sort of potato-esque. You want to split these?"

"No, I consumed several as I ascended just now. You may have all of them."

"Don't mind if I do." Howard settled himself cross-legged on a patch of ground cover near the base of the tree and motioned for Awp to do the same. "Now, you ready for an update on Howard and his traveling Key?"

Between bites, Howard recounted the adventures that had befallen him and Yam since they had set off for the abandoned city four days before. Awp listened closely, an occasional searching question revealing the points that most stirred its interest.

"It is unfortunate that your investigation of the towers was curtailed in such a violent manner," the Hant observed. "Though your experiences after you employed the Key may ultimately yield valuable information."

"You've been around for a zillion years or so." Howard flicked pebbles into the dark pool. "You must've fought on the Red Desert World lots of times. Ever hear anything about those big lightning bugs before? Yam said he thought the checkerboard desert just went on forever."

"Yes, the sand castles and their inhabitants are beyond my experience as well," Awp mused. "Certainly not the Kansas with which I am familiar."

Howard nodded. "And definitely not the Kansas I'm familiar with. Of course, I only spent a couple of hours there when I was sixteen, waiting for a connecting flight." He plucked an ever-gray needle from the ground at his side and began to use it as a toothpick.

"Ah, you refer to that region on your home world for which you have renamed the Red Desert. Still, it is a fact we would do well to remember—that there is more than one Kansas."

"I'll tie a string around my finger," Howard promised. "So, what've you been up to while I was away—and what prompted you to become the Jacques Cousteau of the Fading Worlds?" He gestured at the pond.

"As you suggested earlier, my newfound affinity for depths of water seems to be a by-product of my recent maturation. You may have noticed, for example, that my feet took on a distinctly aquatic appearance during the molt which ended my childhood." The Hant extended a powerful leg and flexed its webbed toes. "I must admit, I had some initial concerns about their altered configuration."

"We all get a little anxious during that period in our lives," Howard said. "I remember when my voice broke for the first time. I pretended I had laryngitis for two weeks, hoping it would change back."

"I believe the nature of the Hant home world itself may be reflected in my current physical state," Awp continued. "Whether I shall ever succeed in following my own memories back far enough to confirm this conjecture remains uncertain. I was attempting to explore the limits of my recollections while I sat at the bottom of the pool. I have managed to come up with some information that may prove useful in our campaign against the Keyholders."

"Alaiya will be happy to hear that. What kind of stuff did you remember?"

"Merely the events of my life, stretching back over many Rounds, including every Turn I fought as member of a battle-gang and every world in which my battle-gang strove. It has not been difficult to extract patterns from the flow of these events."

"Patterns." Howard leaned forward in the dimness, scratching in the clay with a small branch. "Meaning there's a sequence to the worlds that are put in play and the teams that are assigned to them? I thought it was supposed to be random, to keep the warriors on their toes—or their flippers, or whatever.''

''The pattern is vast, becoming perceptible only over the march of many hundreds of Rounds,'' Awp said. ''But it is undeniably present.''

''So you should be able to predict where each team will be on the Fading Worlds from now on.'' Howard nodded. ''We could get there first.''

''The information will undoubtedly be of limited use,'' the Hant cautioned. ''Once the Keyholders realize what we are doing, they need only alter the pattern.''

''Yes, but it could buy us the advantage we've been looking for.'' Howard grinned up at his friend in the moonlight. ''This is great work, *mon vieux*! You should sleep with the fishes more often. Let's go wake up the battlechief and tell her, too.''

They headed back for the encampment, Howard excusing himself for a few moments at the edge of the woods.

''I almost forgot the main reason I came out here,'' he said over his shoulder as he went to stand behind a nearby tree.

CHAPTER VII

Ready or Not

THE BATTLECHIEF WAS ALREADY UP AND ABOUT BY THE
time they reentered the camp. They found her sitting in front of
the small hut she had built for herself near the camp's center,
poring over a collection of fragile-looking paper charts. Orange
light fell past her shoulder from the small cup of firejelly hung
by three delicate chains to one side of the door, and the two
moons washed the scene with cooler illumination. Alaiya was
barefoot, dressed in the black-and-silver vest and shorts the
Breakneck Boys had adopted as their uniform. Half a dozen
narrow metal tubes lay on the ground at her side. She was sitting
with her heels lightly resting on two edges of the central chart
to keep it flat; the others were secured with bits of stone and
wood. In one hand, she held a small wad of Averoy foodstuff.

"You have found each other. Good." She squinted up at
Howard and Awp as they came between her and the moonlight.
"Ahwerd, your shorts are damp. Were you drawn to join the
Hant in its contemplative submersion?"

"No, my brain doesn't work all that well without a steady
supply of oxygen." Howard lowered himself to the ground.
"What are you doing up? I didn't wake you when I left the tent,
did I?"

Alaiya raised an eyebrow. "Even if I had been able to sleep
through the noise you made trying to find your shorts, it would
have been difficult to ignore your knee in the small of my back
as you crawled toward the exit." She rubbed his leg, smiling at
his expression. "I was ready to rise. It is difficult to sleep when
the brain is buzzing with unfinished schemes." She indicated
the overlapping sheets. Several of the Fading Worlds were de-

picted in colored inks on the creased and crumbling pages. "Chinefwa, a Beranot who fought for the Gold Schemers, has a good artistic eye. Several Rounds past, she started making maps of battle sites for her own amusement. She brought them to me yesterday morning with the thought that they might lend some solidity to our discussions."

"Dynamite." Howard leaned over the charts, which were bordered by delicate loops and zigzags that were either annotations or a decorative device. "Awp's brought a few useful insights back from Davy Jones's locker." He gestured to the towering Hant. "Pull up some stone and tell Alaiya what you've found."

Settling its bulk gracefully across from the two humans, Awp described its recent discovery to Alaiya. The battlechief listened with rapt attention, and a grim smile had appeared on her lips by the time the tale was finished.

"Wonderful news!" She sat back against the hut, kneading her neck with one hand beneath her unbound hair. "Can you truly predict the next world to be put in play?"

"If the pattern is followed, it will be that one." The Hant's many fingers moved deftly among the scattered sheets. "In seventeen days' time, the Rain of Blood will confront the Howling Miscreants on the Sinking Swamp World."

"Jeez." Howard rolled his eyes. "Don't those names just make you want to rush right over and join in the fun?"

"Indeed," Alaiya said earnestly. "But we must make sure to arrive before either battle-gang. It is the start of a Lesser Round, so the teams will be fresh from Stillpoint, sent out on different paths to converge at the battle site." She turned to Awp. "Can you locate the place of meeting as well, wise Hant—or do I ask the impossible?"

Awp considered the request. "The terrain of the selected world is largely uniform. However, we know that Howard's Key is guided in part by strong mental images, and that it is not necessary for them to originate in his own brain." It nodded toward Alaiya. "Witness our presence here, on a world that you yourself had only imagined in fantasies evoked by legend. I believe I will be able to visualize the general area clearly enough for Howard and his instrument to deliver a group of us there, if he is willing."

"Hey." Howard lifted the golden Key on its new cord and twirled it in the moonlight. "We run everywhere in the tri-state region. No parcel too bulky, no fare too small."

"The Rain of Blood is a strong, well-seasoned team." Alaiya

narrowed her eyes in thought. "Best to try our luck with the weaker Miscreants. Several warriors remain in the battle-gang from the time of my own membership—Rounds ago, when I was fresh from the Holding. It should not be difficult to persuade them to join us in our strivings; with luck, their comrades will follow, and few lives need be lost."

"What will the Keyholders be doing?" Howard asked. "Don't they have some way of watching the battle-gangs?"

"Uncertain," Alaiya said. "It is known that they observe portions of the actual confrontations—perhaps by employing a Traveler in the vicinity—but they seem to have little interest in the actions of the separate teams before the battle occurs."

"You mean they set this whole thing up and then they don't watch it half the time?"

"We think they watch far less than half the time, though no one is certain. Perhaps they have other amusements to divert them."

"So the battle-gangs fight their hearts out while the Keyholders sit back and flip channels." Howard shook his head in disgust. "You guys need a stronger union."

"What we need is freedom. And now that you have come among us, we at last have a chance of obtaining it for all who fight unwillingly." Alaiya began to carefully roll up one of the maps. "As for the Travelers, you should be able to alert us to danger from that quarter with your demonstrated sensitivity to their presence."

Howard nodded with a grimace. "That's a pretty safe bet."

"What is it that informs you of their nearness, Hawa?" The Hant leaned forward, its complicated eyes flickering as they adjusted to the firejelly's light.

"A strong desire to throw up," Howard said. "Really intense vertigo. It's like my body's on a roller coaster all of a sudden, even though my brain knows I'm standing still." His hand rose and plunged in the air to illustrate.

"Unpleasant."

"Not as bad as actually being caught by one." Howard shrugged. "At least, so they tell me."

"It is said to be most unsettling," Alaiya commented. "A sensation of endless falling that persists beyond the event. Not like the quick blur of the Fade, nor the brief dark passage of Ahwerd's Key."

"Yet it was reported that you passed through a Traveler, Hawa," Awp said. "Back at the Battle of the Black Cliffs, when

I was felled by the mountain gun and you swooped down in your flying suit to vanquish the Dratzul. Those who watched said that when you and your opponent plunged from the cliffside, a Traveler appeared in the air beneath you, and both of you dropped into its blackness.''

"But only the Dratzul was taken," Alaiya amended uneasily. She inserted the rolled map into one of the tubes and reached for another. "Ahwerd fell through somehow to the rocks below.''

"What can I say?" Howard looked from one puzzled face to the other. "I hadn't been showering regularly. Maybe it didn't like the way I tasted and spit me out. It's not something I plan to complain about.''

After another half hour of conversation, Howard's yawns began to outnumber his comments. He excused himself to cross the camp and crawl into his tent for some long-overdue rest. As he lay in the darkness, he mused on how swiftly events could change their shape once they entered the mind. What were now being recounted as his heroic deeds during the Battle of the Black Cliffs survived in his own memory as a confused sequence of almost instinctive reactions to rapidly presented stimuli. It was like the vertigo brought on by the nearness of a Traveler: his brain and body had seemed to act independently.

It's a good thing nobody gave this hero time to think about what he was doing, he thought as he drifted off. I'd probably still be up on that cliffside, pretending to tie my shoelace or something . . .

The sun was mounting the sky when he emerged to find Yamya-mosh seated on a square of coarse fiber, brewing tea at his doorstep.

"Fine waking, Ow-er-bel," the Trilbit greeted him cheerfully. "Wish some morning drink?''

Howard accepted a papery cup of aromatic bigtassle tea and hunkered down next to his friend. "How are you feeling today? You look pretty chipper.''

"Not chipped at all, in truth." Yam patted his midsection. "Think great pinching claws bruised flesh, but caused no damage to bone structure. But what has happened to you?" His eyes widened in alarm as he craned his neck to examine Howard's bare shoulder. "These are surely bite marks! Were you attacked during night?''

"Eh, it's probably just an allergy or something. I wouldn't

worry about it.'' Howard hurriedly pulled on his vest. ''So what's up for today—have you talked to the battlechief?''

''Yes, Lai-ya plans meeting for noon hour to discuss our next actions. With Hant's assistance, we will soon be adding to our number, correct?''

''Yeah, if everything works out.'' Howard watched as Yam poured a small quantity of brown powder into his own cup. ''What's that stuff? Instant cocoa?''

Yam's nose twitched. ''Merely hormonal additives helpful for Trilbit metabolism. Once each Round I must supplement my foodstuff to prepare for any consequences of farrowing-change.''

''No chocolate, huh?'' Howard looked disappointed. ''Hey, want to go jump around in the flowers for a while till it's time for the meeting?''

''Regretfully, I am occupied. I have promised to assist Awp in instructing certain individuals in your Ingliss language. For some to acquire this tongue is simple undertaking—while for others, it is like pulling hen's teeth.''

''I believe it. I still feel like the Ugly American with everybody trying to learn to talk English. You guys know I would have been happy to pick someone else's language for the team.''

''Understood.'' Yam inclined his head. ''But with this mixture of many races and members from different teams, it is necessary to place all on same level. You are strangest stranger here, and your speech is equally foreign to all.''

''Yeah, I know.'' Howard finished his tea and poured himself a refill. ''Those little critters did have their uses, even though I never liked the idea of them lounging around in my head.''

Weeks before, Howard and Alaiya had been warned that the Keyholders might be able to trace their whereabouts in the Fading Worlds by means of their parleybugs, microscopic organisms that all battle-gang members carried in their blood. Residing for the most part in the speech centers of the host's brain, the parleybugs served as interpreters for the many languages used by the warriors in each battle-gang. During their brief stay at the gates of the vanishing city of Stillpoint, Alaiya had managed to secure a small quantity of purge pods—nutlike objects that could be ingested to cleanse the system of parleybugs. The original team members had quickly rid themselves of their parleyblood, and before the latest additions to the Breakneck Boys had been purged, the members of the team had voted to adopt the English of the Nonesuch as their common language. The Hant, who could converse in any language it had ever experienced, was in the unenviable position of translator for all important communication until the team members all achieved fluency in Howard's tongue.

"See, Ow-er-bel?" The Trilbit pointed his muzzle toward the center of the encampment. "Our pupils approach."

Howard looked over his shoulder. Making its way through the hodgepodge of tents and buildings was a small group that included some of the odder members of the battle-gang.

The Keyholders had apparently chosen their slaves with a nod to the necessity of coexistence and cooperation within each team; on the whole, Howard had discovered more similarities than he had expected among the alien races that fought in the Fading Worlds. Most of the beings he had encountered so far were oxygen breathers who used at least one set of limbs for locomotion and another for manipulation. They possessed a variety of sense organs—though visual receptors of one sort or another seemed common to all—as well as a means of producing and receiving audible communication. Aside from these shared attributes, there was still quite a bit of diversity to be found.

Leading the group that approached Howard's tent were a pair of Po'Ellika, shiny, hard-skinned creatures that stood a few inches taller than Yam. They came from the same world as the flounderlike Ga'Prenny, but unlike them they moved across the lavender plain in short, spinning hops. Each Po'Ellika had a single round eye that traveled freely in a narrow groove encircling its tapered head. Below this hung half a dozen boneless arms that normally hugged the body, but could fan out like flails during a spin. The unique style of locomotion that made the Po'Ellika resemble giant tops was powered by a complicated structure at the base of the cylindrical body. From what Howard had observed, they actually seemed to wind themselves up a few turns before every whirling hop. Their one similarity to the flat-bodied Ga'Prenny lay in their vocal apparatus, a series of slits on the upper torso through which they produced the modulated wheeze that served them as speech.

Following close behind the Po'Ellika came a Beranot, its eyes a pair of dark, vertical ovals blinking in slow alternation above the mop of nine-inch tentacles that filled the lower half of its face. The speech of the Beranoi sounded to Howard as though the mouth hidden behind the thicket of tentacles consisted of a glass bowl filled with sharp-edged stones. Like most of the warriors, they were bipeds, with long, powerful arms that attached to their thighs by means of a thin flap of flexible skin. The color of his arm flaps showed that this individual was a male. He shuffled behind the whirling Po'Ellika in the hunched, painful-looking gait typical of his race.

Three Paspers rounded out the group, escorting the others with the catlike movements Howard could only characterize as slinking. Humanoid in general construction, they had handsome faces decorated with ivory fangs and jewel-bright eyes. They were furred in shades of brown and gold, with darker or lighter spots in patterns reminiscent of a cheetah's. Recalling the sand-paper cough of their voices sent a chill down Howard's spine as he watched them bring up the rear as gracefully as lions stalking a herd of antelope.

"Acceptable if we commence our lessons here by your dwelling while we await Hant?" Yam inquired as the group formed a loose semicircle before him.

"Oh, be my guests," Howard said with a bow. The Po'Ellika dipped forward instantly in response, spinning like gyroscopes to right themselves.

"Excellent." Yam turned to his students and clasped his hands at his chest. "Please say good morning to our Nonesuch."

"Gooma-gooma-gooma!" bleated the Po'Ellika, making little whirling leaps straight up into the air. The Beranot produced a noise that sounded like tokens being dropped into a subway turnstile, and the Paspers rasped a chorus of "G'morry, Nuh'suh," as they circled the area in search of the right patch of sun-warmed stone upon which to settle.

"Great, you're all coming along just great," Howard said, patting the Trilbit's shoulder. "And you've got a wonderful teaching assistant in Yam here."

"It was my luck to have heard your tongue in great depth back when my veins hosted parleyblood," the Trilbit replied. "Awp was able to coax memories out of my head that made acquisition of your Ingliss less toilsome." Yam's ears twitched and he lifted his head. "Believe Hant is now approaching."

"Good." Howard slipped on a pair of sandals, crisscrossed the laces over his ankles, and got to his feet. "Well, I'm going to head out for some exercise before the meeting, okay?" He waved to the assembled class. "Later, guys. Keep up the good work."

A chorus of clinking, scraping sounds followed him as he started toward the small rise about a mile away that marked the shore of the flower sea.

For some unknown reason, the pull of gravity in the sea of

bright-hued flowers was only a fraction of that experienced on the lavender plain and in the forest it encompassed. Feeling as though he were on a giant trampoline, Howard leaped and cavorted among the blossoms for an hour of vigorous exercise. He felt a small rush of adrenaline when he sighted the telltale shaking of a patch of flowers not far from him, a sure sign of a predatory slake-like creature underneath the surface. By confining his workout to the high ridges, which were marked by clusters of red and orange blooms, he was able to feel fairly secure; so far the monsters had only been observed in the blue-green depths.

During one of his prodigious vertical jumps, Howard noticed a movement of many individuals toward the center of the camp. Sweaty and invigorated, he bounded back to the stone shore and the unwelcome grip of normal gravity.

A large, circular area in the middle of the camp had been set aside for gatherings. Howard ducked into his tent for a length of fluffy cloth, toweling his hair and face as he walked toward the semicircle of black-clad warriors. Alaiya beckoned to him to join her where she stood with Awp in front of her hut.

"Do you wish to speak first, Ahwerd, or shall I tell them about our plans?"

Howard raised his palms. "This is your ballgame, chief. Go for it."

The meeting proceeded slowly, Alaiya talking for about a minute, then pausing while Awp repeated her words in the various languages used by their teammates. Gradually, she detailed the Hant's findings, then spoke about what they hoped to accomplish with the new information.

"We will go first to the Sinking Swamp World, there to confront the Howling Miscreants and try to win them to our cause. If this is successful, we will repeat the process as many times as we are able."

Questions filtered back from the team members. Would the prospective Breakneck Boys be returned to Field of Flowers? What if the battle-gangs they approached would not join them? What was the ultimate goal of their strategy?

Alaiya was ready with answers. "We will establish a secondary camp to serve as a quarantine for new members until their blood has been purged of parleybugs. It may be necessary to make this a mobile camp to avoid detection by the Keyholders. There is a limit to our supply of purge pods, though I am hopeful we will locate a new batch among the medical supplies of other teams. As you know, the parleyblood can occasionally sour in an individual, necessitating the removal of the old bugs and the infusion of new.

"If a battle-gang refuses to join us, then we will fight and defeat them," she continued matter-of-factly. "Eventually, we will become an army, sufficient in size and ferocity to launch an attack on Stillpoint itself and so destroy the hated Masters in their own nest."

Howard gave a low whistle. "Pretty ambitious," he said softly.

As the Hant translated Alaiya's words, a hum of discussion began among those warriors able to communicate with one another. After a few moments, Arpenwole of the Averoy raised her hand and stepped forward from the small crowd.

"Suppose the Hant has miscalculated in regard to timing," she said rapidly in the language of the Sunset People. "Or suppose the Keyholders initiate an early Fade. We may be caught with the other warriors and sent to the next world."

"Those who have mastered English are expected to use it at these gatherings," Alaiya said quietly.

"I do not like the sound of it. It grates in my throat." Arpenwole tilted her narrow chin, still speaking in Averant. "The Averoy are the largest single racial group among the warriors. You are the battlechief. I believe we should conduct these meetings in our own tongue."

Alaiya appeared to consider this for a moment. Then she turned casually to Howard. "Nonesuch, I request that you use your Key to transport our former teammate to the destination of her choice, as she seems unwilling to abide by the team's decision concerning the use of English. Moreover, should she show evidence of plans to betray us to the slaves of the Keyholders, it is my suggestion that she be killed at once."

"Whoa," Howard said. "Hold on a second, here."

After a brief, whispered conversation with the Averoy woman who stood just behind her, Arpenwole took another step forward, her eyes locked with Alaiya's.

"I withdraw my comments," she said stiffly in English, her face dark with suppressed emotion.

Howard released the breath he had been holding.

"The question was a valid one," Alaiya said. She inclined her head to Awp, who sat nearby. "Is there a chance of such miscalculation, wise Hant? Might some of us be taken by the Fade?"

"It is conceivable that the Keyholders could initiate an early displacement," the Hant replied, after translating the question for his listeners. "But it is my strong suspicion that we Breakneck Boys are no longer susceptible to the Fade, now that the parley-bugs have been taken from our systems. There must be some factor, common to all battle-gang members, that allows them to be shifted from world to world while the local inhabitants remain behind. Parleyblood would seem to be the logical choice."

"Huh. I hadn't thought of that," Howard said with a slow nod. "But it makes sense."

The Hant's calculations placed the meeting between the Miscreants and their opponents about sixteen local days in the future. It was agreed that the Breakneck Boys would spend this time learning to work together as a team. Alaiya discussed available supplies and weaponry with the aid of the Attercack who had been placed in charge of inventory, and a debate followed on possible strategies for confronting the Miscreants.

Howard found his attention wandering as the slow procedure of question, translation, answer, translation, discussion, and translation continued. He was taken by surprise when, after several minutes, Alaiya nudged his side.

"The team has asked for a few words from their Nonesuch before the meeting is adjourned," she told him.

"Ah—right." He rubbed his hands together and faced the crowd. "Well, I've got the utmost confidence in all of you! Now, we've only got a couple of weeks left before the big day, so why don't we just relax and enjoy ourselves while we can?" He turned to the battlechief as the audience began to dissolve into small groups. "How was that?"

"Wonderful," she said. "I had just finished exhorting them to push themselves to their limits in the coming days, sparing no time for anything but training as we approach our crucial test."

"Oh . . . well, that's pretty much what I was saying, too, just in a subtler way. It's called reverse psychology."

"I see. You will have to explain the reasoning behind this practice to me sometime." Alaiya shook her head and moved to confer with the Hant.

The days passed rapidly. Howard continued to receive training in the use of the sword and dagger from Alaiya, while several other members of the battle-gang attempted to instruct him in a variety of weapons and fighting styles. In the mornings, he offered his services as English tutor along with Awp and Yam. Most evenings he spent by himself or with the Hant and the Trilbit. Occasionally, he was able to convince an overworked Alaiya to pause in her duties long enough to accompany him on a quiet walk by the shore of the flower sea.

By mutual agreement, they spoke Averant at such times, and Howard continued to make rapid progress in his mastery of the language. As they strolled in the silver moonlight, Alaiya told him legends from Tai Inimbra, known as Field of Flowers—the home world of her people, which she claimed they had redis-covered. She sang him tales of the goddess Ai'mannan, whose name meant Night Wind, and of Alalarc, her sister and adver-sary, who lived in a house of shadows at the heart of the sun. She told him of the Years of Discord, an ancient time when Averoy had turned against Averoy, summoning monsters to wage war upon their kin, and of the long peace that followed. Mixed with the stories of bloodshed and tragedy were gentler tales of wonder and discovery, and songs of fabulous quests on the world of flowers.

While he listened to the stories, Howard scanned the horizon, thinking of the deadly slakes—creatures believed bred by the Keyholders alone—that roamed the depths of the flower fields, and of the hidden perils that lurked in the abandoned cities. Was this truly the home world of Alaiya's people? Her faith seemed unshaken, and one night she spoke quietly of her dream to some-day bring the rest of the Sunset People here from Noss Averatu, the Holding where her people had dwelled since their impris-onment by the Keyholders millennia ago.

As the day approached, Howard made brief scouting trips to the Black and Blue World with members of the team. They had decided to establish the first interim camp there, so that the Keyholders would not be able to trace the battle-gang back to Field of Flowers by means of the parleybugs in any new recruits.

A band of ten warriors was chosen, including the battlechief and the Nonesuch—two more than the average team. Alaiya made her selections from among the races she knew to be rep-resented in the Howling Miscreants. In the end, she chose two Averoy—Arpenwole, who made no secret of her dissatisfaction with the current governance of the Breakneck Boys, and the dark-skinned warrior known as Omber Oss—as well as two tall-crested Attercacks; Chinefwa, the Beranoi mapmaker; a Ga'Prenny; an Intzwam; and a white-maned Domeny named Faweet.

* * *

Howard sat in front of his tent with Yam the evening before their departure. He was waiting for Alaiya to join him after she concluded her last-minute preparations.

"Are you looking forward to this encounter with Howling Miscreants, Ow-er-bel?" The Trilbit was weaving floor mats of fibers collected from the fields beyond the forest.

"No, but my stomach's telling me it's going to happen soon." Howard rubbed beneath his vest. "You know that feeling you get when it's time for the big final and you've spent the last two weeks doing everything but studying?"

"You do not feel well prepared for tomorrow's activities?"

"Yam, I don't know how to prepare for something like this. Ever since I've been on the Fading Worlds, things've just happened to me, mostly without any warning. It's different when you have time to stew about it. Let's face it, I'm no warrior. This is the kind of thing you've been doing all your life."

"In truth, I wish this farrowing-change were not upon me. It is an inconvenience at this time, and I will miss participating in the raid." The Trilbit looked thoughtful. "But you should not feel concerned about your own performance. You are the None-such."

"Right. That says it all, doesn't it? No use moping about it, I guess. I'll do what I do, ready or not." Howard stretched his arms and began to crack his knuckles methodically. "So, do you have any insights about this Sickly Swamp we're going to? It's a new world for me."

"Lai-ya has most probably informed you of its several peculiarities," Yam said. "Keep always in motion, lest you fall beneath surface slime. Avoid acid pools surrounding fungal growths, and be watchful of airborne vermin. Eat no insects with scarlet markings." The Trilbit shrugged with his face. "This is all that comes immediately to mind."

"Sounds like good advice," Howard said. "Alaiya also told me to bring some filterfluff. She said it works for your nose as well as your ears, and there might be a few smells I'd want to avoid."

"Unfortunate you cannot exchange your nose for mine, Ow-er-bel." Yam rubbed his plush muzzle. "The Sinking Swamp World is savored by those of my race as a treasurehouse of rich and delightful scents. A pity that you will not appreciate them."

"Well, we'll see. Maybe Earthlings and Averoy have different tastes in odors. I sure can't stand their food." He folded his arms behind his head and leaned back against the tent pole with a sigh. "What I wouldn't give for a box of saltines and some Velveeta right now."

"You long for your home world?"

"Oh, off and on. Mostly off. I wasn't that thrilled with it when I lived there. Have I ever told you about income tax, or chain letters—or garbage trucks at five in the morning?"

"Trilbit Holding is also imperfect," Yam said. "With blasting caves and whirr-stings, and always a pelagose under the grainpile. But it was also my home, and one day I hope to walk high slopes and catch tang of ripe marshweed beneath amber clouds again."

"Hey, say the word, pal." Howard straightened and put his hand on his friend's woolly shoulder. "I'm serious—any time you're ready to give up this warrior stuff, the Key and I'll whisk you off to your hometown. Of course, I'd miss you if you took off—but I could always visit."

The Trilbit patted Howard's hand. "Fine noble offer, Ow-er-bel. Not yet ready to forsake this life of adventure—or to leave my good, good friend." He began to pile coarse fibers on the unfinished mat. "And now my body tells me that I must go lie flat for a few hours. Wake me, please, before you depart."

"Sure thing. I hope you come out of this soon." Howard folded himself a small cushion out of a length of thick cloth and inserted it between his back and the tentpole. He leaned back again as his friend ambled into the darkness between the cook-fires.

He was awakened a few hours later by Alaiya's touch on his arm. After a quiet promenade along the flower coast, they retired to her hut for the night.

CHAPTER VIII

Several Stinks

HOWARD'S EYES BEGAN TO WATER AS SOON AS THE NEW world appeared in front of them. Then the smell hit the back of his throat and he started to gag.

Thick with decay and sharp with ammonia, the overpowering stench of decomposing animal and plant matter was mixed with currents of nauseating sweetness, as if he stood in a storeroom full of rotting fruit in the middle of a slaughterhouse. Retching, Howard fumbled the filterfluff out of his belt pouch, ripped it in two, and stuffed the pieces into his nostrils. Then he clamped his mouth shut and tried to put off breathing until he started to feel light-headed.

When he finally gave in, he was amazed at the effectiveness of the fluff. As long as he inhaled only through his nose, it might have been the clear air of the Black and Blue World that filled his lungs. He made a mental note to open his mouth as infrequently as possible on this world.

Howard's vest and shorts had been plastered to his skin almost immediately by the oppressive heat and humidity. It felt like a boiler room. He wiped his forehead with the back of his hand and looked around. The atmosphere swam with eddies of mist, and he shuddered, certain that each current hosted its own particular blend of revolting smells.

With the filterfluff barricading his nose, Howard found himself becoming aware of the considerable visual beauty of the Sinking Swamp World. He stood in a large clearing surrounded by thick tropical underbrush. Fan-shaped leaves topped curving trunks, no thicker than Howard's wrist, that arched thirty feet in the air, the space beneath them heavily curtained with vines and creepers. The vegetation ranged from bright aquas and turquoises to shades of darker blue, and exotic ivory and yellow blooms speckled with scarlet festooned the bases of many plants. There was a golden glow to the air. The sun itself was hidden by a layer of rapidly moving clouds, its light filtering down in broad shafts that permeated portions of the drifting vapor with swirls of radiance in which millions of tiny sparks appeared and vanished in an eyeblink.

Alaiya had released his arm and stepped away as soon as they had arrived. Now she returned to prod his shoulder.

"Move!" she said. "You begin to put down roots."

Howard looked down to see his legs sinking slowly into blue-green quickslime. The mud sucked voraciously at his boots as he tried to lift his feet, prompting a few moments of concern. Then Alaiya grasped his upper arms and wrenched him out of the slime, resuming her own restless back-and-forth hopping as soon as he was free. The other members of the team remained in the loose circle in which Howard had transported them, but they were in constant motion, each warrior in its own fashion. Nearest to him, the two Averoy and the humanoid Domeny jogged lightly in small circles on the mud, while the Attercacks raised and lowered their splayed toes like lizards dancing on a hotplate. The Beranot managed a shuffling dance, the Ga'Prenny a hopping undulation of its entire body. Only the Intzwam, which was apparently as lightweight as its attenuated physique suggested, was able to remain standing in the same place for almost a minute before its narrow feet began to sink into the muck.

"Over there!" Alaiya pointed to a grouping of large, bone-colored growths that Howard recognized from the Hant's description. Of various heights, ranging from ten feet to fifty, they were shaped like gigantic golf tees. Howard had been told that they were actually an edible fungus—though the gray-white pools that ringed their bases were infused with a deadly concentration of corrosive acid.

"We must scale one of the growths," the battlechief said. "It will be a while before the Miscreants arrive. In the meantime, this ceaseless motion in such heat eats up energy we may need later."

She led them onto a narrow, sandy strip that bordered the shallow algae pool in which they had found themselves. The pathways, which were only slightly firmer than the quickslime, crisscrossed the visible area of the swamp. They made their way rapidly to the edge of a scum-surfaced acid lake some hundred and fifty feet in diameter, from which the half-dozen golf tees thrust up like spikes toward the clouds.

At Alaiya's signal the Domeny stalked past Howard, clutching in its strong, brown fingers a transparent pouch filled with greenish powder. It poured a small quantity of the substance into its palm, then flung it in a straight line onto the poisonous-looking liquid in front of them. Within seconds, a six-foot hummock of lime green gel rose out of the pool, growing wider and flatter as the powderbridge extracted moisture from the complicated chemistry of the lake. The Domeny crept cautiously along the newly made bridge and repeated its actions at the far end.

The process took about five minutes. When the powderbridge stretched to the base of the nearest fungus tee—a thirty-foot specimen with a mottle of beige color winding the length of its trunk like pale lace—Alaiya led the rest of the warriors out onto the sticky, slightly yielding material.

The Ga'Prenny, whose name Howard had so far found unpronounceable, carried a coil of slender rope strapped to its broad back. With moisture sluicing from its smooth hide, it fastened a small grapple to one end of the line and hurled it in an arc up over the flared rim of the towering fungus. The top of the tee was softer than the trunklike sides; the hooks caught at once, and the rope grew taut.

The Attercacks went up first, swiftly scaling the thin line. The Averoy and Domeny followed at a slower pace, Chinefwa the Beranot using her powerful arms to cling to Arpenwole's back. The Ga'Prenny was next, and the Nonesuch brought up the rear. As he was shinnying awkwardly up the rope, thinking dark thoughts of high-school gym classes, Howard was startled to see the Intzwam skitter past him up the central column of the fungus. When it reached the top of the stem, the sticklike creature turned without halting and crawled upside down to the flared rim, where it vanished quickly onto the top. Howard felt a little shiver travel up his spine.

Omber Oss was waiting when Howard finally arrived, panting and streaming with sweat, at the lip of the fungus. With a wide grin, the dark-skinned Averoy warrior reached down and hauled his leader up over the edge.

Alaiya began to dole out the contents of their armory—in actuality the large pack carried by Dokkalin, a tall Attercack whose crest was dyed to resemble a rainbow in bright segments from red to violet. Each warrior already possessed a hand weapon of its own. In addition, Alaiya had assigned certain unique devices or substances to the individuals she judged best able to utilize them. Howard raised his eyebrows hopefully when the battlechief neared him, but Alaiya shook her head, handing a small pouch filled with black, marble-sized spheres to Chinefwa instead.

"You have your sword, Ahwerd—and you have the Key." She pointed to the golden object on his chest. "And that is the most powerful weapon in our arsenal."

"I know. So why do I feel like I was invited to come along just because I'm the only one who could borrow some wheels?" He sat down cross-legged on the spongy surface of the tee and watched glumly as the other warriors performed exercises to prepare themselves for possible battle.

Alaiya patted his head. "I am certain that you understand," she said. "If we lose the Key, then all is lost. That is why I would like you to remain up here when we descend to confront the Miscreants."

"Yeah, yeah," Howard muttered to himself. "You kids go on and have a good time. I'll just sit here and keep the station wagon running."

They waited. After a while, Howard used his machete to carve two horizontal lines on the impressionable surface of the tee, crossing them with two vertical lines. It did not take him long to teach Oss and Chinefwa the rudiments of ticktacktoe.

Halfway through their fourth tournament, the Beranot raised a webbed arm and called Alaiya over to inform her that it was nearly time to leave their refuge. Only the Beranoi and the Hant still had reliable internal clocks; the other warriors had lost their time-sense with the purging of their parleybugs. Howard glanced at the pale band still visible against the tan on his left wrist and sighed.

The warriors silently descended the tee, leaving Howard behind. The powderbridge had been placed so that neither it nor the rope would be visible from the side of the clearing where the Miscreants were scheduled to appear.

Howard moved to the edge of the tee and stretched out on his stomach, supporting himself on his elbows as he peered down at the clearing. The Breakneck Boys took up prearranged positions behind clumps of vegetation. Howard watched as the nine warriors stood in careful concealment, eyes trained on the blue jungle, all the while keeping their lower extremities in motion, at varying tempos and as quietly as possible. From his vantage point, they looked like a bunch of children who refused to give up their hide-and-seek game in order to take the bathroom break they desperately needed.

Long minutes passed. At last, there was movement in the vegetation at the edge of the clearing. Gestures rippled down the line of Breakneck Boys as the Howling Miscreants slipped into view one by one. They were dressed in uniforms of pale brown. As they made their way single file along one of the sandy central paths, Howard nodded at the accuracy of Alaiya's choices for her own team members; the Miscreants consisted of three Ga'Prenny, an Averoy, two Beranoi, an Attercack, and a Domeny. The brown-clad warriors were well into the clearing, in an area where the sandy paths narrowed to a hand's width and they were forced to pick their way carefully through the algae-covered pools, when Alaiya gave her signal. The Breakneck Boys stepped silently out of hiding, their weapons drawn and at the ready. The Miscreants reacted in panic and confusion, shouting to one another as they tried to maneuver in the treacherous quickslime. It made for a strange tableau—the line of startled Miscreants and the encircling cordon of Breakneck Boys, all engaged in the ceaseless motion necessary to prevent them from sinking below the surface of the swamp.

The battlechief had chosen the site of her ambush well: the Miscreants stood trapped between the approaching Breakneck Boys and the edge of the acid lake. Alaiya called out to the brown-clad Averoy, who shouted back at her, motioning to his teammates. According to Alaiya, the current leader of the Miscreants was a Ga'Prenny, probably the largest of the three who hopped and undulated below, necklaces of red and gold beads draped across the front of its dull uniform.

Alaiya sheathed her dagger and approached the enemy leader with her own Ga'Prenny in tow. There was a brief skirmish when one of the Miscreant Beranoi attempted to launch his own attack on the Breakneck Boys. Howard fingered his Key anxiously as a small projectile launched from one of the Beranot's wildly swinging arms narrowly missed Alaiya's head. In the end the rebel was subdued by his own team members, and Alaiya began her negotiations with the Miscreant Ga'Prenny, aided by her flat-bodied translator. The other Breakneck Boys moved closer, and a general cacophony ensued as they delivered prepared messages of peace and goodwill to members of their own kind among the Miscreants. Soon the clearing was filled with the yowling, clanking, and wheezing Howard had come to identify with meaningful discourse on the Fading Worlds.

Finally, Alaiya raised her face toward the tee on which Howard lay and motioned for him to climb down and join the group. Feeling like a child summoned to meet visiting relatives, Howard got to his feet and started toward the far side of the great disk, already wincing at the image of himself inching clumsily down the swaying rope while the crowd watched. Halfway to the edge, it occurred to him that there was a way he might make a slightly more dramatic entrance into the midst of the two teams. Holding the Key out from his chest, he walked back to the other side of the tee. He was about to call out to Alaiya to prepare her for his imminent miraculous appearance when he caught a glimpse of sudden motion. Looking out over the crisscross of slender trees, he saw figures dressed in brilliant orange moving stealthily through a small sandy area separated from the clearing by a wall of interwoven vines and dark blue underbrush. He saw complicated silver weapons being handed out as silent orders traveled along the line of orange-clad warriors from an exceptionally tall Attercack, who gestured imperiously with its four arms as its followers slipped into their places. Looking down at the Breakneck Boys, whose backs were to the newcomers, Howard realized that he was witnessing the last few seconds of preparation before the launch of a massacre.

Howard took a good look at the line of enemy warriors, fixing the pattern in his mind. Cupping his hands around his mouth, he let forth with a single wild war whoop. Then he closed his eyes and turned the Key. Less than a second later he was standing unsteadily in the middle of the interim camp on the Black and Blue World, and two startled Breakneck Boys dressed in black and silver were turning to look at him.

"Hi, guys," Howard said. "Just passing through." Then he concentrated on his next destination, took a quick breath, and turned the Key again.

He appeared about three feet in front of the gray-skinned leader of the Rain of Blood, looking into an expression of utter and profound surprise. Hearing Howard's cry from the top of the tee, the towering creature had apparently started its warriors forward. Now it skidded in the quickslime, striving to halt before it collided with the strange apparition that confronted it.

"Care to rethink this move?" Howard asked the baffled Attercack. "My team has some excellent entry-level positions, and we're willing to match your current benefit package." He was giving the Key another turn even as the Attercack stumbled back to raise a deadly-looking spear tipped with an odd corkscrew device. In an instant Howard was on the Black and Blue World again, his heart pounding wildly. The Domeny and Ga'Prenny who had witnessed his recent appearance had been joined by a third Breakneck Boy. The three broke off their ex-

cited conversation to stare in bewilderment as Howard winked
in and out of existence yet again.

This time he appeared in front of a burly Dratzul located to the
far left of the Blood's leader. The creature bellowed in shock and
aimed a small pistol-like weapon as Howard vanished once more.

Back to the Black and Blue World, then on to the next enemy,
in the middle right of the advancing line. Howard stuck his
tongue out and shook his head rapidly from side to side at an
enormous Ga'Prenny holding whirling, whiplike devices in each
flexible, three-fingered hand. A twist of the Key sent him back
to the interim camp, his head swimming as he strove to hold on
to the zigzag pattern he had established in his mind.

The next warrior to be confronted on the Sinking Swamp World
was of a species he had never seen before—its body was a bulging
sack of pinkish, highly elastic skin that seemed to be packed with
an assortment of randomly protruding bones. The thing shrieked
when Howard appeared in front of it, dropping the sword it was
holding in one of several clawlike appendages.

By his seventh trip to the Black and Blue World, a small crowd
had gathered. Howard gave a ragged smile as they waved and
cheered him on during the brief seconds he remained in their midst.

Then he was once more standing before the leader of the Rain
of Blood. To either side of him, the attacking line surged with cries
of astonishment and rage. He heard other sounds behind him; he
hoped the Breakneck Boys had discovered the stalled ambush.

The Attercack still held its spear poised to strike. Howard
pointed his own machete at the Attercack's crest, a carefully
trimmed brush of six-inch quills colored in alternating patches
of pink and charcoal.

"Interesting dye job," he said, beginning to tremble with
fatigue and dizziness. "Definitely a 'fifties' look."

The Attercack gave a rattling scream and swung its weapon
down to within an inch of Howard's head. Yellow sparks spat from
the corkscrew tip, and the air began to quiver with intense heat.

"Hey," Howard said. "I wasn't criticizing! Sure, it's a fashion risk, but you seem like the kind of guy who could pull it
off." He clutched the Key, ready to continue his plan of chaotic
distraction for as long as he was able. There was a low humming
sound from behind him, and the Attercack's head jerked back
suddenly on its tall neck, a shiny black ball the size of a marble
embedding itself with a dull thud in its left eye.

Looking over his shoulder, Howard saw Chinefwa winding
up her sinewy arm for another throw as the curtain of vines and

underbrush was ripped apart by the appendages of a dozen warriors, some in black and some in pale brown uniforms. Noise
and motion were everywhere. Howard stared around him, trying
to take in the scene, as screams and the sounds of strange weaponry tore the air. He was staring downward, watching his boots
sink slowly into blue-green slime, when Alaiya appeared at his
side. "I'm really tired now," he muttered as she put her arms
around him. "Do you think you could find me a place to lie
down where I won't get killed?"

He awoke to an overwhelming feeling of déjà vu. He was
lying on top of his bed-mound on the Red Desert World while
a reek of dissolving flesh rose from the body of the Trull warrior
hidden among the carnivorous fronds below. But the sky was
wrong. Howard rubbed his eyes and squinted at the swiftly moving clouds above him as shafts of golden sunlight flashed and
vanished. The air swam with humidity.

The smell was right. He brought his fingers to his nose and
discovered that the filterfluff had become dislodged from his
right nostril. He must have been snoring for some time before
that, at any rate; the nauseating odor seemed to have coated his
mouth. He smacked his lips in disgust.

He rolled over onto his side and stretched, trying to keep his
jaw clenched shut through the yawn that followed, and noticed
faint markings on the surface beneath him. Looking closer, he
saw that they were the remnants of one of his recent ticktacktoe
victories. Seeing the healed tissue reminded him that he lay on
a living organism. Alaiya had said the fungus was edible. Howard wondered idly how it tasted, though his stomach rebelled at
the thought of ingesting food amidst the stench of the Sinking
Swamp World.

He heard a noise that might have been voices and got slowly
to his feet. Most of his crushing fatigue had vanished, though
the world still rocked a bit when he moved. He had no idea how
long he had slept. His boots and belt had been removed and laid
with his sword by his side. He groped for the Key where it lay
beneath his loose vest and cupped it in his palm; at least he
could be sure the others had not left the world without him. He
padded to the edge of the giant golf tee and peered down.

Alaiya stood with her back to him on a lower tee about twenty
feet away. Facing her were two warriors. It took Howard a moment to realize the significance of their bright orange uniforms,
another moment to see that Alaiya was holding them at swords-

point. Reluctant to distract her, Howard watched silently as she removed something from her belt and passed it to one of the captives, directing the warrior with gestures to apply it to its comrade. Howard guessed that it was the twiglike substance known as tanglewood, an organic restraint with which he himself had been bound on more than one occasion. When the arms of the smaller of the warriors, a Domeny, had been secured to her satisfaction, Alaiya suddenly pointed past its teammate with a cry of astonishment. As the blue-crested Attercack turned to follow her gesture, she reversed her sword and clubbed it neatly at the base of its narrow skull. The warrior sank to its knees, and Alaiya went briskly about the task of binding its four arms behind its back.

"I'd sure hate to get on your bad side," Howard called as she finished her work and rose to her feet.

Alaiya turned and saluted him with her sword. "You have rejoined us!"

"Yup. I've been thinking about making myself a mushroom omelet." He lowered himself to a sitting position near the rim of the tee. "Only we don't have a frying pan or any eggs." He tipped his head to the two prisoners. "What's going on?"

"About half the Rain of Blood declined to accept our offer of friendship following the death of their leader. I sent the others off to look for them while I remained here with you. A short time ago I looked over the edge and saw these unlucky ones skulking below." She gave the Attercack a light kick with her boot, and it stirred and made a soft gargling sound. "After I subdued them, I decided to cast another grapple and bring them up to this growth, so as not to disturb your well-earned slumber."

"I appreciate that." Howard watched as she knelt to apply the binding root to the ankles of the Domeny. "You caught these guys all by yourself?"

Alaiya gave the Averoy hand-shrug. "There were only three of them."

"Three?" Howard frowned.

"The Pasper is new to the Fading Worlds," she said. "He had difficulty understanding that he had no hope of defeating me." Leaning to one side, she directed Howard's gaze to a large algae pool some distance from the acid lake. A twisted form lay in the center of the muck, its jet black fur coated with thick green-blue slime. "A pity, as he bears unusually attractive coloration for one of his race."

"Is he dead?" Narrowing his eyes, Howard thought he saw a trickle of dark crimson against the orange uniform.

"No, his wounds are not life-threatening in themselves. But he has fallen onto a coil of rotten vine, and that is all that keeps him from sinking beneath the quickslime. Should he change position or make any attempt to extricate himself, he will surely experience a rapid descent."

"Oh. Are we going to take him with us, then? There's always a chance we could talk some sense into him."

"If you like." Alaiya smiled and shook her head. "You are a forgiving sort of creature, Ahwerd—always ready to hold out your hand to all manner of devious mis-robe. I used to think that was a flaw in your nature."

"And now?"

Another shrug. "Perhaps there are things we are learning from each other." She turned back to her captives, checking their bonds as the Attercack lifted its long neck groggily and rose to its feet in a series of awkward jerks.

"Is everybody else okay?" Howard asked, scanning the empty clearing and the blue jungle beyond it. "Were there any casualties on our side?"

"None. The recruiting effort went better than we could have hoped, thanks to your timely intervention. We gained the entire membership of the Howling Miscreants, as well as four skilled warriors from the Rain of Blood. You seem to have a great talent for descending to our rescue whenever the battle turns against us. Perhaps you should be stationed on high ground during every time of conflict."

Howard laughed, dangling his legs over the edge of the tee. "Pure luck," he said. "Personally, I think I'd do better with the USO." He strummed an imaginary guitar and snapped his fingers. "Doo-wa, sh'bop-bop! Want me to sing you something while you work, soldier?"

Alaiya shuddered expressively, her back turned as she tightened the Domeny's restraints. "Thank you, Ahwerd, but I have already experienced your singing."

"Oh. Too much of a good thing, huh?" Howard fastened his belt around his waist and began to draw on his boots. "Well, how about a recitation? What would be appropriate for this pungent paradise?" He spat carefully into the acid lake and surveyed the landscape. "I know—here's something I memorized during my single miserable semester of grad school." He cleared his throat and lifted his arm dramatically.

"In Köhln, a town of monks and bones,
And pavements fang'd with murderous stones
And rags, and hags, and hideous wenches;
I counted two and seventy stenches,
All well defined, and several stinks!
Ye Nymphs that reign o'er sewers and sinks—"

"Ahwerd!" Alaiya stood with her eyes wide, her ivory-golden arm outstretched as she pointed at him with her sword.

"Ah, I take it Coleridge isn't your cup of bigtassle. Well, let's see . . ." Howard leaned back and into the spreading shadow of something huge and dark.

"What is—" He blinked and twisted on the smooth surface of the tee, trying to make sense of the shape that loomed behind him.

Dropping silently toward him through the glowing mists was what appeared to be a gigantic spider hanging from a hot-air balloon. It took him a moment to realize that it was all one creature, an impossible floating monster some twenty-five feet in length from the top of its bulging gasbag to the tips of its dozen whiplike arms.

Howard stumbled to his feet and stared as the thing glided toward him above the surface of the tee. Its skin was moist and black, with a pattern of scarlet ovals girdling the distended air sac. Six blood-red eyes encircled the bottom sphere, and below them hung the flexing tentacles, the longest of which was nearly Howard's height. As it began to close the few yards that remained between them, the thing made a loud hissing noise. It bobbed slightly from side to side as it floated nearer, and Howard's gaze was drawn to the bright, hypnotic pattern on its air sac. He shook his head and tried to think, still disoriented by the effects of his recent ordeal. On the other side of the tee, past the mass of coiling purplish black arms, lay the grapple and the rope. Beneath him was the acid lake. He felt for his sword, then spotted it several feet away on the spongy surface.

"Ahwerd!" Alaiya's voice was raw with emotion. "The Key!"

As he turned to her, the spider-balloon gave a hiss that sounded like the airbrakes of a tractor-trailer and dropped several feet with frightening swiftness. Snakelike tentacles struck at him as he tried to lift the Key away from his body, snaring it and his right arm in a constrictor's grip. Then the creature began to rise. Pain lanced through Howard's shoulder. A clear fluid ran from hidden openings near the base of the sinuous arms; Howard's skin burned for a second where the liquid touched it, then lost all feeling. He felt his feet lift from the surface of the fungus as the spider-balloon rose into the golden mists.

"Ahwerd, look at me!"

He tried to control his panic, twisting his neck to stare down at the lower tee. Alaiya stood with her sword arm raised.

"You will catch my sword! I know that you can do this! Ready now—" She reversed the blade and tossed it lightly in his direction. Howard lunged against the pull of the monster, his left arm straining outward. As the flat of the blade struck the back of his hand and began to fall, two powerful tentacles encircled it.

"I missed!" he shouted to Alaiya. "I missed it!" Something shot through the air a foot above his head, burying itself solidly between two of the crimson eyes. Arms writhed frantically about the base of Alaiya's dagger and the creature dipped and yawed. Recovering, it began to rise faster, a hollow, windy sound coming from inside it.

The sword still hung wrapped in several nearby tentacles, its blade pointing upward at a forty-five degree angle. As Howard saw the disk of the tee begin to spin below him, he reached out with his left hand and grasped the hilt. His fingers slipped and burned as the numbing fluid bathed them. With a choked cry, he gave the blade a sharp twist and with all his strength drove it upward into the bottom of the gasbag.

There was a screech like a steam whistle, and an incredible variety of internal structures spewed from the pulsing wound, all of them dark and coated with clear liquid. Numbness played over Howard's body like a cold flame as the smooth surface of the tee rose to pound his back.

He lay still for a long moment, the world whirling about him. Then he used his elbows to drag himself laboriously from beneath the deflating carcass. It seemed only seconds before Alaiya was kneeling over him, cradling his head in her arms. Howard lifted his left hand with difficulty and pointed toward the ruined monster. The battlechief's dagger still protruded from the ring of filmy red eyes, and the hilt of her sword was visible in the pulpy mess beside it.

"Thanks for the loan of your stuff," he said in a shaky whisper. "Remind me to clean it up a little before I give it back."

CHAPTER IX

Small Change

WHEN THEY RETURNED HALF AN HOUR LATER, THE warriors had the single remaining fugitive from the Rain of Blood with them. They stowed the sullen-eyed Domeny on the middle-sized golf tee with its two fellows, then climbed the tallest growth and assembled for mutual introductions and a discussion of their next move.

Most of the feeling had returned to Howard's limbs, though at the moment he would have welcomed a few more hours of numbness. Limping slightly on Alaiya's arm, he went to greet the newcomers. At the battlechief's suggestion, he was trying his best to look stern and omnipotent. "They must learn you are not to be treated with other than awe," she had said.

One of his nose filters had worked loose again, and he suddenly got a strong whiff of the Sinking Swamp World as he was being presented to the erstwhile battlechief of the Howling Miscreants. Howard turned away, gagging, and jammed the fluff awkwardly back into place, wincing as bruised muscles protested his sudden movements. He sighed.

The Ga'Prenny approached him hesitantly on bowed legs. It made noises that sounded like someone trying out an accordion for the first time.

"Keyholder!" translated the Breakneck Boy Ga'Prenny who stood at his side. "O mighty, mighty Keyholder!"

"Not really," Howard said. "Just an incredible simulation."

The Miscreant blinked its two vertically positioned eyes doubtfully when Howard's comments were conveyed to it. It wheezed and hummed for a while.

"You pop in, out, come, go like Keyholder," it insisted through the translator.

"I know that, but I'm not a Keyholder. I just happen—well—to be holding a Key." Howard frowned. "I know it seems like a subtle distinction, but, believe me, it makes a world of difference."

The two flounderlike warriors sang back and forth for a few minutes.

"Interesting language," Howard commented to Omber Oss, who was watching the exchange from nearby. "Sounds like the dueling harmonicas from that travelogue about Southern waterways." Oss nodded politely.

"Okay, I tell her you not serve Keyholders," the Breakneck Boy translator reported. "She seem almost believe, think inside maybe trick." The flat body leaned toward Howard in a confidential manner. "You give big present, she believe. You got shelterstone, amoeba suit?"

"No gifts." Alaiya interposed herself smoothly between Howard and the translator. "If she does not wish to join us, she is welcome to share the fate of those we battle."

"Wait a minute, hold on." Howard raised his hands between the two. "Maybe a little dramatic gesture would help things along. Say your word for 'Keyholder' again, okay?"

The translator produced a sound like an out of tune saxophone. Howard imitated the noise as best he could, screwed his face up in exaggerated distaste, and spat dramatically onto the pale fungus. "Yuck!" he said. "We hate the Keyholders!" He looked at the team leader hopefully. "Does she get the picture?"

"Ahwerd." Alaiya put her hand on his shoulder and spoke quietly into his ear. "On their Holding, the Ga'Prenny prepare food for ingestion by spitting enzymes onto it. When performed in conversation, the act communicates great reverence or admiration for the topic under discussion."

"Ah." Howard glanced at the two Ga'Prenny, who were engaged in a round of agitated honking. "I don't suppose you know what I'd have to do in order to indicate the opposite opinion?"

Alaiya gave the Averoy sniff of negation. "It is not an activity you could successfully perform without serious damage to some important body parts." She squeezed his shoulder. "You have made a strong impression with your actions during the raid. Best to leave further negotiations to those already skilled in the various tongues. You may trust me that your viewpoints will be well represented.''

Howard shrugged and stepped to the edge of the tee as the familiar Babel of wildly different languages rose behind him. Several hundred feet away, the black-furred Pasper still lay curled on its side in the algae pool.

''Look—'' Howard turned back to Alaiya. ''If you people don't need me for a while, I'm going to get that guy some help. It bothers me to see him lying down there when he might be in pain.''

Alaiya looked surprised, then went to speak briefly to a member of the Rain of Blood through a Breakneck Boy interpreter. She returned to Howard's side. ''His teammates agree that he is young, and most likely confused by recent events. He may offer no resistance if you attempt to assist him.'' She raised her eyebrows slightly. ''Or he may open your face with his claws.''

''I'll be okay.'' Howard slipped his curved sword into its sheath. ''I'm going to bring him to the Black and Blue World before he sneezes or something and finds himself on the bottom of that pool. I'll be back before you know it.''

He threaded his way through the crowd and descended the rope with frustrating slowness, panting with exertion by the time he touched ground. He made his way around the acid lake, skipping awkwardly to avoid sinking. Glancing upward at the top of the tee, he saw that he was being watched by dozens of curious eyes.

He reached the algae pool and waded slowly into the muck. The Pasper watched him silently with eyes like matched opals. When Howard was almost within touching distance, the fallen warrior reacted to his presence for the first time by raising his upper lip in a protracted hiss.

''Whoa.'' Howard felt the hairs stand up along his arms. He backed away slightly, conscious of the mud sucking at his boots. From above and behind him, he heard Omber Oss call, ''Ahwerdbel, are needing assistance?''

''No, we're doing fine,'' he yelled back, trying to keep the annoyance out of his voice. He scowled at the motionless Pasper. ''Look, buddy, you're going to have to stretch, or scratch, or do something, sooner or later.'' He spread his arms, speaking in a soothing tone. ''I'm being nice, see? My sword's tucked away where it can't hurt either of us, and I have only your best interests at heart. But my legs are sore and I won't be able to stand here treading slime forever, so I suggest you let me touch you and we'll both get the heck out of here . . ." He leaned forward as he spoke, inching his left hand toward the matted fur of the Pasper's upper arm. The opal eyes followed him, but the mouth remained shut, two points of white protruding slightly below the bifurcated lip. Howard felt his feet begin to settle into the muck as he stilled all movement but the slow progress of his left hand.

At last Howard's fingers grazed the mud-caked shoulder. "All right," he said with a soft release of breath. "This is good." He looked down. Blue-green quickslime was creeping toward the tops of his boots. He moved the back of his hand gently along the black-furred arm, making sure to maintain solid contact as he used his right hand to draw the Key from his vest. The Pasper's eyes grew wide when Howard extended the golden object on its thong, anchoring it in his left hand as he gripped the filigreed handle with his right. He gave a reassuring smile. "We are outta here," Howard said as he turned the Key.

The world went black and stayed black. Howard found himself at an odd angle, his feet jammed against something hard in front of him. He was holding onto the Key and the Key was attached halfway up a vertical surface, forcing Howard to stand hunched like a water-skier. The Pasper moved convulsively near his legs, the fur of his arm slipping from under Howard's hand. He dropped to the ground with a muffled yelp. After a few moments, Howard could make out an eerie, reddish glow coming from some distance away. As he blinked in confusion, he noticed a patch of shiny material on the wall in front of him. His shoulders slumped wearily.

"Oh, God, not again." He reached down for the Pasper. When his fingers touched the soft fur, the warrior gave a strangled cry and jerked his body away. "Oh, for—get back here!"

Howard stretched his left hand out toward the almost invisible figure, but kept his right still wrapped around the Key, which seemed to be jammed in the lock of the door to the Executive Washroom. The Pasper backed up against the opposite wall and sat staring at him, gemstone eyes an eerie yellow-green in the light from the distant exit sign.

"Come here," Howard whispered. He held out his left hand, reluctant to release the Key. "God, you remind me of my aunt's cat, sitting there like that. Give me a dog, any time. I wish I had an electric can opener—that's the only thing Speedy would come running for."

There was a sharp cracking noise at the far end of the corridor.

Howard looked up in alarm to see something large move in the shadows beneath the exit sign.

The Pasper had turned its attention to the source of the noise. Holding his breath, Howard released the Key and lunged forward, grabbing the sleek arm and yanking the warrior back as he groped behind him. His fingers closed on the cool metal handle. He squeezed his eyes shut and gave it a twist.

Bright daylight flooded his eyes when he opened them seconds later. High above, iron-colored clouds massed like great vessels in a cobalt sky, and jagged black peaks ringed the horizon. Howard sat down heavily in the rose-red moss and exhaled a long breath. At his side, the Pasper stood frozen, eyes darting from side to side.

"This is our stop," Howard said. "Welcome to the Black and Blue World—we hope you enjoy its quaint shops and Old World charm. Please remember your luggage when you leave the train." He heard anxious voices nearby. Turning, he watched black-suited warriors race toward them from the interim camp. He leaned back onto the feathery moss and sighed as the cool breeze blew over his face and body.

In fifteen minutes, he was back on a fungus tee on the Sinking Swamp World, his uniform soaked and sweat dripping regularly from his nose and chin.

He had arrived in the middle of a debate concerning the disposition of the remaining prisoners. There was a brief hiatus while those warriors unfamiliar with the Nonesuch discussed his miraculous return in low, excited tones. To play it safe, Howard had brought himself back to one of the sandy pathways. This had seemed more prudent than appearing on the tee itself, running the risk of startling one of his teammates into an inadvertent plunge into the acid lake. When he reached the spongy surface of the tee, Alaiya took him aside for a moment to fill him in. On the other side of the small crowd—which now numbered more than twenty warriors clothed in uniforms of black, brown and bright orange—Arpenwole declaimed in halting English, while members of the Breakneck Boys strove to translate her words into a variety of alien tongues. The silver-haired Averoy warrior, who had apparently attempted to kill the fourth fugitive during its capture, was arguing vehemently for the speedy demise of their unwilling guests, declaring that they would never be worthy of trust, and could cause only grief if they were brought back to the Breakneck Boy's encampment.

Surprisingly, Alaiya refused to share her own opinion, deferring the matter entirely to the judgment of the Nonesuch. "We risk anarchy if decisions are not limited to a selected few."

"Yeah, or even an outbreak of rampant democracy." Howard walked to the center of the group and lowered himself with a grunt to sit cross-legged on the yielding fungus. Most of the warriors instantly assumed their own equivalents of a sitting position. Arpenwole grudgingly joined them, after a disdainful look to either side.

"Well," Howard said, "it looks to me like we have a couple of options." He tapped the index finger of his left hand. "We can haul these three to the Black and Blue World, where—from what you tell me—they'll probably do their damnedest to try to escape back to the Keyholders. Or—" He touched his middle finger. "We can make it easier on all concerned and just leave them right here to wait for the Fade and a chance to make their way back to Stillpoint."

Arpenwole raised an eyebrow and pointed to his third finger. "You have not mentioned slitting the mis-robes' throats, and so putting an end to this problem here and now."

Howard shook his head calmly, examining his palm. "That option doesn't exist," he said.

A babble of conversation ensued as Howard's words made their way through several translations. He raised his hands for attention.

"Listen to me, you who claim you are willing to follow the Nonesuch. The Keyholders kill without a thought. To them, loss of life means only sport and entertainment. Warriors who know no other existence kill because they are ordered to do so by those who control their lives. But in this battle-gang—which I hope will be the last battle-gang to be established in these Fading Worlds—we take life only to protect ourselves and our teammates. This is our first law. If you can't abide by it, you have to go elsewhere." He allowed his eyes to wander over the score of faces, then slapped his palms on his thighs and pushed himself to his feet. "Take your time, think it over. Let us know when you've decided." He motioned to Alaiya, leaning heavily on her shoulder when she came to his side.

"I'm so sore," he whispered. "Let's go sit down over there and pretend we're discussing something incredibly profound."

"Your talk was very forceful." Alaiya supported him without appearing to as they walked to the other side of the tee. "I was amazed to hear such resolve."

"I'm cranky and I'm sore and I'm really tired again," he said, once more seating himself. "It makes me impatient with long discussions."

"You should attain this state more often," Alaiya said.

After a while, another Averoy approached, seating himself across from them at Howard's nod. He was of a racial type different from the Averoy Howard had already seen, with kinky golden-brown hair and narrow black eyes set above the high cheekbones of his red-brown face. Alaiya introduced the man as Kormender, an old acquaintance from her days with the Howling Miscreants.. "He also knew Sermantry, who died at the Black Cliffs," she said. "They were children together on the Holding."

"Ah. Pleased to meet you." Howard held out his hand. After a moment's hesitation, the other man took it, murmuring a few words of polite response in Averant.

"So, how do your teammates feel about this new situation in which they find themselves?" Howard asked in the same language. Kormender's eyes widened slightly.

"Some of the newer recruits are not so certain," the warrior said slowly. "They have not yet had time to become sick of fighting, and may fear they are being tricked into dishonor."

"I hope they learn to trust us," Howard said. "We will need their help."

"Yes." Kormender nodded his agreement. "The Redborn has told me some of what you have already accomplished, and what you hope to do in the future. It is a great striving, an undertaking undreamed of for many generations."

In time other members of the group, both old and new, came to join them. All of the new warriors had decided to cooperate— at least for the time being—and allow themselves to be transported to the interim camp, there to be purged of their parleybugs before journeying on to Field of Flowers.

Howard had requested another hour of rest before using his Key again. As the Breakneck Boys gathered for their departure, the three orange-suited prisoners were relieved of their bonds and their belts. Howard watched from the edge of the tee, smiling at the amazement on the faces of the captives when they learned that their lives were to be spared.

Alaiya paused for several moments at the base of the fungus growth, doing something to the trunk with her sword, before ascending the tee one final time. She wore a small smile when she took her place by Howard's side in a wide ring of warriors.

"What were you up to down there?" he asked. "Defacing the local monuments?"

"I was leaving a message in the written tongue used by all battle-gangs," she said. "It will heal in a matter of days, but perhaps some servant of the Keyholders will come upon it first. It was the thing you once told me about: the peering face and the words underneath. Of course, I had to modify it slightly to fit the occasion."

Howard was mystified. "What on Earth are you talking about?"

"Here, you have learned enough warrior speech." Alaiya scratched rapid characters in the soft fungus at their feet.

Howard narrowed his eyes at the crude letters. "The Breakneck Boys . . . once occupied . . . this location." He shook his head with a laugh. "Let me finish it!" Drawing his own sword, he moved the point higher and sketched part of a round face in the fungus. The face had an exceedingly large nose, most of which hung over the front of a wall or fence, which Howard had represented with a simple horizontal line. "Kilroy would be proud," he said, sheathing his sword and placing Alaiya's hand on his arm. "Can we go now?"

"One more thing." She extended her blade again, tongue poking past her teeth, and added a small V beneath the nose. Then she carefully drew an odd-shaped, sticklike object directly below the spot where the two diagonals met.

"What's that?" Howard asked.

"You cannot tell?" Alaiya looked around, then reached up and solemnly tweaked his nose. "That is your Key."

Howard stopped to check on the black-furred Pasper before leaving the quarantine camp. Kimmence, an Averoy woman with purplish skin who had been Arpenwole's teammate in the Exacting Cyclone, assured him that they were taking good care of the feline warrior. "Sleeping now," said Kimmence, tugging with her left hand at one of her black curls. "Seem full of shock when you bring here, later better. Small wound to chest, to leg." She made the Averoy hand-shrug. "His race take many time long for purge pod. You come back two, three day, maybe ready move."

The cleansing pods had been administered to all members of the two newly-converted teams. Due to the varying metabolisms of the warriors, it would be three local days before the last new Breakneck Boy was declared free of the parasitical interpreters.

Leaving behind three of his black-suited followers to assist those already present in the camp, Howard returned with Alaiya and the others to Field of Flowers.

The sun was spreading banners of coral and maroon above the dark line of trees when they arrived in the center of the encampment. Howard went straightaway to the Trilbit's small hut. A coarse fiber curtain cloaked the doorway. Howard stood outside for a moment, listening for the distinctive sound of his friend's snore. Finally, he tapped lightly on the doorjamb. "Yam? You in there?"

"Ow-er-bel!" There was a brief rustling; then Yam's blunt muzzle poked past the curtain. "You are back safe and round."

"Sound," Howard said. "How about you—how're you doing?" He bent to give the little warrior a cautious hug. "Still under the weather with this farrowing-change thing?"

"Over with." Yam reached back inside the hut and withdrew two of the fiber mats. "Now feeling round as a dollar."

"Sound." Howard sighed with relief. "So that's it—you're all back to normal?" He squinted at Yam in the deepening twilight. "You know, I didn't want to pry, but I wasn't too sure what was happening with this change stuff. I thought maybe you were going to pull an Awp on me and end up seven feet tall or something."

"Small change only, Ow-er-bel." Yam brought forth a water sack and a small porcelain pot. "Natural way of Trilbit body: once, twice each Round, adjustments occur. Much appreciation for your concern, however." The small hand paused above a canister of aromatic leaves. "Tea?"

Howard gave Yam a capsule version of the events of the day, pausing at the end before mentioning his return trip to the hallway of the Matrix Building.

"Back to your home world again, Ow-er-bel?" Lines creased the Trilbit's velvet brow. "Have you consulted the Hant for an opinion on these strange happenings?"

"I haven't said anything to anybody yet, except you," Howard confessed. He drank the last of his tea and rubbed the cup thoughtfully against his cheek. "I didn't want to start people worrying. Anyway, it only happens when I'm not concentrating. I'll just have to remember to keep my mind on the road from now on."

"Hopeful that is sufficient remedy—" Yam gave a cavernous yawn. "Would not wish you lost in this dark corridor."

"I don't think that's likely to happen." Howard paused for

his own protracted yawn, then laughed. "Whoa. Day's catching up with us. Looks like we could both use some shut-eye." He handed over his cup and pushed to his feet with a groan. "Tell you what—breakfast at my place, sometime before noon. Deal?"

"Deal." Yam stifled another yawn. "Pleased you came through this day safe as a dollar, Ow-er-bel."

"Likewise."

On his way to his own tent, Howard looked for Awp. The Hant had established no fixed abode, sleeping only rarely and preferring the bottoms of the forest pools for its periods of meditation. Howard was pleasantly surprised to see the towering creature heading in his direction as he neared the center of the encampment.

"Greetings, Hawa. Alaiya tells me you have spent a most productive day."

Howard gave a rueful laugh and patted one of the massive arms. "Yeah, productive of bruises, anyway. I'm glad I ran into you. I'm heading for the sheets right now, but there are a few things I'd like to run by you tomorrow, if you're planning on being above water."

"Certainly. I have been isolating berry pigments for the past few hours. Tomorrow morning, I am hoping to make watercolor sketches of the flower sea. We can meet at the shoreline north of camp if you wish."

"Sounds great. Well, I'm glad I caught you." Howard turned toward the center of the camp, where cheerful cookfires blazed. "I spent sometime over at Yam's little hacienda. I was kind of concerned, but the patient seems to have fully recovered from whatever was going on."

"Indeed," the Hant said. "She assured me of that when I visited her this afternoon. Have a pleasant evening, Hawa."

Howard had taken several steps into the shadows between two tents before he stopped and turned around. "Hey, Awp," he called to the retreating figure. "Did you just say 'she'?"

"Indeed." The Hant returned to their meeting place, a thoughtful expression on its broad, pale face. "Hawa, am I correct in assuming that you are ignorant of the ramifications of the farrowing-change among Trilbits?"

Howard stood for a long time without replying. "Boy," he said finally, shaking his head as he started off once more in the direction of his tent. "You don't get days like this very often."

CHAPTER X

Green Eggs and Yam

HOWARD ROSE EARLY, MAKING HIS WAY TO THE SMALL promontory that faced the flower sea while the sun was still half-hidden behind the horizon.

He sat with his legs drawn up in front of him, gnawing on the wad of Averoy foodstuff he carried in his belt. Visions of breakfasts past tormented him as he chewed the bland substance, filling his thoughts with eggs over easy bracketed by crisp bacon with a stack of fragrant pancakes waiting nearby; Frosted Flakes and sliced bananas swimming in cream; biscuits melting with butter and jeweled with the deep purple of grape jelly; a single, perfect blueberry Poptart . . .

He swallowed one last greasy sliver with a sigh and replaced the foodstuff in its pouch. He knew he should be grateful for this creation of the Keyholders, even if the motivation behind it was to keep their in peak fighting condition. If consumed in small portions, and allowed to regenerate sufficiently between feedings, one lump of the substance could theoretically last for many years, providing the warriors with both food and water. Each race had its own special blend, keyed to the requirements of the species.

Howard leaned back, hands clasped at his knees, letting the brisk morning winds from the endless meadow blow over him with their mint-scented currents. His vantage on the sloping rocks was too cool for the shorts and sandals that were his only garments, but he made no move to return to his tent, only hunching his shoulders a little against the bite of the breeze. He jumped slightly when the broad hand fell on his shoulder.

"Pardon me, Hawa. Am I disturbing you?" The Hant stood behind him, arms laden with homemade art supplies.

"No, I was just watching the sun come up." Howard cleared his throat and looked up. "Ah. Portrait of the artist as a young Hant."

"Yes, I am experimenting with painting as a form of meditative aid. Contrary to your jesting characterization, I am technically no longer a young Hant. As I have found myself disinclined to participate in combat since my maturation, I have been exploring ways of opening up the potential of my mind. It seems likely that any future contributions I will make to the Breakneck Boys will result from such endeavors."

"Hmm, not exactly art for art's sake." Howard began to crack his knuckles. "Look, don't feel you have to hunt for ways to contribute to the group just because you're not into fighting anymore. You do more than your share. I don't know if you've noticed, but I'm not exactly G.I. Joe myself."

"Thank you, Hawa." The Hant unfolded a broad square of pale material that seemed to have had its origins in tree bark. "Rest assured, however, that I also plan to derive enjoyment from the manipulation of form and color."

"Okay, then, as long as you have some fun." Howard turned back to watch the ceaseless tide of wind rippling through the multicolored blossoms. Far out in the level expanse, a lone butterfly the size of a bald eagle dipped and wheeled above a patch of reddish flowers. "It's certainly a pretty world."

"Indeed, it is, Hawa." The Hant lowered its bulk to the stone at his side, setting out a smooth bark palette and a number of small pigment cups made from nutshells. It considered the vast field of color for a long moment, its complicated eyes extending and retreating like camera lenses, then raised a brush fashioned of evergray needles and fell to work.

They sat together in silence for about fifteen minutes, the Hant busily mixing and daubing colors onto its canvas while Howard watched the play of sunlight on the swaying blossoms.

"Please understand that I am quite capable of conversation while I paint," the Hant said finally, pausing between strokes to clean the brush with its wedge-shaped tongue. "Have no fear of disturbing my work when you are ready to begin our discussion."

"Discussion?" Howard raised his brows.

"You mentioned last night that you wished to speak with me. And there is trouble in the air this morning," Awp said. "Quite literally. You discharge your emotional turbulence in the form of pheromones, electrical activity, temperature fluctuations . . . I have been observing your distress since my arrival.''

"Jeez." Howard drew his legs in closer to his body. "I feel like a major polluter, here. Sorry about the interference.''

"I am making no complaint. My artistic efforts are undoubtedly enriched by your volatile condition.'' The Hant added a mass of clouds to its horizon, using a series of bold diagonal strokes in shades of plum and indigo. Below, the painted flowers bent to the east as if swept by a giant hand. "However, I repeat that I am open to dialogue should you wish to talk to me.''

"Well, now that you mention it, there may be one or two small items bothering me.'' Howard scratched his shoulder and grimaced, feeling as though glowing fireworks shot from his body with every movement. "I've had a few unexpected detours lately . . .'' He told the Hant in detail about his two unscheduled appearances in the corridor outside the Executive Washroom.

"I can appreciate your increasing concern,'' Awp responded. "You fear that the Key may not always be trusted to obey your conscious wishes.'' It shifted position and cocked its head at the mounting sun, eyes vibrating. "Given our lack of knowledge of the origins and functioning of the device, however, it is difficult to determine whether it is in fact your own longing to return to Earth which sends you there periodically, or the influence of some outside agency.''

"You mean someone else could be sending me back there . . . Jeez, I hadn't thought of that. Do you think it's possible for the Key to be controlled by another person while I'm holding it?''

"As you know, Keylore is currently a field of limited scope among the warriors. Many have tried to unravel the secrets of the Keys—and of the other products of Keyholder science—but such undertakings have met only with frustration until now.''

Howard nodded. "Alaiya told me people have been injured or killed trying to analyze Keyholder technology.''

"Indeed. Kimmence of our own team lost the lower portion of her right arm in an attempt to disassemble a firebug projector.''

Howard looked down at the gleaming golden shaft that lay against his skin. "Believe me, I have no desire to take this baby apart. It's the same way I always felt about my car: I didn't give a damn what was under the hood as long as it got me where I wanted to go.''

"There is an option I might suggest we explore before it becomes necessary to attempt more dangerous measures,'' Awp said. Howard listened as his friend spoke on for several minutes; then he got to his feet.

''Well, you're probably right, and I'll think about it—especially if things get any worse. This has helped a lot, old buddy. Nice picture, too. Exciting.'' He shaded his eyes in the direction of the soaring butterfly. ''I think I'm going to go loosen up for a while, okay?''

Awp leaned away from the square of bark to examine its work as Howard pushed off from the jut of lavender rock and bounded into the flower sea with seven-league steps. Reaching forward with its wide white hand, the Hant wiped the canvas clean in two measured swipes. ''Now, perhaps, we may try for a more sedate composition,'' it murmured to the retreating back of the Nonesuch.

The sun was high overhead when Howard started back to the encampment. Spotting a small gray-white figure seated near his tent, he winced and made a sudden detour, heading toward the camp's center and the hut of the battlechief.

He found her seated with Chinefwa, going over landscape details on a brightly colored map. The drawing showed a maze of islands set in a dark green ocean. It was a world to which Howard had never traveled, and he sat at the edge of the consultation, only half paying attention. After a short time, the map-maker excused herself, gathering up her scrolls with a respectful nod to the Nonesuch and shuffling off toward her own hut.

Alaiya raised an eyebrow at him when they were alone.

''Good morning,'' he said.

''Good afternoon.'' She removed her foodstuff from her belt, took a small bite, and held the grayish wad out to Howard. ''Hungry?''

He drew back in distaste. ''I've eaten, thanks.''

They sat in silence, Howard drawing lines in the dust with a twig of soft, silvery needles while Alaiya nibbled at the foodstuff.

''It's getting pretty hot,'' he said after a while. He tilted his head toward the doorway of the hut. ''Out here in the sun, I mean.''

''Do you think so?'' Alaiya frowned. ''I am very comfortable.''

''Oh. I just thought it might be a little cooler inside.''

''Quite possibly.'' She took a final bite and returned the foodstuff to its pouch. ''Perhaps your sensitivity to heat is greater than my own.''

''Yeah, maybe. Well.'' He sat staring at the smooth stone of the plain, his chin resting on his fist. Alaiya put her hand on his shoulder and rocked it lightly. "Ahwerd, do you wish me to accompany you inside the hut?"

"I wouldn't want to disturb you if you're busy or anything."

She nodded in the direction of the departed Beranot. "Now that you have chased away my one appointment of the afternoon, my schedule is reasonably flexible."

"Great."

They stretched out next to each other on the floor of fresh evergray boughs. "Back rub?" Howard asked. Alaiya removed her vest and turned onto her side.

"Did you sleep well last night?" Howard began to knead her shoulders.

"Quite well. And you?"

"Yeah, very well."

"Ya-mosh was here a few hours ago. The two of you had planned to meet this morning."

"Yeah . . . I got sort of tied up talking to Awp out at the shore."

"I see." Alaiya inhaled deeply as Howard moved to her middle back. "She seemed well."

"Mm." Howard scowled in the dimness. "So, did everybody know this was going to happen but me?"

"If you are referring to the farrowing-change, it does not always alter gender. Thus, an accurate prediction would have been impossible." She turned over onto her back and reached out to stroke Howard's arm with the back of her hand. "Has it occurred to you that your English is somewhat deficient in pronouns, Ahwerd?"

"Excuse me?"

"I mean no criticism. But language shapes the way we view things. In Averant, for example, we have three primary pronouns that are commonly applied to the things of the world. Do you remember the teaching examples?"

"Sure. The rock, the bug, and the child. Three different kinds of 'it': not alive, alive, alive with intelligence."

"Correct. And those are the distinctions it is possible to convey in my tongue without resorting to more complex constructions—the suffixes needed to form the indicators of size, coloring, gender, and age."

Howard put his palm on top of hers. "Alaiya, why are we having a grammar lesson?"

"I am no linguist, Ahwerd. I am merely pointing out that in your language, you need to know the gender of a sapient being before you may comfortably discuss it. You see a living thing that does not seem to reason and are satisfied to say 'it.' But as soon as you believe a creature capable of intelligent thought, you must gift it with gender.''

"Mm," Howard said. "We tend to be a generous people in that area.''

"I do not doubt it. But did you know that among the Trilbit the primary identifiers relate to scent? By Ya-mosh's standards, our own species is considered practically noseblind, indifferent to distinctions that are quite significant to the Trilbit." She shifted position again in the bed of soft needles. "I imagine it would be quite disconcerting for her if you were suddenly to undergo a change in scent the rest of us might not even notice.''

"I don't suppose this is just a hint that I should be showering more," Howard said.

Alaiya smiled. "I do not mean to lecture you, Ahwerd. I am just pointing out that—were your English not so insistent on inquiring after the reproductive capabilities of every thinking being—you would never have begun calling Ya-mosh 'he,' and so could have avoided the strangeness of having to accustom yourself to 'she' at this time.''

"I know, I know. It's funny, I remember thinking Averant was a little . . . removed in that area—at least when it came to other humans. As if you were skirting the issue when you talked about folks, where with another person from Earth, we'd have to get right down to it.''

"But to what purpose?" Alaiya propped herself up on one elbow, genuine curiosity in her voice. "Is it truly necessary to know instantly whether you will be able to produce offspring with every member of your own race you discuss?''

"Well, no, not when you put it that way.''

"And with members of different species altogether . . .''

"I know. The big joke is, Yam looks exactly the same to my eyes. Of course, what would I have expected to see?" He nodded. "High heels, long eyelashes, and a big pink bow, probably, like Daisy Duck. God, what an idiot!" He began swatting himself on the side of the head with a handful of evergray boughs.

Alaiya placed her hands on his chest. "Ahwerd, do not scold yourself. You are a captive of your language, and it is a prison from which few ever escape—" She paused. "Ahwerd, what are you laughing at? Do you not agree with me?''

"I agree with everything you've said. Of course, being the modern kind of guy that I am, I hope that I was really more bothered by the fact that I *could* be bothered—even a little bit—

by something like this, than I was actually bothered by it at all. That, plus the fact that I don't as a rule like being surprised. Follow me?''

''Not at all. And I still do not see the reason for your laughter.''

''Oh, that's just because I started wondering if you realized the full implications of all this stuff you've been saying about my native tongue. I mean, there I was—perfectly willing to have Averant—or Ga'Prenny, or Neehant or Ya'trril—established as the official language of the Breakneck Boys. But no! You folks had to make a firm commitment to learn my nosy, imperfect language, and now I guess you're just going to have to try to live with it—without turning into a bunch of narrow-minded, gender-obsessed Earthlings in the process!''

''Hmm,'' Alaiya said after a few moments of silence. ''I had not considered this point.''

''Oh, cheer up,'' Howard told her, burrowing down into the nest of boughs by her side. ''I'll be here to help you get through it.''

Howard left the hut and hurried back toward his own tent. When he got there, Yam-ya-mosh was still seated on one of two fiber mats she had brought with her, her small woolly head resting on one shoulder as she snored quietly. Howard leaned over and gently shook the sleeping warrior.

''Ah, Ow-er-bel, you return!'' The Trilbit rubbed her eyes. ''Pardon for slumbering at your doorstep.''

''Yam, I'm the one who should apologize. I blew off our meeting, and I'm sorry. I had a small attack of confusion to fend off.''

Yam nodded wisely. ''Always important to attend to one's health.'' She looked at the bulging pack behind her. ''Would you mind entering your dwelling for a few moments, Ow-er-bel? I have a thing to prepare.''

''Sure.'' Bemused, Howard went into the small tent and sat on the floor until he heard Yam's cheery call.

When he emerged, he found the Trilbit busily engaged at a small cookfire. Several shallow bowls sat on the ground at her side, and a plump brown loaf warmed on a stone next to the fire.

Howard sniffed the air in amazement. ''What is all this?''

''Hearty breakfast!'' The Trilbit beamed up at him. ''You have mentioned your dissatisfaction with Averoy foodstuff on several occasions. For some time, I have been searching for items you might possibly prefer. This bread I made from herbs and grains gathered in the land beyond the forest.''

"Bread?" Howard got slowly down on his knees and inhaled above the fragrant loaf. "I don't believe it," he murmured, eyes half-closed in pleasure.

"Here is honey for the bread, manufactured by a small insect from the orchards, similar to a whirr-sting." Yam handed him a bowl filled with dark amber.

"Oh, my God." Howard dipped a finger into the sticky confection, then tasted it. "It's incredible. What's this?"

"These are fungus growths I picked in the forest. The Hant has made certain they are safe to ingest, and I believe they have a pleasing flavor. Lai-ya told me this morning you were wanting a mushroom omelet on the Sinking Swamp World."

"Omelet—you have eggs?"

"They are not quite as you described them to me, I am afraid." Yam tipped the third bowl so that Howard could see its contents. "On the small side, and rather more chartreuse than yellow, but I hope you will find them satisfactory."

Several minutes later, Howard mopped up the remaining traces of egg from his plate with his third piece of freshly baked bread, popped the morsel into his mouth, and sat back with a dazed look on his face. "Oh, Yam," he said.

The Trilbit blinked and peered into Howard's eyes. "Ow-er-bel? You do not feel well?"

"I feel great. It's the most wonderful meal I've had in months—years! Thank you." Howard leaned forward and gathered his small friend into his arms.

Someone coughed lightly. When Howard opened his eyes, Alaiya was standing next to the tent.

"Odd." She tilted her head to one side and inspected his face with narrowed eyes, her lips quirked in a half smile. "You do not seem unhappy. Yet I had recently heard that you do not approve of surprises."

"Can't believe everything you hear." Howard grinned at his clean plate.

"Then you enjoyed the meal?"

"Oh, Alaiya, you don't know." He pushed Yam out to arm's length and shook his head at her. "And they say the best chefs are men—ha!"

CHAPTER XI

The Brindled Intzwam

THE HANT CALCULATED THE INTERVAL BETWEEN THE raid on the Sinking Swamp World and the next opportunity for recruitment at approximately eight local days.

Howard grudgingly resumed his training regimen in martial arts and weaponry, managing to learn enough basic skills in each discipline to satisfy his instructors—though never displaying the inspired bloodlust necessary to truly excel.

On the second morning, he decided to skip practice in favor of an early visit with Yam to the quarantine camp on the Black and Blue World. "What's the good of being Nonesuch if you can't cut class once in a while?" he remarked to the Trilbit before turning the Key.

Half a dozen of the new recruits were lounging nearby when the two appeared beneath the deep blue sky. Understandably reluctant to materialize in the midst of a crowd of people or objects, Howard always tried to visualize himself in a relatively empty area on the world of his destination. It had begun to seem, however, that the Key itself had enough sense to prevent him from ending up half inside someone else's body or belongings. Howard suspected that part of the device's function was to search for an unoccupied space of appropriate size before allowing its wielder to fully enter the target world. He and Yam arrived a good ten feet from the latest Breakneck Boys, who evinced a variety of reactions to the unanticipated arrival of their new leader.

Most affected was the black-furred Pasper Howard had rescued from the algae pool on the Sinking Swamp World. Moments after spying his benefactor, the catlike warrior had sprung across the sward of rose-colored moss, uttering a rough-voiced exclamation, and attempted to throw himself on his knees at the feet of the Nonesuch.

Yam-ya-mosh, interpreting the Pasper's enthusiastic greeting as an unprovoked attack, immediately interposed her small body between Howard and his admirer, legs spread in a fighting stance and sword held ready. The scene grew more chaotic when the Pasper—who had apparently not yet fully recovered from his recent wounds—twisted his left leg halfway into the kneel and threw back his sleek black head in a bloodcurdling screech of pain.

The Trilbit cocked her sword arm, a snarl on her lips, and prepared to eviscerate the yowling warrior. Something caught at her wrist from behind. Yam turned in surprise to see the Nonesuch shaking his head, face red with embarrassment. Looking acutely uncomfortable, Howard stepped past his protector and helped the whimpering Pasper to his feet.

"Thanks anyway, Yam. I get the feeling this guy is more of a menace to himself than he'll ever be to me." Howard dusted bits of moss and twigs from the warrior's new black vest. "You all right, fella?"

The Pasper murmured something that sounded like "Piano rhumba, Nuh'suh."

"I see." Howard nodded and turned hopefully to the small ring of onlookers that had gathered. "Anybody here speak Pasper?"

Kimmence of the Averoy detached herself from the crowd. "Two Pasper stay back on Field of Flowers," she said in her accented English. "One more here, it go look for rockskin on mountain ridge. Pasper love sweet taste."

Howard followed the woman's gaze to the black foothills that reared behind the camp. "I thought we'd agreed everybody would stick together over here in case of trouble."

Kimmence gave a humorless smile. "I warrior, not jailkeeper. We tell rule, give purge pod. Soon language all different. Try tell rule again, bad understanding. Nonesuch blink in, blink out." She waved her left hand back and forth. "Maybe Nonesuch stay camp here with us all time, can keep new ones obey his word."

"You're right, the system needs work." Howard scanned the onlookers. "How soon can the rest of these people travel to the other camp? Once it's safe to take them over there, we can start them right in with English classes. Plus, there'll be more people available to translate."

"Those two ready now." The Averoy woman gestured with the stump of her right arm toward a pair of stoop-shouldered Beranoi. "Purge pod quickly go through body that race." She pursed her lips. "Other Averoy ready. Sarsi tomorrow, maybe Intzwam, too. Hard to know with Intzwam—always bad understanding with that race."

"Fine. I'll come more often and we'll try to keep things moving. I appreciate the difficulty of your task." At a slight rasping sound, Howard glanced down. The Pasper, whom he had been supporting with his arm as he spoke with Kimmence, had apparently drifted off to sleep while still standing, his chest vibrating in something midway between a purr and a snore.

Kimmence allowed herself a small grin. "That one drug for pain to leg and chest. Nervenumb mix funny with purge pod. Pasper take many sleep."

She helped Howard carry the unconscious warrior to the central tent, where they deposited him in a nest of rough blankets. The Pasper woke for a moment to blink up at them, claws extending reflexively to tug at the wool; then he promptly fell back to sleep, the tip of his pink tongue protruding slightly past his lips.

Howard and Yam had each brought a pack from Field of Flowers, laden with supplies requested by the quarantine camp. A rotund Sarsi named Huliper Apperdoy approached them while they were unloading.

"Pardon, Nonesuch, more purge pods needed. Now left enough for cleansing eight more warriors, maybe nine." It fingered its abdominal pouch beneath its loose vest as it spoke. "Use up uniform, also. Now left two complete. Soon maybe need hand out scraps."

"Hmm. We'll have to hope we come across a cache of pods in some other team's supplies. It's too bad that substitute Awp came up with turned out to have so many side effects. It's pretty hard for folks to concentrate on learning a new language when half of them are hallucinating and the rest can't stop throwing up." Howard rubbed the back of his neck. "As for the clothing, we can try to collect some spare outfits from the others. Most of our uniforms have extra pieces, anyway, to allow for changes in environment and weather. We could probably patch together some of those. If worst comes to worst, people can just keep on wearing their old stuff as far as I'm concerned. I'm not real big on uniforms."

"Maybe problem some warrior wear color old battle-gang," the Sarsi suggested.

"Seems true, Ow-er-bel." Yam turned from setting out a parcel of wooden eating utensils. "Keeping old uniforms might well encourage factions within group."

"Yeah, that makes sense," Howard agreed. "Well, I'll look into it. Anything else?"

"No big problem." The fat marsupial hesitated, twining curls of moss in its long, prehensile toes. "Maybe little problem Intzwam." It gestured past the tent flap. "Intzwam hard to know thoughts. Now have three out by water stream. All night standing. Maybe fight. Now one Averoy watch."

Yam and Howard located the trio of stick-thin warriors facing one another on the far side of a narrow brook some distance from the camp. Kormender turned to greet them as they came up to stand by his side.

"You will excuse my Averant speech, Nonesuch," the copperskinned warrior said. "The purge pods have only just rid my blood of parleybugs, and I look forward to beginning my acquisition of your tongue."

"Of course," Howard replied in the language of the Sunset People. He nodded toward the three spindle-legged figures posing like statues in the mossy field. "One of the Sarsi thought there might be some trouble here."

Kormender frowned. "It is difficult to say. The Intzwam are an odd race, introduced fairly recently to these Fading Worlds. They fight well as a rule, though somewhat unpredictably. But they are almost always segregated, no more than one to a battlegang, due to the strong reaction they occasionally have to others of their kind."

"Do you know what's behind this strong reaction?" Howard asked.

"Ow-er-bel!" Yam had wandered closer to the stream's edge to study the nearly motionless trio. "One is brindled. See there?" She directed Howard's gaze to the farthest warrior. Faint bands of darker color marked the light beige skin on its naked chest, back, and thighs. "Intzwam come in three kinds: smooth, spotted, brindled." The Trilbit shook her head in disapproval. "Not good to mix."

"There is said to be a mutual animosity of some sort among the different types," Kormender amplified. "I have heard rumors that the bandings represent various genders, but this has never been corroborated. The Intzwam themselves do not invite inquiries about such matters, which they consider intensely personal."

Howard puffed out his cheeks. "So these three guys must have all come from different teams, right?"

"Correct. When you brought us here from the Sinking Swamp World two days ago, we had a pair with us: a Smooth from my own team and that Brindle—formerly a member of the Rain of Blood, as you can see by its orange headband. They seemed to ignore each other until yesterday, when you brought over new warriors from Field of Flowers to replace those who had served here for a few days. Among these was the second Smooth Intzwam. No one noticed exactly when they left the camp, but Apperdoy found all three of them out here last evening, standing much as they are at this moment. We have been watching them intermittently since then, but they seem to have moved only slightly.''

"Has anybody tried talking to them? Have the new ones already been purged?''

The Averoy spread his hands. "Purge pods were indeed administered to my former teammate and to the brindled member of the Blood. The Breakneck Boy Intzwam seems oblivious to our queries.''

There was a slight movement from across the stream, and the three warriors began a strange, coordinated shifting of position. Twiglike arms flexed, legs bent almost imperceptibly, and lean torsos rotated in exaggerated slow motion as they adjusted their stances, each one's motions in perfect sync with those of the others.

"Weird,'' Howard said with a small shiver. He exhaled a deep breath and walked several paces downstream, then leaped lightly across the water. He cautiously approached the once-more frozen aliens, stopping several feet away from the tableau to clear his throat.

"Beware the heel-spurs if they attack, Ow-er-bel,'' Yam called from the other side of the brook. "It is said that waving one's hands rapidly in front of their eyes will sometimes disorient them.''

"They are weakest at the knee joint and the collarbone in terms of sword thrusts,'' Kormender added.

"I'm hoping for a somewhat less physical exchange,'' Howard said, inching closer to the three. "Thanks for the tips, though.''

Each Intzwam stood at one vertex of a perfect equilateral triangle, the slits of its angled eyes seemingly focused on the empty air between its two fellows. This placed the Brindle with its back to the stream, while the Smooths stood between it and a wide meadow bordered by an arm of dark forest. Howard looked from one to another, trying to decide where best to impose his presence. Finally, he stepped into the line of sight of the Breakneck Boy Intzwam, who was distinguished from the other Smooth by the black and silver headband that clasped its narrow skull.

"Pardon me," Howard said.

At the sound of his voice, the Intzwam facing him made a tiny motion with one of its skeletal fingers. The second Smooth turned its head a millimeter in the direction of the first. Then, with a swiftness that left Howard gaping, the Brindled Intzwam darted between the other two and began to race toward the woods in a series of zigzagging leaps.

"Hey—" Howard stood looking after the skittering figure. The Smooth closest to him made a brief flailing motion with its forearms, then collapsed like a folding chair onto the ground, while the other circled around behind it in three delicate steps and froze into position with its arms upraised above its companion's bowed head.

Howard turned to Yam and Kormender, who stood wide-eyed on the other side of the brook. "Hey, we can't let him run off like that!"

"Too fast, Ow-er-bel!" the Trilbit called. "No way to stop."

Howard made a quick decision, then turned back to stare at the retreating Brindle, which was nearing the line of dark trees. "Hi-yo, Silver," he said, pulling the Key from his vest. "Gold, I mean." He gave it an urgent twist.

A plain of smooth lavender stone pressed for an instant against his sandals. "And away!" he called, squeezing his eyes shut and turning the Key again.

He reappeared directly in the path of the leaping figure. Its legs jabbing the moss like broomsticks, the Intzwam came to a teetering halt in front of him. Howard raised both his arms, swaying slightly from side to side. The Brindle's slitted gaze flicked rapidly left, right, left, right.

"Ha! Didn't expect this kind of chase, did you?" Howard took a half step toward the quivering creature.

The Intzwam contracted its body and launched itself at him.

"Gah!" Howard flung his arms up in front of his face and stumbled backward. Something that felt like a pool cue poked him on the upper chest and then the right shoulder; his scalp crawled as an impossibly light foot balanced for a long moment on the crown of his head. Then it was gone, like a leaf taken by the wind. He twisted around in time to see the creature hop over a low wall of scarlet underbrush and vanish into the forest.

Howard scratched the top of his head vigorously with both hands for a few seconds, then turned and made his way slowly back to the little stream.

CHAPTER XII

Thousand Islands

THE HANT WAS INVITED TO THE BLACK AND BLUE World for the purpose of interrogating the two remaining Intzwam. Alaiya made the trip back, as well.

The creatures' language consisted of a range of voiceless vibrations that sounded to Howard like a deck of cards being shuffled at various speeds. The pair of Smooths circled the Hant ceaselessly during the inquiry, moving with the same slow-motion gait they had employed earlier. As he watched, Howard was reminded of an insect that he had run across in the woods near his home once or twice as a child. "It's called a walking-stick," he told Alaiya, watching the scene over his shoulder. "Kind of like a praying mantis crossed with a twig."

At last Awp stepped between the two warriors, leaving them to continue their circuit around a patch of empty meadow, and joined his friends where they sat on the banks of the little brook.

"I do not believe a mind could swim in much more foreign seas and still be considered intelligent by our measurements," the Hant commented thoughtfully.

"Everybody seems to feel that way about them. Funny that the Keyholders chose them to fight alongside the rest of you," Howard said. "Were you able to find out anything about what's been going on?"

"Pieces, strands." The Hant splayed the many fingers of its large moplike hand. "The Intzwam method of ordering occurrences does not match our own. Indeed, their very perception of the passage of time is quite unique. If you will allow me half a minute to collate the information, I will present my reconstruction of the sequence of events . . . ." It remained silent for exactly thirty seconds. "Well. The Smooth Intzwam from the Howling Miscreants did not attempt to kill the Brindle from the Rain of Blood upon first meeting because there existed the small chance that the two might form a breeding dyad. For its part, the Brindle made no move against the Miscreant Smooth because Brindled Intzwam recognize the existence of members of the other phyla only when they are present in numbers of two or more. When a certain amount of time passed without the formation of a dyad, the Smooth began preparations to dispatch the Brindle. At this point the second Smooth arrived. Now it became imperative for the Brindle to acknowledge the reality of the other two, while the Smooths found it necessary to postpone the former's murder until they could ascertain whether or not a breeding *triad* would occur. They had apparently just concluded this evaluation when you interrupted them earlier today."

"Whoops," Howard said. "You mean it's my fault we won't have hundreds of little Intzwam swarming over the camp in a few months?"

"No, from what I was able to learn, the triad had also failed to materialize. The two Smooths were merely waiting for the proper opening so that they might fall upon their brindled companion and disassemble its body. Your distraction of one of them disturbed the stasis and provided the Brindle with the opportunity it needed to escape with its life."

"I see." Howard rubbed his chin. "And what happens now? Are Moe and Larry here just waiting for the proper moment to tear each other limb from limb?"

"No, the remaining pair has recently succeeded in forming a dyad." The Hant turned to watch the glacial dance of the two stick figures. "Soon they will perform whatever actions are required to consummate the union."

"Yikes." Howard followed the Hant's gaze. "You mean I was right about this place becoming an Intzwam kindergarten?"

"There is little chance of that, Ahwerd," Alaiya said, stirring her bare feet in the cool stream water. "Did you not know? Our foodstuff contains a component which prevents conception. Without the antidote from Stillpoint, no member of a battle-gang may reproduce."

Howard's jaw dropped. "No, I didn't know that."

"It does not appear to be a concept which the Intzwam themselves have grasped," the Hant said. "Though I explained the matter to them in some detail, they are proceeding with their mating as if a successful outcome were inevitable."

"Perhaps they have no choice," Alaiya suggested.

"Indeed," the Hant agreed. "It may be a mandate of their physiological construction that they must follow a pattern of this sort to its conclusion, once it is set in motion."

"Or," Howard said, trying to glance discreetly over his shoulder, "they might just be in the mood for a good time."

"A possibility," the Hant conceded. "Although a somewhat remote one, as the recipient of a viable fertilization typically has its visual organs and lower limbs forcibly removed by its partner at the onset of the pregnancy."

Howard whistled softly. "An argument for serious birth control if I ever heard one."

A search of the nearby forest failed to turn up any sign of the missing Brindle. Howard transported his friends to Field of Flowers, along with the new members of the Breakneck Boys whose bloodstreams had been cleansed of parleybugs.

The next day, Howard returned to the quarantine camp. According to Kimmence and the others, no one now remained on the Black and Blue World who carried active parleyblood. It was deemed safe to close the interim camp and bring the last of the group to the permanent base on Field of Flowers.

"We'll be back to set up shop again in another week or so—after the next raid," Howard told Kimmence. "Maybe by then the Brindle will have wandered back into the area." At the last minute, they decided to leave a message for the Intzwam in the written warrior speech, promising it protection from its fellows if it returned to the team. "Maybe this will work," Howard said, watching as the Averoy woman scrawled the words with brightly colored marking sticks on a smooth black outcropping near the center of the temporary camp. "I hate to lose somebody if it's not necessary."

Kimmence looked doubtful. "Not sure Intzwam can read warrior writing," she replied with an Averoy shrug.

Howard returned in two days with Yam for a brief search of the area, and again in four. There was no sign of the Brindled Intzwam on either visit.

The next world scheduled to be put into play was called Thousand Islands. Alaiya conducted a meeting the night before the raid, during which all members of the expanding battle-gang were encouraged to share information or experiences that might prove useful to the twelve Breakneck Boys chosen to actively participate. Howard listened with interest.

The battle site was located in the middle of a great ocean. Many of the Breakneck Boys believed that the entire planet was covered with water, though none of them had ever had the means to travel beyond the zone of combat. The only known landmasses on the world were a large central island, several miles across, and the numerous smaller ones that surrounded it.

The big island was shown in some detail on Chinefwa's map, with a heavy circle in black for the temporary presence of Stillpoint, the roving city that the warriors inhabited between assignments. The hundreds of smaller islands were illustrated by a hazy nimbus of intersecting circles sketched around the central isle. Dozens of erasures showed that Chinefwa had attempted to keep track of the islets for several Rounds before giving up. "They move," Alaiya had told Howard. "The Keyholders have some way of changing their positions between Turns."

It was decided that they would make their appearance on Thousand Islands somewhat earlier in the Turn than they had traveled to the Sinking Swamp World.

"There is evidence of treachery among the Keyholders themselves," Alaiya stated to the group. "Several Turns past, the Meticulous Victors surprised my team hours before the scheduled battle. Only the Hant and I survived the attack. Only days ago the battlechief of the Rain of Blood attempted to lead his followers in the same sort of cowardly ambush. In both cases, I believe the team leaders were given secret information concerning the whereabouts of the opposing battle-gang."

Early in the day of the raid, Howard transported Kimmence, Kormender, and three others to the Black and Blue World to prepare the interim camp.

Howard had decided that the Black and Blue World was his favorite—though he refrained from telling Alaiya he preferred it to Field of Flowers. He filled his lungs with sweet, cool air as the jagged mountains and rose-red meadow grew solid before his eyes. Then the Attercack on his right suddenly cried out, gripping Howard's hand convulsively. The Nonesuch followed the gaze of the long-necked saurian and felt a tingle of shock.

The body of the Brindled Intzwam was suspended several feet above the ground, neatly impaled on a saw-edged, spearlike implement that had been driven into the moss some fifteen yards from where they stood. Howard and the others walked slowly to the site of the gruesome exhibit. Beyond the murdered creature lay the remnants of their camp: the large tent they had left

behind had been ripped to shreds, and the cache of buried supplies had been unearthed and despoiled.

Howard looked from the tattered canvas to the corpse, his
mind whirling.

"Could there have been another Intzwam?"

"No. Look there." Kimmence directed his gaze to the black
rock face where they had left their message. The bright characters of warrior speech had been smeared away. In their place
was a single massive symbol, drawn in thick lines of silver-gray
that shone like a snail's track: a triangle resting on one point
with three concentric circles inside. To Howard it looked like a
baleful eye staring out at them in scornful amusement.

"The Keyholders?" he asked softly. Kimmence nodded, her
face ashen beneath her purplish complexion.

"How they know?" The Attercack paced the meadow, its
four arms pawing the air in agitation as it swung its long neck
back and forth to scan the nearby mountainside. "Battlechief
say parleybug gone, Keyholder cannot find—how they know?"

"Here is the answer," Kormender said in Averant. He was
kneeling at the base of the jagged spear. Three small shapes lay
half-hidden in the moss below the contorted jaws of the Intzwam.
"It must have had these in its throat pouch," he told Howard as
the others gathered around him. "Death caused their ejection."

"Purge pods . . ." Howard lifted one of the brown objects.
"It never swallowed them." He shook his head, then looked
around. "We'd better get back to Field of Flowers."

News of the Keyholders' presence on the Black and Blue World
threw the main camp into an uproar. The two Smooth Intzwam
were immediately examined to make sure that they had ingested
the purge pods allotted them, their indignant protests sounding
like baseball cards ticking in the rear wheel of a bicycle.

"We're just lucky we didn't show up any sooner," Howard
told Alaiya. "I got the feeling the Brindle hadn't been dead all
that long."

The battlechief had remained grimly calm through the chaos
that followed Howard's return. "We must proceed with the understanding that the Keyholders are now aware of our activities—at least to some degree." She rubbed absently at the small
scar at the edge of her upper lip. "In one way, this is good
news—for it seems to confirm that we are invisible to their meth-
ods of detection so long as we purge ourselves of the parleybugs." She lifted her head to scan the lavender sky. "They were

drawn to the Black and Blue World, after all, not to this one. We must find some way to secure another supply of the pods before long . . .''

"But doesn't it also mean they could be waiting for us on Thousand Islands? Suppose they just start shooting the minute we appear?''

"It is a possibility," she agreed. "But my instincts tell me they will do all that they can to avoid disrupting the scheduled battle. We have an additional advantage in that they cannot predict where we will materialize on the big island. As long as we time our visit to occur after Stillpoint has moved away from the world and before the teams have clashed, I believe we will be reasonably safe." She looked at him from under raised brows. "But that is only my belief. No one truly understands the Keyholders' motivations. The wisest course of action would undoubtedly be to postpone our next recruiting raid for several Turns. Unfortunately, during that time the Keyholders may decide to reorganize the schedule of battles. Once they do that, we find ourselves at a serious disadvantage.''

"I get the picture." Howard nodded. "No guarantees. So— where shall we set up the next quarantine camp?''

There was an unusual sharpness to the air of Thousand Islands, part salt tang and part something else. Howard swung his head quickly from side to side, searching the immediate area. He smiled grimly as he noticed that the other members of the team were engaged in the same activity. Maybe I'm starting to develop a warrior's reflexes, he thought. Or maybe just a potential target's nerves.

They were standing about thirty feet from the shore on the large central island. An emerald ocean stretched away like a sheet of glass under the windless, rose-pink sky. Howard turned his gaze farther inland. The reddish surface of the island resembled a carelessly tossed blanket; ridges and gullies made a maze of the visible land. Barrel-thick clumps of pale green spikes crowded the hills, some of them rearing five or six feet above the coarse sand. All in all, an ideal setting to hide an army waiting in ambush.

To Howard's right, Omber Oss hoisted Yam-ya-mosh onto his shoulders for a better view; on his left, a pair of Po'Ellika did their part to scout the surrounding dunes by hopping vertically into the air, the spinning cylinders of their bodies achieving a height of twelve or fifteen feet before dropping back to the sand. "No see bad!" one of them squeaked to Howard, the single eye circling freely in its groove like a blue-black marble. Howard touched his forefinger to his brow in thanks and made his way down the gradual slope that led to the shore.

The water was dark, perhaps as the result of microscopic plant growth, and it was impossible to see deeper than a few feet. Howard had been warned that ravenous creatures waited to feed just beneath the placid surface. Yet another variation on the ubiquitous slakes, he supposed, keeping an eye out for black tentacles as he approached the quiet shoreline.

The rust-colored curves of small islands were visible out to sea, but gauging their size was difficult from where he stood. There was an odd feeling to the place that Howard struggled to pin down. Was it the scale that seemed wrong? Some distance down the coast, he saw the beginning of a chain of little islands leading out from the shore—one of the jumping-off places Alaiya had mentioned when she described the way battles were conducted on Thousand Islands.

As was customary on most worlds, the two opposing teams were released from the gates of the mysterious city of Stillpoint at different times. Each followed its assigned route from the center of the island down to the shore, where the islet chains came close enough to the big island in several places to permit access to the warriors. Traveling from one small landmass to the next was relatively easy, either on foot or with the aid of powderbridge. The teams moved outward, hopping from islet to islet till they finally encountered one another. But Alaiya claimed that the configuration of the small chains was altered for each battle, the overlapping archipelagoes forming a great puzzle of intersecting paths and unexpected dead ends. Often a team racing toward its adversary would abruptly run out of islands. Then it was necessary to turn back and start again at an intersection, wasting valuable time and energy while the enemy had the opportunity to choose the place of confrontation. "Depending on which team moves more swiftly," Alaiya had concluded, "the battle itself may take place on an island capacious enough to hold both teams—or on a spot of land with barely enough room for two individuals. It is, in the end, a very exhilarating situation, one with little room for error."

Howard left the shore to seek out the battlechief, whom he found conferring with Chinefwa on a nearby ridge.

"We are in luck," she told him. "Stillpoint has retreated sufficiently to prevent its sending additional troops against us. Now we must see if the Noise and the Assault have already encountered one another. According to Chinefwa's map, we may be able to find a useful vantage point atop this terraced area."

The battle-gang began to climb a series of steep furrows leading to a hump of higher ground. Howard looked around him as more of the world came into view. He could not shake the growing conviction that the world of Thousand Islands had been created—or at least reshaped—to fit the Keyholders' needs. There was an unnatural feel to the surroundings which contrasted noticeably with the Sinking Swamp and the Black and Blue World. "It's like a giant theme park," Howard murmured to himself as they neared the highest terrace. "All that's missing is Mickey and Donald selling tickets."

The Breakneck Boys fanned out over the rounded dome that topped the hill, searching the visible segments of the maze of islets for signs of other warriors.

"We are not in a good position, after all." Alaiya came to stand by Howard's side. "The island is too large, and its terrain too varied. Great portions of the ocean are hidden from us." She gnawed a knuckle, then shook her head in frustration. "Ahwerd, it may be necessary for us to leave and come back again several times before we are able to find the other teams. Even then, it will be a matter of luck for us to come between them. The island chains are too tangled to unravel from this close to sea level. If we had only had some way of seeing the entire picture—a great flying machine from which Chinefwa could have drawn a hundred detailed maps." She laughed ruefully. "I am growing used to miracles in your company," she said, laying her hand on his arm. "We must do with what we have."

Howard had been staring up at the pink bowl of sky while Alaiya spoke. Now he turned to survey the nearest clump of islets with a look of calculation on his face. "You know, what we have just may be able to do the trick . . ."

"What do you mean? The flying suit remains lost in a sand castle on Kansas—badly damaged, you said." She searched his face. "Surely you have not hidden wings from me all this time."

"I don't think I need wings." His fingers toyed with the thong around his neck while his eyes resumed measuring the heavens. "I think I've got something better." He gave a short nod and shifted his gaze to her face. "Only I have to do it now, before I really reason it out and lose my nerve. Wait here—I'll be back real soon!" He gave her a quick kiss on the mouth and stepped back, pulling the Key from beneath his vest and closing his eyes in concentration as he gave it a turn.

The scented breeze of Field of Flowers washed over him for a second. He opened his eyes long enough for a few deep breaths, shut them again, and turned the Key.

When he opened his eyes a second time, he was afraid his heart would stop. It was a sensation unlike any he had ever experienced.

Howard hung, apparently motionless, high in the empty air above the world called Thousand Islands. Breathing was difficult; he gulped cold air into his lungs as his staring eyes took in the panorama stretched out below him. The large island lay beneath him and to the right. It was about the size of a postage stamp. He was too high to make out the figures of the Breakneck Boys, and he doubted they could see him, though he thought he could recognize the high ground where they must be standing. Surrounding the big island were dozens of intersecting chains of tiny islets, like rough necklaces overlaid one upon the other on a bed of green velvet. While his conscious mind was busy grappling with the unreality of his situation, he felt the complicated pattern of the islets slip automatically into his brain. As yet, he had no sensation of falling, though the wind whistled constantly past his ears and his clothing flapped noisily. His knuckles were white around the shaft of the Key. He was afraid the thong might be torn from his neck if he loosened his grip. Through the fear and strangeness, a sense of quiet wonderment was filling him, and he lifted his eyes to the rosy vastness that surrounded him.

When he looked down again, he knew without a doubt that he was falling. The big island had grown to the size of a wallet photo. A tiny clot of black figures stood to one side of the raised ground at its center. He turned his attention to the islet maze, forcing himself to focus on his task. A moving strand of purple showed him the location of one battle-gang; an irregular spot of crimson betrayed the other.

The sensation was dreamlike. With effort, he tore his eyes from the slowly expanding scene beneath him and squeezed them shut. He left a cry of sudden terror hanging in the air behind him as he turned the Key.

Long seconds passed before he finally appeared gasping at Alaiya's feet on the high ground of the island. He was curled up into a fetal position, his hair hung in wild disarray, and his black uniform was covered with streaks of thick golden powder.

"Ahwerd!" Alaiya knelt next to him. He lay on his side with his mouth open, his dark eyes wide. "What is it? Where have you been?"

As she pulled him into a sitting position, he gestured helplessly, still breathing in short spasms. "Up there," he said finally, pointing at the sky above them. "Getting the big picture."

Alaiya brushed gold pollen from his face. "What are you talking about?"

Howard explained his trip to the sky above the emerald sea as coherently as he could. He started to tremble when he reached the part where he had turned the Key as he fell toward the island.

"It suddenly occurred to me, just before I turned the thing, that if I was dropping like a stone through the air when I left Thousand Islands, wouldn't I still be falling just as fast when I hit the stone plain on Field of Flowers?" He paused to take a shuddery breath. "At the very last instant, I visualized the air above the flower sea instead of the ground next to the encampment. I figured the lighter gravity might give me a better chance of surviving." He gave a shaky grin. "The next thing I knew, I was bouncing around in the blossoms like a basketball. It took me a little while to get my bearings, and then I came back here."

"A foolish risk, Ahwerd." Alaiya gripped his shoulders sternly. "You must promise me you will not try any new maneuvers with the Key without thinking them through first."

"Sure thing." He brushed long, dark hair out of his eyes. "Now let me up and I'll show you what I found out."

Howard used Chinefwa's map to describe what he had seen. "Here we are, right?" He squinted at the eastern horizon, then rotated the map several degrees before setting down his forefinger. "The guys in red were down at this location a minute or two ago, in the middle of a chain of rocks that curls out like this. Over here are the purple ones—the Dreadful Noise, right? They're picking their way out along a real thin section, waiting to reach the spot where the islets get bigger again." Howard accepted a marking stick from Chinefwa and began to sketch rapidly as he spoke. "What they can't tell from their vantage point is that the larger islands that they're heading for are actually part of another strand, and that the chain they're following is about to end right out here. So they're going to have to double back real quick, or the Well-Mannered Assault will have them trapped on this skinny little stretch of rocks where they'll have no room to regroup. At that point, the Assault can just sit back and pick them off one by one."

Alaiya studied the map, her eyes shining with excitement. "This is incredible, Ahwerd. If you can transport us to somewhere along here . . ."

"Yeah, there's a sizable rock right there that'll put us practically on top of the Noise. Then we'll be the ones who have them cornered, instead of the Assault.'' He handed the map back to the Beranot and gestured for the Breakneck Boys to link limbs in a circle. ''Shall we?''

The team materialized at their destination in the green sea after a quick trip to Field of Flowers. The chosen islet was a chunk of upthrusting rock some fifty feet in diameter, with a broad, flat rim that girdled the central peak. According to Howard's aerial glimpse of the chain, the string of smaller rocks across the islet from their arrival point would bring them directly to the Dreadful Noise.

With Alaiya's permission, Omber Oss pushed into the lead as the Breakneck Boys slowly rounded the central column of rust-colored rock. ''Two other Averoy—one of them his close comrade—fight for the Noise,'' she explained to Howard. ''If Oss is able to speak with Shing at the outset, the negotiations may proceed more smoothly.''

They peered around the rock. The opposing team was where Howard had said they would be. About a hundred yards down the chain, eight warriors in plum-colored uniforms threaded their way slowly along a series of narrow islets. As they watched, the lead warrior turned to those behind it with a hoarse cry. ''They've just discovered the dead end,'' Howard said. After a brief discussion, the Dreadful Noise reversed direction and began heading back toward the rock where the Breakneck Boys waited. Oss craned his neck, examining the approaching band intently, then slumped back in puzzled disappointment.

''Shing is not among them,'' he reported to Alaiya. ''And there is a new Domeny I do not recognize.''

''There are many reasons for a warrior to be replaced,'' she whispered in the language of the Sunset People, holding his eyes with her own. ''Temporary illness, approved leave for further training, perhaps even a promotion to a better team.''

''There is another reason much more common than those,'' Oss replied quietly, moving back to yield his place to the battle-chief. He gestured to the other team. ''Quickly now—before we lose the advantage.''

Alaiya stepped from behind the curve of rock, the rest of the Breakneck Boys following to line up in loose ranks behind her. She raised her arms and called her greetings in Averant to the slowly moving warriors. A small, silver-haired Averoy stared at her in consternation as the battle-gang ground to a halt; then he turned to interpret her message to his comrades.

The team leader, a mountainous Sarsi, called sharply to the

Averoy from her place at the rear of the battle-gang. The silver-haired warrior was turning back to Alaiya when the next to last warrior in line—a squat, three-horned Trull with iridescent skin the color of oil on blacktop—gave a high screeching cry and hefted a bulky instrument to its shoulder. The tip of the weapon flared with incandescent light. There was a shout of rage from the team leader, and the Sarsi lunged forward, attempting to knock the weapon out of the Trull's hands. The Trull twisted beyond the fat marsupial's reach, and there was an abrupt flash of bright light.

"Firebug!" someone yelled behind Howard. The Breakneck Boys scattered. Howard watched as something like a glowing bee arced through the air toward him; then Alaiya was gripping his arm and pulling him off to one side. "The Po'Ellika!" she cried urgently. "They must have room to move!"

Howard heard a whirring sound. He twisted his neck in time to see a small cylindrical shape launch itself toward the firebug like a frog after a moth. The glowing pellet swerved, narrowly eluding the spinning warrior. At that moment, the second Po'Ellika leaped into the air. Howard gaped as the top of the creature's head snapped back as if on a hinge to reveal a huge, yawning mouth. There was a crackling sound, and the firebug was gone.

The enraged Sarsi leader cuffed the rebellious Trull, sending the dinosaurlike warrior sprawling at the edge of the tiny island. Murky water churned as the Trull's arm slipped momentarily beneath the surface, and then the warrior rolled back from the edge with an anguished cry, purplish fluid streaming in a dozen places from its dark hide.

Easing its bulk cautiously forward past its followers, the Sarsi bawled a question to the Breakneck Boys, its own weapon raised. Huliper Apperdoy moved to Alaiya's side and whispered softly into her ear. The Dreadful Noise moved uneasily on their narrow pathway, a thirty-foot stretch of land made of three widely spaced islets temporarily connected with bright green powder-bridge. After his brief conference with Alaiya, the Breakneck Boy Sarsi stepped forward and spoke at some length in the guttural language of his race.

With Apperdoy acting as interpreter, a hurried dialogue ensued between Alaiya and the other battlechief. After several minutes, the plum-suited Sarsi raised a fat hand and turned to bark a few phrases to her restless warriors, who responded somewhat hesitantly by lowering their weapons.

"Good," Alaiya said. "We have them."

CHAPTER XIII

Second Thoughts

THE TWO TEAMS MOVED SLOWLY BACK ALONG THE string of tiny islets, half a dozen Breakneck Boys walking at either end of the line of new recruits.

After the incident with the Brindled Intzwam on the Black and Blue World, they had decided to establish the next interim camp on the red-orange desert of Kansas. Kimmence and her coworkers had been deposited there to set up shop a few hours before the raid. But before the team traveled there, they were headed toward the shore of the big island. Alaiya had requested time to explain to the members of the Dreadful Noise the unusual manner in which they planned to depart from Thousand Islands, and Howard preferred to turn his Key somewhere he could keep an eye on all his passengers. With twenty warriors spread out over fifty feet of narrow rock, it would be too easy for someone to break contact and get left behind.

An occasional scouting leap by one of the Po'Ellika reported no sign of the Well-Mannered Assault. Alaiya theorized that they had become hopelessly lost on their own section of the island-maze and were backtracking somewhere beyond their view. "Just as well," she said. "One team each raid is quite enough to handle."

Howard agreed. His impromptu skydive had left him with a nervous tingle in his stomach, only made worse by the touch of seasickness he was beginning to feel as he neared the end of the long march. He tried to remind his body that he was actually walking on solid ground at all times and that the ocean itself had remained all but motionless. But the sensation grew stronger as he finally made the leap from rock to shore, and he stood for a moment with his hand on his belly, waiting for the world to stop revolving inside his head.

"Ahwerd?" Alaiya, still several yards back in the islet chain, was watching him with concern. "Are you all—"

"Oh, God—I know what this is!" Howard took a convulsive breath and lifted his head, gooseflesh prickling along his arms as he scanned the high ridge before him. "Everybody!" he shouted over his shoulder. "Stay where you are! Don't come any—"

The world exploded with sound and color as a line of crimson-suited warriors poured over the ridge and raced screaming toward him down the beach. Behind him the two teams milled in confusion—the Breakneck Boys, who had divided into two groups to escort the Noise, calling to one another in garbled English over the general din.

"Everybody link up!" Howard bellowed, leaping onto the narrow spit of rock and trying to edge backward to rejoin his teammates.

One of the crimson warriors paused to discharge a firebug projector. Again a Po'Ellika leaped into the air to intercept the burning missile, its slender head snapping open like an old-fashioned cigarette lighter as it devoured its prey. Strange projectiles shot back and forth over Howard's head as he reached back to clasp the hand of Omber Oss.

The red-clad warriors were within yards of the islet on which he stood when their war cries faltered and then died. Howard saw expressions of awe and dread on those faces he knew how to read as they spread out into a cautious semicircle on the coarse sand. For a hopeful second he thought they were staring at him, but then the sensation of vertigo and nausea doubled in intensity and he heard a hollow, booming sound that sent a chill through his bones. Looking over his shoulder, he saw a tall oval of absolute blackness hanging in the air just behind the last Breakneck Boy in line. To Howard's horror, he recognized the small shape hurrying to catch up with the others on the narrow island. "Yam!" he called. "Get away from it!"

The twenty warriors were closing ranks in a ragged line halfway between the shore and the black apparition. As the Trilbit scrambled to join the Breakneck Boy in front of her, Howard realized that they were being herded. But there was no time to ponder the motivation behind the strategy. "Link up!" he called again as bodies pushed together.

There was a high-pitched cry from the middle of the line.

Howard watched helplessly as the purple-suited Trull wrestled fiercely with its Sarsi leader, disconnecting the far half of the group. On the other side of the Trull, Faweet, a white-maned Breakneck Boy Domeny, moved forward in the peculiar glide of his people and hurled the Trull sideways off the rock with a series of arm and leg movements too rapid for Howard to follow. The emerald sea boiled as something beneath its surface eagerly responded to the gift.

The Domeny reached out a glossy brown arm and completed the broken link with the Sarsi. Howard made a quick scan of the line. The Traveler boomed again and rushed toward Yam-ya-mosh, a thin halo of painfully bright light bordering its rippling darkness. Howard shut his eyes in panic and turned the Key—

—And tried to turn it back again, as something occurred to him—

There was a moment of nothingness, then an awful wrenching sensation; Howard hung suspended in darkness, in the heart of an explosion, as colors streamed past him with a roar so loud it seemed to destroy one sense while opening up another. Years passed while he waited there.

Finally, there was bright pain and the absence of sound, and the agony resolved itself into sunlight. He blinked and his eyes were his own again. The silence was divided into discrete moments. Between the moments came noise, sounds of movement, bits of speech.

The sun beat down on his face. The noises seemed to be confined to an area behind him. He turned around.

He stood at the bottom of a pocket valley, ankle-deep in the sand of the Red Desert World. The top half of a weatherbeaten tent was just visible on the rim of the slope to his left. Stretched out in a crooked line behind him were twenty figures dressed in black or purple. As he watched, the line wavered and broke into smaller fragments, then into individuals. Several of them came toward him and he realized that he knew them, pulling up memories as if from a great depth to match the faces.

"Alaiya, Yam . . ." He swallowed dry air. "You're all right." Suddenly exhausted, he slumped down to his knees.

"Ahwerd?" Alaiya looked frightened. "What has happened to you?"

"Why is your face so different?" asked the Trilbit, putting her small hand on his shoulder to peer into his eyes. "Did something go wrong?"

"I wasn't concentrating . . ." Howard rubbed his hand over

his face, discovering a trickle of blood under one nostril. "The Traveler was almost on top of you, and all I could think of was getting off those islands, away from there. This time I'd already turned the Key—I was already in between—when I realized I didn't have a destination in mind. I knew where we'd end up." He leaned forward wearily. "I tried to change it—I forced it to bring us here." Alaiya knelt by his side, supporting him. "Learned a lesson about the Key, anyway," he murmured, as his mind tilted and slipped downward into sleep. "It charges a high price for second thoughts . . ."

CHAPTER XIV

Weekend Getaway

MIXED IN WITH THE MEDICAL SUPPLIES OF THE Dreadful Noise had been a small quantity of purge pods. About half the allotment was used to cleanse the systems of the seven warriors who had survived the raid on Thousand Islands.

"We have enough left over to convert one more team," Alaiya told Howard, Yam, and Awp, who had gathered for an informal conference at the shore of the flower sea. The first moon was climbing the sky past ranks of silvered clouds as they sat around a small, crackling fire. "If that battle-gang also happens to carry a supply, then an additional raid becomes possible."

"What if they don't?" Howard asked. "Suppose the next three or four teams aren't packing any—do we have any other options?"

Alaiya had been pacing slowly along the ridge of smooth stone as she spoke. Now she stopped and stood facing the moon-lit blossoms, hands clasped behind her back. "We can go to the source," she said quietly. "We can attempt to enter Stillpoint itself and obtain a new supply."

"Much danger in that undertaking," Yam said. The Trilbit laid another bough of aromatic evergray on the fire and rubbed her ear. "Will Keyholders not sense this Key's presence in their own stronghold?"

"Perhaps there is another way to enter, without endangering the Key or its wielder." Alaiya turned to face them. "At the end of each Turn, the Gate is opened and all who wait beyond are free to pass through."

Howard frowned. "Don't they have somebody at the door,

checking IDs?'' he asked. ''I can't believe it's that easy to waltz inside.''

''The Keyholders send agents from time to time, to mingle with the warriors assembled outside the Gate,'' the Hant commented. ''They seem to take a special interest in the tale-tell, when surviving team members recount the glories of their battles. Occasionally, one of the Masters will attend in person.'' It blinked its complicated eyes thoughtfully. ''There is a slim chance a group of Breakneck Boys could pass unnoticed, but only if they were well disguised as survivors of decimated teams.''

''I did not say it would be an easy task,'' Alaiya said. ''At any rate, we are merely speculating at this point. Perhaps it will not even be necessary.''

''I am a member of this team,'' Howard said. ''If you do decide to go in at some point, I'll be there with you.''

Alaiya inclined her head formally. ''Thank you.''

''No problem.''

The Trilbit and the Hant excused themselves after a short while, leaving the Nonesuch and his battlechief to tend the fire.

''I wish we had some marshmallows,'' Howard said, poking idly at the embers with a pointed stick. ''They taste so much better over a campfire—black and flaky on the outside, gooey and scalding hot in the middle.'' He smacked his lips.

Alaiya stared into the heart of the small blaze. ''Perhaps soon you will be able to obtain some of these,'' she said quietly.

Howard laid down the stick. ''Has Awp been blabbing to you again?''

''No. But it has occurred to me that the most logical way to deal with your involuntary trips to your home world would be to go there intentionally.''

''Yeah, that was Awp's advice, all right. It does seem to make sense. After all, I do have a few loose ends to tie up, and I could use another watch and a new pair of sneakers. I mean, if there's some deep, unconscious urge that keeps dragging me back there, it seems like the only way to handle it is to face it—get it out of the way.''

''Or accept it.'' Alaiya picked up the stick and balanced it in her hand like a weapon. ''Like the other warriors, I was raised on a Holding—a world where members of my race were imprisoned thousands of years ago, after having been taken from their home by the Keyholders. Though Noss Averatu is the place of my birth, it is not the birthplace of my people, and so it does not have the same meaning for me as your Earth must have for you. If the pull is strong enough, perhaps you will decide to remain on Earth.

"Aw, jeez." Howard moved closer to the fire. Orange light played over his arms and legs. "Is that what you've been thinking?"

Alaiya said nothing.

"Look, Awp told me we may have to sit out the next recruitment opportunity—is that right?"

Alaiya cleared her throat. "According to the Hant, the next battle site to be brought into play is the Sunless/Moonless World. It is true that without certain specialized equipment and supplies, we would stand little chance of operating effectively in such an environment."

"Great—that means we have some time off, whether we like it or not. So I've got a proposition for you. I've been putting off asking you because I was afraid you'd say no." He watched her face closely in the flickering light. "What do you say we tired executive types leave the Breakneck Boys in the hands of our capable staff and have ourselves a small weekend getaway in Greater Metropolitan Boston?"

"Weekend getaway?" Alaiya frowned.

"Yeah. According to my calculations, it's definitely either Sunday or Thursday back home, so if we leave tomorrow, I figure we have a fifty-fifty chance of actually hitting it. Now, I can't promise you luxury accommodations on such short notice—or even that there'll be a decent Stooges film festival in town—but I'm sure we'll be able to find something to entertain us." He leaned forward and lifted her chin with his fingers. "Alaiya? What do you say?"

"You truly wish me to accompany you to your home world, Ahwerd? You do not ask this merely out of a sense of duty?" Her expression was wary. "If you would prefer to go alone, I will make no objection."

"And miss the opportunity to see your reaction to rush hour on the Southeast Expressway—Oreo ice cream—automated teller machines—microwave popcorn?" He grinned and rubbed his palms together. "This is going to be great!"

They chose the following evening as their time of departure. Howard had borrowed some bark-paper from the Hant, and he spent the morning making lists of places to see and items to obtain on the trip. He was sitting cross-legged outside his tent with a marking stick between his teeth when Yam came trotting up.

"Wha' y'think?" He removed the stick and scribbled a notation at the bottom of his current list. "Will it be possible to find a Mr. Bubble T-shirt in Harvard Square, or is that something you have to send away for?" He eyed his friend's plump belly critically. "I wonder what size you take—Adult Small or Child Hefty?"

"Toenippers, Ow-er-bel!" Yam dropped to the ground before him, slightly out of breath.

"Beg pardon?"

"Toenippers! While awaiting your recovery on Kansas three days past, I went looking for toenippers in red desert. They favor shallow sand at base of outcroppings—especially smooth white ones called toothrock."

"Oh, the little crablike things. I remember. About the size of a saucer, right?" He framed a small disk in the air. "I tried to catch some once—thought they might be good to eat."

"Very good, Ow-er-bel!" The Trilbit rolled her black eyes. "Grub-tasty, as we say. I was also unsuccessful in my attempt to capture one. It gives my finger a bad pinch. Painful! Then it seems to melt right down into sand before I can grab it again. Something lights up in my memory, but not clear enough for identification. Then, this morning, I am sitting in my dark hut and suddenly two and two are combined for me!" She extended her arms to either side. "Our big hosts in the sand castle cellar, all shiny in dark and slicing through walls—they are giant toenippers!"

Howard narrowed his eyes. "You're right," he said. "I bet you're right! If we'd seen them in the daylight, they probably would have looked just like them. What do you think—are the little ones their babies? I wonder if they glow in the dark, too? Jeez, Yam, I'm glad we didn't eat any . . ."

"Is continuing puzzlement, Ow-er-bel. Few days ago, when you bring us back to Red Desert World—where are sand castles? Where is low flat land? On my search for toenippers I see only same up-and-down, nowhere any different. Later, I talk to other warriors—no one has seen this strange place."

"You got me." Howard tugged at his chin with his thumb and forefinger. "But there's something funny going on there, all right. And as soon as things settle down around here, my dear Dr. Watson, you and I are going to get to the bottom of it."

"Prefer not bottom next time, Ow-er-bel." The Trilbit shivered. "Too cold and black. Better next time we climb on top of sand castle."

Howard tapped his marking stick on the lavender stone. "I'll make a note of it," he said with a sober nod.

Howard was halfway to Alaiya's hut when he became aware of something following him. It was just a feeling, at first. Then he started to hear small sounds in between his own light footsteps, and catch glimpses of something dark flitting behind the tents. He changed his route, deliberately heading between two closely built huts, then halting midway to steal back the way he had come on tiptoe. Circling around the outside of one of the small buildings, he crept up behind the black figure that crouched at the far end.

"Boo," he said softly.

The Pasper sprang a good yard and a half into the air, twisted, and landed almost, but not quite, on his sandaled feet. Clutching the corner of the little building, he stared at Howard with fanged mouth gaping, all the hairs on his head and arms standing erect.

"Looking for me?" Howard asked.

"Nuh'suh!" Trembling, the Pasper went down on his knees.

The Nonesuch grimaced. "Don't do that." He beckoned with his hands. "C'mon—up, up."

The feline warrior rose slowly to his feet.

"That's better. Now, did you need to see me about something?" Howard tapped his wrist. "I'm a little pressed for time."

Gemlike eyes locked on Howard, the Pasper gave his own forearm a careful tap.

"Oh, yeah." Howard sighed. "I forgot you just started English classes. Look—do you have a name?" He placed his palm against his chest. "Howard," he enunciated carefully. "Howard."

"Rrowrr?"

Howard shrugged. "I've heard worse. Now you—who're you?" He jabbed his finger at the warrior with a questioning look.

The Pasper raised his own pawlike hand and set it hesitantly on the small patch of white fur that lay just below his throat. "C'mu." Howard caught the faint scent of fish on his breath.

"Nice to meet you, C'mu." He extended his hand and lightly grasped the black paw, hoping the Pasper would keep its wicked-looking claws withdrawn while they shook. The Pasper watched him closely, his arm limp. The padded palm felt like warm leather.

"Well, I do have to be somewhere." Howard started to move away, but paused when he saw the look on the warrior's face. "You want to come with me? "Here, c'mon." He took the black-furred shoulder and guided the Pasper along. "Maybe I can teach you to say bon voyage by the time we get to Alaiya's."

The C'mu stood just behind Awp and Yam in the circle of well-wishers, his expression wavering between worshipful and bewildered as he joined the others in waving good-bye.

At Howard's side, Alaiya smiled, her face calm while her hand clamped his arm like a vise. A trickle of sweat started down her forehead while she waited for the Nonesuch to turn his Key. Both of them were dressed in several layers of black trousers, vests, and overshirts. On their backs were small supply packs. Howard had done his best the previous night to tally up the time he had been away from Earth; his estimate had been somewhere between six and seven months, including the almost four weeks he and Alaiya had lost while making a single trip from the Black and Blue World to Field of Flowers. "That's it," he had concluded, checking his figures for the third time. "Seven at the max—which puts the calendar at about mid-March back at the old homestead." He shivered. "That's the tail end of winter and it can still get mighty chilly, so we're going to have to bundle up."

They had borrowed extra garments from the team members to insulate themselves against the cold. Howard felt hot and uncomfortable under the warm sun of Field of Flowers, like a child dressed by an overcautious parent. He looked down at his wrists, half expecting to see mittens dangling there.

"Well, what do you say—are we history in this town?" He stretched his mouth in a comical smile at the Breakneck Boys and closed his eyes. His fingers moved on the shaft of the Key.

The air became much cooler and developed a flat odor. Howard opened his eyes to dim reddish light and slowly eased the Key from the lock of the Executive Washroom. He started to move away, then paused and stepped back to the door. "As long as we're here—" He juggled the crystal knob experimentally and turned to Alaiya with a sigh.

"Locked, of course. Someday I'm going to figure out how to get past that door without being bounced all over the universe in the process."

"This is truly your world, Ahwerd?" Alaiya's hand still clutched the crook of his elbow.

"This is it." He pulled the collar up on his outermost shirt. "Good thing we added the longjohns. It must be forty below outside, if it's this cool in here with the heat on." He slipped his hand into hers. "Ready to face the cold, cruel world?"

There was a sharp noise at the far end of the corridor, followed by the sound of a heavy door opening. Howard yanked Alaiya's arm, pulling her after him on the soundless carpeting. Something gleamed on the left a few yards down the hallway. They took several quick steps toward the source of the noise, then ducked into a half-open doorway. Holding his breath, Howard eased the door slowly shut, twisting the knob to prevent it from latching. Behind him was a broad window, and beyond it shone the glowing city lights he had seen from the hallway.

He stood braced against the door, still holding the knob. "Ahwerd," Alaiya breathed into his ear. She pointed to the crack at the bottom of the door where pale light shone suddenly, disappeared, then returned again as if someone were making sweeping arcs with a flashlight. Howard stared at the doorknob in the dimness, afraid to release it, praying that whoever was out there would not try to turn it. The sliver of light suddenly winked off. Half a minute later they heard a heavy, muffled sound that might have been a door closing.

Howard drew Alaiya closer and set his lips against her ear. "I think they're gone. We'd better give them a few minutes to make sure."

They waited silently in the darkened office, Howard keeping his ear pressed to the crack between the door and the wall. Minutes later, when he turned to give Alaiya the all-clear, he found her on the other side of the room. She was leaning with her hands on the low windowsill, staring out at the glittering city.

"Oh, Ahwerd," she said softly as he came to stand at her side. "It is vast. Larger than the dead city on Field of Flowers, greater even than Stillpoint." She turned her head slightly, so that her clean profile lay against the jeweled darkness. "What are your people, that they inhabit such a place?"

He put his arms around her shoulders and looked out with her, tightness gathering at the back of his throat as he saw the world through her newcomer's eyes for a few moments. "A people no different from your own, Alaiya," he said in Averant. "Brave and deceitful, kind and merciless, foolish and wise."

They left the office and made their way down the long corridor. Howard forced himself to open the heavy door with excruciating slowness. There was a stairwell on the other side, with concrete steps leading up and down. A tiny white light burned high on the wall in a cage of metal. He shut the door carefully behind them. "This is going to take a little while," he told Alaiya softly. "We're about sixty flights up, if I remember correctly. It's a safer bet than taking the elevator, though, if we want a shot at getting out of here unnoticed."

After they had gone down a few flights, they discovered small numbers stenciled in red paint on the back of each door.

"I had not realized we were so far above the ground," Alaiya said many minutes later, as Howard halted them on the landing whose door was marked with a single vertical bar.

"There's still a desk with an all-night guard between us and the front doors," he said, moving to the top of the next flight. "We'd better see what the garage is like. Maybe we can slip out there."

The stairs led to an abrupt dead end three floors down. Howard and Alaiya descended the last dozen steps into a dark, square-sided well. The little light lay smashed above them in its protective cage. Howard opened a pouch in his belt, dabbed up a bit of bluish gel, and spat on the end of his index finger. A tiny orange flame leapt from his fingertip. "There." A small G had been scratched rather than stenciled on the unpainted metal door. Howard tried the handle.

"Locked." He moved his miniature torch to show a quarter-inch gap between the door and the metal frame. "I wonder . . ."

Alaiya touched his arm. "Let me."

Howard was surprised to see that Alaiya had included Silversting among the items in her pack. As he held his finger near the door for illumination, she inserted the narrow blade below the lock and drew it carefully upward. There was a small click, and the door leaned toward them. Howard wiped his finger back and forth on the concrete wall a few times to extinguish it, then grasped the handle and pulled slowly inward. Alaiya slid the dagger into a clip at her belt.

The garage was a long, low-roofed cavern. Here and there, blue bulbs hung like luminous insects from the ceiling, and in the distance a trio of red exit lights burned against the wall. Alaiya hung back slightly as they left the stairwell. "It reminds me of the pit beneath the dead city," she whispered, her breath warm on Howard's cheek.

He smiled. "Listen—Massachusetts is one of the few places I can personally guarantee to be slake-free these days."

They proceeded through the dark expanse, their footsteps echoing hollowly. A few automobiles were scattered about the garage. They stood alone or in pairs among the empty lines, patches of chrome and glass agleam in the dim blue light. Alaiya regarded them curiously as they walked past.

They saw no signs of life. The glassed-in booths sat empty at the foot of the upcurving exit ramps. "Some of these places go on automatic after a certain hour," Howard murmured. "Stay late enough and you get to leave for free."

They were nearing the exit signs when Alaiya touched his arm. "I heard something. Back there." Her fingers sought the hilt of Silversting.

Howard stood still for a few seconds, listening. He heard a distant scrabbling sound from the direction they had come. The noise stopped. "Probably a cat after a rat," he said with a shrug. "Or a dog after a cat." They began to ascend a narrow walkway behind an iron railing that paralleled the spiraling ramp. The air grew warmer as they rose through the dimness. "In the garage, they have the heat on full blast," Howard said, as perspiration began to bead his forehead. "Figures."

Howard calculated that in another turn and a half they would reach street level. "It's probably not too good an idea to be seen walking out of this place." He stopped at a doorway set into the wall beneath a blue lamp. "I wonder if there's a smaller pedestrian exit . . ."

A steep flight of steps led them to a battered-looking door with a crisscross of metal threads set into its thick glass window. A streetlight shone greenish-white beyond. Howard tried the knob. It hesitated, then turned with a muffled click. "Bingo," he said softly. Behind him Alaiya repeated the word in a reverent whisper.

"Okay, button up." He clasped her hand. "Time to hit the streets." He pushed the door outward, and the two stepped through onto a sidewalk littered with scraps of plastic and a sprinkle of broken glass. It was like walking into an oven.

"Whoa—what's going on?" Howard tugged at his collar fastenings and peeled open his outer shirt, gasping in the heat. He and Alaiya removed their packs and began to strip off the extra layers of clothing, their bodies dripping with sweat.

Someone gave a low whistle of appreciation. Looking up, Howard saw a man in a tank top and cutoffs walking with loose-limbed rhythm along the sidewalk across the street. "Hey," Howard called, "what month is this?"

The stranger lifted a tiny black earphone from the side of his head. Tinny music with a driving beat leaked into the stifling air. "Say what?"

"What month is it?" Howard repeated. "What's the date?"

The man spat on the sidewalk in disgust and popped the earphone back into place. "Enda July, shithead," he said as he turned the corner and disappeared.

"Thank you," Howard called after him. He finished stuffing the extra garments into his pack and straightened. He and Alaiya were dressed alike now in black vest and shorts. "Damn, I forgot to bring my sandals." He inspected his tall boots unhappily as Alaiya bent to tie black laces around her calves. "I gotta find a pair of Reeboks, like soon."

"The man told you it is July," Alaiya said. She hefted her pack and rose to her feet. "This is a different month from the March you had expected, correct?"

"Yeah, about four months different." Howard wiped his forehead and looked around. A chain-link fence enclosed a small, blacktopped playground on the other side of the street. Shirtless teenagers chased a basketball under a cone of yellow light that was alive with circling insects. "I don't understand how I could've been so far off." He looked at the sky. No stars were visible through the city haze. "I wonder what time it is. It can't be that late. Those kids are making too much noise for after midnight—somebody would have called the cops by now." He strapped on his pack. "Let's see if we can find out."

They followed the fence around the corner to the site of the game. A tall, red-haired boy of about eighteen rose from the ground and guided the ball through a hoop of warped metal from which several inches of tattered string hung like Spanish moss. Howard leaned against the fence while the boy's teammates slapped at each other's palms. "Hey, anybody have a watch?"

The redhead turned from his friends and looked at Howard. He cocked an eyebrow at the combination of shorts, vest, and high black boots. Then he seemed to notice his own wrist.

"Wow," he said, lifting his forearm in amazement. "Looks like *I've* got one." He turned back to his teammates, shook his arm. "Hey, look—*I've* got a watch!"

Howard smiled. "Would you mind telling me the time, then?"

He spread his hands. "As you can see, *I* don't have one at the moment."

The tall player shook his head sympathetically. "Doesn't life just suck?" he said. He bounced the ball across the blacktop to a skinny boy with coffee-colored skin and moved away from the fence. "Play ball, you sucking sores," he called to the group.

Howard sighed. As he pushed back from the fence he realized that Alaiya was no longer standing in the shadows behind him. He heard a chorus of delighted yells from inside the playground and swiveled back in time to see her step through an opening in the fence several yards down and walk purposefully onto the blacktop. The players closed around her in a loose circle, gesturing and making a variety of low-voiced propositions as she headed for the red-haired leader.

"Oh, my," the boy said, watching the movement behind her loose vest as she stepped into the cone of bright light. He slammed the ball heavily into the midsection of the boy to his left and took an exaggerated, sliding step toward Alaiya, his long fingers clutching the air in front of him at chest level. "Whatever can I do to sweeten *your* night?"

Laughter erupted from the onlookers, followed by a round of detailed suggestions. The ring tightened slightly about her, several of the boys closing ranks to partially block Howard's view.

"Time," Alaiya said reasonably. She pointed to the boy's freckled wrist, gestured to the fence. "You can tell that man over there the current time. Now."

"Oh, the *time*. Now, that's *easy*." He rolled his eyes and took another long step forward. "It's just plain gonna be the *best* time you *ever* had."

On the other side of the fence, Howard gave a sigh and leaned forward to rest his forehead against the cool metal.

Alaiya made a small fluid motion and Silversting appeared in her right hand. She raised the dagger until it glinted in the harsh yellow light. "A second chance," she said softly. "Then we take the watch *and* the arm."

The redhead scratched his cheek and swallowed with difficulty, his eyes on the silver blade. At the edge of the light, a stoop-shouldered boy with long black hair and pockmarked cheeks took a quiet step into the shadows behind the hoop and bent quickly to the ground. Alaiya turned, stepped lightly through a gap in the crowd, and melted into the shadowed area after him. There was a choked cry. Seconds later, she returned to the circle of yellow light, the black-haired boy stumbling ahead of her. A long piece of twisted metal dropped onto the blacktop from his right hand, which seemed to be hanging at an odd angle from his wrist. White-faced, he pushed his way between two of the others and left the circle.

Alaiya had returned Silversting to her belt. Her hands were empty as she came back to stand before the boy with the watch. "Time," she reminded him.

He blanched under the red hair and stumbled back, his eyes darting to his wrist. "It's nine-thirty!"

"Is he lying, Ahwerd?" Alaiya asked without taking her eyes from the boy's face.

"Nine thirty-four!" He held his wrist up for her to see. "I meant nine thirty-four."

"Yup, that sounds about right to me," Howard said. "I think we can leave now, dear." He motioned with his head for Alaiya to join him and pried his hands from the fence links. Deep red welts crisscrossed his palms. "Thanks a lot, guys," he called over his shoulder as he ushered Alaiya down the street. "Enjoy your game!"

"I have displeased you by obtaining the information you sought," Alaiya said after they had walked in silence for a few blocks. She peered into his face as they neared a well-lit intersection. "Please explain the error in my actions."

"It's not what you did, it's how you went about it," Howard said patiently. "We were raised to be polite in my family—not to terrorize schoolchildren with broadswords."

"I am always exceedingly polite," Alaiya said indignantly. "It is when politeness fails that only the foolhardy hesitate to implement a different level of persuasion. As for schoolchildren, I was half their age when I began my warrior training." She slid the dagger from her belt. "And Silversting, as you know, is hardly a broadsword."

"Put that thing back in your pack—please?" Howard looked around nervously. "I'm sure parading a weapon like that through the streets without a permit is deeply and sincerely illegal."

Howard tried to employ his body as a screen while Alaiya removed her pack and stowed the dagger inside. A pair of young Asian women hurried by, giggling behind their hands as he stood whistling next to the yellow-painted post of the crosswalk light.

"It appears that your clothing is earning us more attention than my battleknife," Alaiya commented when she had finished. "Or perhaps it is your attempt at bird noises that is bringing such amusement to the passersby."

"Can we walk now?" Howard asked. "If we want to make it to Cambridge while it's still early enough to drop in on my former landlady, we've got to get to the nearest subway station as soon as possible."

"Fine. *I* am not preventing us from reaching this place." Alaiya walked briskly down the sidewalk ahead of him. "I have a question," she said over her shoulder. "What is a subway station?"

"It's where you get the subway. That's a method of transportation, like a bunch of troop carriers hooked together. It's very dirty and noisy, but if you're lucky it takes you from one place to another. In order to get on it, you have to go down underground and put some metal tokens in a slot—damn!" He smacked his fist into his palm and stopped walking. "We don't have any money! We can't ride the subway without money." He stepped to the edge of the sidewalk and stared out at the noisy intersection with abject horror. "My God, what have I done to us? We're in America now—we can't do *anything* without money!"

He felt a hesitant touch on his arm. Alaiya stood next to him. "Is there a way to obtain this money—following the customs and laws of your people, I mean?"

Howard gave a wan smile and covered her hand with his own. "No, not in time to get us where we need to go."

She looked thoughtful. "Is there any other way to reach our destination besides this underground carrier?"

"Buses, cabs—all take money. We're left with walking, and that's going to take forever." He shrugged in defeat. "There's a medium-sized river and a whole lot of city blocks between us and Harvard Square, but it's the only option I can think of—other than thumbing."

"Thumbing." Alaiya examined her hands with interest. "Is that some form of personal combat? What does it entail?"

"Oh, you stand over on the side of the road and stick your thumb out like this. Then some nice person in a car stops and gives you a lift."

"Let us try that, then." Alaiya practiced the gesture a few times, glancing back and forth between her hand and Howard's. "It would seem preferable to walking this great distance."

Howard shook his head. "Forget it. This is Boston—there *are* no nice people in cars here."

Alaiya sighed. "I am afraid that when it comes to dealing with your own worldkin, your philosophy is filled with contradictions,'' she said. ''This 'thumbing' approach appears to be polite enough. I am suggesting we employ it.''

''Fine.'' Howard checked the sidewalk behind him and sank down onto the curb. ''You can try it, if you want. I'll be here gathering my strength for our hike. Just give me a holler when you're ready to call it quits.''

Alaiya surveyed the traffic patterns for a few minutes. When the light turned green, she took a step out into the intersection and raised her thumb.

There was a squeal of brakes as a small silver convertible peeled out of the center lane, cutting diagonally in front of a line of cars and swerving to a stop inches from Alaiya's outstretched arm. A burgundy sports car pulled over and slammed on its brakes directly behind the convertible, its driver tooting his horn and waving for her attention. Farther up the street, three men riding in a white van with landscapes painted on its side shouted for her to wait while they attempted to back up through the intersection.

Alaiya brushed her hair back with one hand as she leaned over the convertible and spoke briefly with the driver. She straightened up and returned to where Howard was sitting at the curb, his fingers cupped around the lower portion of his face.

''Ahwerd, is it customary to accept the first offer when thumbing, or must I speak with each of them so as not to insult the various competitors?''

''Alaiya, Harvard Square is that way. These cars are all heading in the opposite direction from where we want to go.''

''I see. One moment.'' She walked over to the silver convertible and conferred again with the driver, then came back to the curb. ''I do not believe this will be a problem.'' There was another screech of brakes, followed by a chorus of angry honking, as the convertible darted out and made a rapid U-turn just as the light changed. The driver beckoned to Alaiya from the other side of the street.

''Fine,'' Howard said, pushing to his feet. ''Does he realize I'm coming along?''

''Yes, although I had the impression he prefers to convey one passenger at a time. At first he offered to come back for you somewhat later, but I insisted—politely—that we required simultaneous transportation.''

Howard waved the other prospective good samaritans on their way, and they crossed the intersection to the silver convertible. The driver was a well-dressed man in his late forties, with a brown mustache and hair that matched his car. He lunged across the passenger seat to open the door for Alaiya. Howard removed his pack and squeezed into the narrow backseat.

Alaiya's eyes roamed the city ceaselessly as the little car negotiated the heavy traffic. The driver seemed to be conducting a nonstop, one-sided conversation with her while Howard sat glumly in the back, separated from them for the duration of the twenty-minute drive by the blare of the car radio and the noise of the street. He leaned forward as they finally coasted into the Square. "This'll be fine, friend. Thanks a lot."

The driver pulled over reluctantly, his first acknowledgment of Howard's presence in his car. Howard climbed out and stood waiting on the curb while Alaiya allowed the man to shake her ivory-golden hand, which he seemed unwilling to return to her. At last, she exited the car and came smiling back to Howard's side. "What a generous and congenial individual," she announced, waving as the man give a final toot of his horn and drove away. "That was Harrison R. Frantzen, known as 'Skip' to his friends. Look, he has given me his residence number in case we cannot find lodging for both of us in the same dwelling and I find myself in need of a place to sleep."

"How considerate of old Skip." Howard took the small white rectangle from her hand, turned it over. "Mm, investment counseling. Here, let me hold on to this for you." He crumpled the business card into a small wad and jammed it into the pocket of his shorts.

CHAPTER XV

Square Times

IT WAS TEN PAST TEN ACCORDING TO THE BIG DIGITAL clock on the building across the street. "We made good time, anyway." Howard's spirits started to rise as he looked around the Square. People in various stages of undress thronged the red brick sidewalks, and music prowled through the humid air from half a dozen unidentifiable sources.

"Let's sit down for a minute." He led Alaiya to a low, angled concrete wall that separated an open-air café from the sidewalk. They sat between an elderly woman reading from a worn paperback edition of Emily Dickinson and a pair of teenage girls in tiny skirts who were arguing the merits of picking the scabs on their knees. " It toughens your skin," the blonde said, turning to Howard for corroboration as he and Alaiya boosted themselves up onto the smooth concrete. "Tell her."

"Hey," Howard said. "Let sleeping skin lie. What do you want, knees the size of cantaloupes?"

The blonde closed her jaws on a sphere of pink bubblegum, making a sound like a gunshot. "Who asked you? You think Nature doesn't need a helping hand now and then? I bet when you have a cold you just let your nose fill up till it runs out your ears, you're so scared to blow it."

"Allison, you are so *gross!*" her friend said, slapping her lightly on the shoulder with a gap-toothed orange comb. "I don't know her personally, mister," she said to Howard. "The city pays me to sit here with her so it don't look like she's talking to herself."

Howard turned back to Alaiya, shifting his body slightly to

give them some privacy. She was watching the passersby in fascination.

"Hey," he said. "Back at the playground. I'm sorry I wasn't very appreciative. This is a completely new deal for you. God, if you'd yelled at me every time I made the wrong move back in the Fading Worlds, you'd have lost your voice the first week." He lifted his shoulders, then let them fall. "I don't know, it's so strange being here. There are things about this world that feel so comfortable, but . . ." He looked around at the noisy crowd. "I think it's harder for me to do stuff here, because I already know the consequences of my actions—you know what I mean? On the Black and Blue World, or Kansas, or Field of Flowers, I just do what feels right, but here . . . here I'm not the Nonesuch, and it's not so easy." He tapped his fingers on his thigh a few times. "Anyway."

Alaiya pushed the hair back from the side of his forehead with her fingers. "Is your former dwelling near this place?"

"Yeah, not far at all. Prime real estate, too, this close to the Square. Luckily, my landlady owns the whole house. After her husband died, she decided to rent only to people she liked, and she kept it low enough that I—being one of those fortunate people—was able to afford the place." He glanced up at the clock again. Segmented numbers a yard high proclaimed the time to be 10:17. "We should get over there. I don't exactly know what to expect, but I had this idea she might've held onto some of my stuff when I disappeared. It's been what, ten months now. I don't know . . ."

He took Alaiya's hand and led her toward a wedge-shaped concrete promontory that separated two busy streams of traffic. In its center sat a small store, the windows crowded with magazines and out-of-town newspapers. "Let's stop over there for a minute," he said. "Headlines we can read for free. I want to check out the state of the world while I get up my nerve to face Mrs. Flowers." The muggy breeze surrounded them with the scent of pastries and coffee as they crossed a small side street. "Oh, God," Howard said, "Maybe she'll have doughnuts."

A band of pale adolescents clattered and rocked their skateboards over the uneven brickwork of a sunken area near the newsstand, while a more sedentary group sprawled on the nearby benches, sharing cigarettes and practicing rudimentary grooming behavior on each others' hair. Most of them were dressed in black from top to bottom, but an occasional maverick had added an accent piece in olive drab. The majority had dyed their hair either black or henna-red, with a strong minority favoring shaven heads. Several of the latter sported tattooed blue spiders on their fuzzy scalps.

Alaiya looked with interest from her own black vest and shorts to the clothing of the nearest youths. "Surely a team affiliation of some sort is denoted by this uniformity of attire," she said to Howard as he browsed at a rack of brightly colored magazines outside the newsstand. "Is this a form of local battle-gang? Look—that boy is crested like an Attercack!" She pointed out a cadaverous youth whose skull was bisected by a strip of drooping spikes dyed the bright lime green of newly set powderbridge. "But, truly, none of them appear to be in anything approaching fighting condition," she mused. She looked beyond the black-clad group to the crowded streets and shook her head somberly. "Nor, for that matter, do many of your people seem physically well cared for. They have a loose and mealy look to them."

"You'd never guess it from the amount of money shelled out to health clubs every year," Howard said absently, resisting the urge to unfold one of the newspapers stacked in rows on a low wooden counter under the window. "Hey, that's funny." He lowered his head, squinting in the flickering light from a nearby fluorescent tube at some small print near the top of the first page. He drew the newspaper from its pile and scrutinized the upper right-hand corner. Shaking his head, he flipped several pages under the watchful eye of the young employee seated on a stool at the door to the shop. With a strange look on his face, he returned the paper to the counter and reached for another one. "I don't get it . . ."

"Hey, pal, is not li'bry." The worker had dark skin and a strong Middle Eastern accent. "You wanna know son'tin', jus' fifty cent."

"Is this right?" Howard held up the second paper, pointing at the date with a black-smudged forefinger. "Is this today?"

"Yah, is fresh news, all fresh." The man reached out his hand for the newspaper and Howard released it with nerveless fingers. "You wanna take?"

"No, I don't have any money." Howard turned from the counter and took several steps away. Alaiya followed him curiously as he went to lean against the first in a curved line of public telephones set on rusting metal posts.

"Ahwerd, what distresses you? Is the writing not to your liking?"

"It's the date," he murmured, leaning heavily against the plastic and metal frame. "It's not the right date."

Alaiya glanced back at the newsstand. The young worker, once more perched on his stool, lifted his hands at her in a shrug. "It is March after all, then?" she asked Howard.

"No, it's July—it's just not the July I was expecting." He rubbed his hand down from his forehead to his chin, rested it at his throat. "I figured I'd been gone six, seven months, tops." His face was pale. "Alaiya, it's been nearly *two years*!"

She guided him to a seat on a jut of graffiti-scrawled concrete near the phones.

"At least it's Thursday," he muttered as Alaiya squeezed in next to him to avoid a fresh-looking wad of purple chewing gum. "I got that right, anyway."

"Do you think it could be the same phenomenon we experienced when we brought the Hant's overskin back from the Black and Blue World? We lay between the worlds for some period of time without knowing it."

"Yeah, but Awp said that was because I'd been fooling around with the second band on the Key, and managed to activate some sort of Directory function. I know I didn't do that this time. I just turned it like I always do. And anyway, that was only a month or so we lost—this is over a year . . ."

"So, what're you two made up for?"

Howard and Alaiya looked up to find a girl of fourteen or so standing by the phones, her arms folded on her chest. Her round face was the color of skim milk beneath straight black bangs streaked diagonally with daffodil yellow. The hair on the sides of her head had been razor cut into small furrows and tinted lilac to match her lip gloss, and she was wearing half a dozen silver rings in each ear and an additional two in her left nostril. A three-inch expanse of delicate silver bracelets concealed one wrist, while a score of black rubber rings clung to the other skinny forearm. Her sleeveless black shirt had been ripped apart along the seams, then put back together again inside out with the help of a box of safety pins. Torn black mesh stockings climbed out of black spike heels to cover her pallid legs in spiderwebs.

"Excuse me?" Howard said.

"No, don't tell me." She raised her palms. "They're filming a movie here, right? Mom and Dad switch brains with their kids and become cool for a day. So Winona Ryder and River Phoenix are running around somewhere dressed like stockbrokers, right?'' She scanned the nearby street, then shook her head in disgust. ''God, it bites how Hollywood has to to sanitize everything. I can *not* deal.'' She leaned forward suddenly and wrinkled her nose, sniffing the air between them. ''You do smell like you haven't been inside a shower in a while, but that's not gonna come across on film, unless they do scratch-and-sniff like in that John Waters movie. So—even though the ponytail's not too bad, and I like her scar—from a purely visual angle we're talking verisimilitude zero here.''

Howard tilted his head to one side and squinted up at her. ''Who are you?'' he asked. ''And why are you talking to us?''

''I need a light.'' She produced a thin, brownish cigarette from somewhere and waved it at him. ''You guys got a light?''

''Sorry, we don't smoke.''

Alaiya had been watching the girl in fascination. Now she glanced at Howard. ''Smoke, from a light-casting device?''

''She wants to make some fire so she can inhale the smoke from that thing,'' he explained.

''It is fire you are seeking?'' She gave Howard a small nudge. ''Ahwerd, if this child is in need of fire—''

''Yeah, 'Ah-werd.' '' The girl batted eyelashes that looked as if they had been dipped in tar. ''Give the child some fire for her butt.''

Howard clicked his tongue, then flipped open a pouch on his belt. Taking the cigarette from her nail-bitten fingers, he touched the tobacco end gently to the blue gel. He held up the cigarette to within a few inches of the girl's lips. ''You have to spit on it,'' he said. ''Go ahead—just a little bit.''

''Sick.'' She smiled with half her mouth, then pursed her lilac lips and spat carefully on the blue smear. A tiny flame leapt into the humid air.

''Wow, magic.'' She took the cigarette between her first two fingers and blew out the fire, then stuck the filter end into her mouth and took a deep drag. ''Pee-yuke!''she said, screwing up her face. She flipped the cigarette over her shoulder, bracelets jangling as she wiped her mouth with the back of her hand. ''That stuff is squamous. What are you, some kind of anti-smoking terrorists?'' Behind her, a thin, elderly man in a tattered suit jacket reached down and retrieved the smoldering, purple-stained stub. He had a length of dirty clothesline knotted around his collar in place of a necktie, and wore a pair of expensive-looking socks but no shoes. He tipped an imaginary hat at the girl's back and hurried off with his prize.

"No, we're travelers from another world," Howard said. "I'm Howard, and this is Alaiya. She thinks your friends are loose and mealy."

"Edith Kodaira." The girl looked over her shoulder. "If you're talking about those two, the tall guy calls himself Blot. I can't remember the other one's name, but I'm pretty sure it's not Louis or Mealy." She rubbed at the corner of one eye and brought her knuckle away smeared with black. "So, what world exactly are you from?"

"Oh, lots of them." Howard grinned as Alaiya watched him, wide-eyed. "When we get bored with one, we just hop to the next one. We're here on Earth for a little weekend getaway, only we don't have any money with us, so it hasn't been a great success so far."

"Squamulose. I've got a couple bucks I could give you, but I really don't want to set up that kind of dependent relationship. I make most of my money from the TV crews. I've been interviewed for three homeless specials so far this year."

"You have no residence?" Alaiya asked.

"Sure, I live with my mom. She's at Harvard. I'm half Japanese, can you tell? The other half's Connecticut Yankee—my dad's at Yale, yuk yuk. I'm just homeless for TV. It's a professional persona, so to speak. Of course, I never actually lie to them, I just edit—makes it more of a challenge."

"So what's the attraction here? Edith Kodaira could be home helping her mom correct papers." Howard spread his hands at the circle of lounging teenagers. "Why has she fallen among punks?"

"Actually, I prefer to think of myself as a proto-nihilist. I just started coming down here a few months ago to research the possibility of nothingness as a viable life-style."

Howard grinned. "Any conclusions yet?"

"The jury's still out." Edith scratched her elbow. "In the meantime, I pass among my subjects as one of them." She tugged on one of her nose rings. "Look, self-mutilation. Do I know how to lose myself in a part? I do keep a certain clinical distance, though." She popped open the Walkman clipped to her waist and showed Howard a cassette labeled with magic marker on masking tape: *Conquering the Gag Reflex—The World Tour.* "It's actually Mozart's *Horn Concertos,*" she whispered. "But don't tell them. I'm just starting to win their trust, and I'm still in sort of a vulnerable position here—y' know, like Jane Goodall?"

"Ahwerd." Alaiya touched his arm. "Do you not think we should be continuing to our destination?"

"Yeah, you're right." Howard pushed to his feet and held out his hand to the girl. "Edith, I want to thank you for a diverting several minutes. Alaiya and I have just found out we've lost about a year between planets somewhere, and I think you helped prevent me from going into temporal shock or something."

"A year, huh? Well, you know what they say—one year's pretty much like the next. You probably didn't miss much." She looked down at his outstretched hand, glanced around, and gave it a quick shake. "Let's try to make this look like you're passing me an illegal substance, okay? Otherwise, my gentle cousins will think I'm collaborating and toss me from a tree." She turned and took a few steps toward a short, bald-headed boy with tiger stripes tattooed on the side of his face, but then stopped and walked back to stand before Alaiya. "I just want you to know that I'm planning on looking exactly like you in a few years." She rubbed the side of her lip with a forefinger. "Maybe I'll start with the scar."

They walked down a succession of tree-lined side streets. The farther they went from the Square, the more Howard noticed people looking at them out of the corners of their eyes as they passed on the sidewalk. He stopped before a three-story house painted gray with white trim. A single light shone from a large bay window on the ground floor. Taking a deep breath, he went up the wooden stairs two at a time and pushed the buzzer. They heard sounds of movement through the open windows. Finally, the door opened a crack and a watery blue eye stared out at them above the curve of a thick metal chain.

"Mrs. Flowers? It's—"

The door slammed shut. Howard looked around at Alaiya, a pained expression on his face. "I'm not sure she got a good look at me. It's kinda late, too. Maybe I should—"

There was a rapid jingling sound and then the door swung inward. "Well, did you go out without your key, Howard?" The white-haired woman in the doorway had a round, kindly face and a bulldog's jaw. Peering up at Alaiya through thick lenses, she ushered them into the small foyer, pausing to lock the door behind them. She led the way to a small living room lit by a floor lamp with a blue-green shade. A tiny circular fan hummed from its perch on a stack of paperbacks in one window.

"How have you been, Mrs. Flowers?"

"Oh, this and that, Howard, this and that. Let me get some tea, now." She waved them toward the couch and disappeared into the kitchen. They heard glasses being set out on a counter, and the clink of ice cubes. Mrs. Flowers returned bearing a small, round tray with three tall glasses and a pitcher of amber liquid. "I know Howard likes plenty of lemon and sugar with his tea. Now what do you take, Miss . . ."

"Redborn," Howard said. "Helen Redborn. You like lemon and sugar, too, don't you, Helen?"

"Yes." Alaiya nodded, glancing uncertainly at Howard. "I would appreciate those items."

"Fine." Mrs. Flowers bustled back into the kitchen.

"Helen?" Alaiya raised an eyebrow.

"I don't know. I couldn't think. I was afraid she'd want to know where you were from if you told her your real name. Anyway, she likes the name Helen. She used to have a parakeet named Helen."

Mrs. Flowers reappeared with a sugar bowl and a saucer of lemon wedges. Alaiya watched Howard prepare his drink before carefully duplicating his actions.

Howard took a long swallow from his glass and slumped back into the couch. "Dee-licious. You don't know how long it's been since I've had iced tea, Mrs. Flowers."

"I know how long it's been since you've had mine," the elderly woman said. "Two years come September."

Howard straightened up. "Yeah. I'm really sorry about that." He eyed the ceiling. "I suppose you rented out my apartment."

"Yes, I ended up giving it to my nephew."

"Oh, that's good." They sat in silence for a minute. Alaiya looked around the dim room, taking cautious sips of tea.

"See, the thing is . . ." Howard bit his lower lip indecisively, then shrugged and leaned forward. "Mrs. Flowers," he said in a confidential tone, "have you ever heard of the Federal Government's Witness Relocation Program?"

"Why, yes. As a matter of fact, they had a movie on the television about it just last week. Some unfortunate young woman happened to see her employer toss his business partner out of a very high window. Well, a few days later she was an entirely different person, managing a very pleasant-looking little diner out in the Midwest somewhere. Do you know, they even found her a new boyfriend, and the most adorable beagle puppy—" She put her hand to her mouth. "Why, Howard, is that where you've been?"

He looked uncomfortable. "It's part of the deal that you don't talk about it." He nodded his head toward Alaiya, who had poured one of her ice cubes into the palm of her hand and was studying it intently. "Miss Redborn here is working on my case."

Mrs. Flowers nodded sagely. "You may not believe this, dear, but I had you figured for FBI the moment I laid eyes on you. I'm no stranger to the government, you know—my husband ran a small barber shop that was frequented by city council members." She shook her head. "The tales he brought home."

"I'm sorry I left so suddenly," Howard said, warming to the topic. "But you know what it's like—bounced from one place to the next. And there's always somebody there to make sure you play by the rules." He tilted his head in Alaiya's direction and rolled his eyes.

"Oh, of course. How interesting it must be to have a whole new identity!" Mrs. Flowers peered at him in the greenish lamplight. "I suppose most of those muscles are fake, then. Do they force you to wear that ponytail?" She raised her hand. "I know, I know, you're not allowed to say." She raised her brows at Alaiya, giving Howard a conspiratorial look. "You and I need some more tea, Howard. Would you care for some, Miss Redborn?"

"No, thank you." Alaiya slid the ice cube into her mouth and began to chew it somewhat noisily.

Howard followed Mrs. Flowers into the kitchen. "I'm not in town for very long," he said as she poured brown powder into the pitcher. "I just wanted to say hello, and see if by some miracle you might've held on to any of my stuff."

"Why, of course." She swirled the pitcher under the cold water tap. "Most of it's in the attic. Except for the mail, which I keep in the hall closet." She led him back into the living room. "Oh, and Morley's been taking care of your goldfish for you."

"Mail? You've kept some of my mail?" Howard stood in the doorway. "Could I see it?"

Mrs. Flowers excused herself, returning with a large cardboard box filled with stacks of envelopes and folded papers in different-colored rubber bands. She handed it to Howard, who looked down open-mouthed while she cleared a doily and a bowl of wax fruit from the coffee table.

"Now, this pile is all first-class mail. Over here are the bills—I've only kept the latest in some cases, the ones stamped third or final notice." She switched on a small lamp hanging on the wall behind the couch. "I weed out the circulars regularly, too.

No out-of-date announcements or coupons. I didn't think you'd mind.''

"Mrs. Flowers, I'd marry you, if I didn't already have a wife and seven kids somewhere!'' He grinned up at Alaiya, who had gone to inspect the assortment of knickknacks over the fireplace. "I love mail!''

Twenty minutes later, he pushed back from the coffee table and stretched. A stack of half a dozen pieces of mail sat before him. On the floor, the cardboard box held the rest of the items. "That's it,'' he called.

Alaiya stuck her head around the doorway to the kitchen. "One moment, Ahwerd. We are tasting tapioca pudding.'' A minute later, she came back into the room, licking her lips as she joined him on the couch. "A most unusual texture.''

"Look, first and foremost, I got a new bank card.'' He waved a small plastic rectangle in a soft white envelope. "I wonder if they noticed how restrained I've been about touching my account lately? There's also a new credit card that arrived about a year ago. Luckily, there's no annual fee with this one, or they would've cancelled it by now.'' He shuffled through the pile. "This is an invitation to my fifteenth high-school reunion, which is technically my seventeenth reunion, because it took Ellen—she was the editor of our yearbook—two years to find anybody to serve on the committee with her. Look—she actually included a list of the ten most uncooperative people she dealt with.'' He snorted. "Sounds like my class, all right. According to this, it's scheduled for this coming Sunday. 'Come to the Big Bash. Renew old friendships. Count the wrinkles and the kids . . .' Right.'' He dropped the card into the box of wastepaper. "Won't be needing that . . . Oh, here's something odd. It's a postcard from my sister out in California.'' He held up a hand-colored photo of a stuffed alligator partially dressed in a tuxedo. " 'Dear Howie—Something funny I need to ask you about. Don't panic: it's probably no big deal, but I'd appreciate a call. We also have to make a decision soon about the house.' Blah-blah-blah—she gives her phone number—'Love, Anne.' '' He tapped the card against his chin. "The odd thing is, it's dated the week I . . . went away.'' He raised his brows at her above the top-hatted reptile. "And according to Mrs. Flowers, she never wrote again.''

Mrs. Flowers insisted they stay the night. Howard and Alaiya took a walk down to Massachusetts Avenue, where they entered an automatic teller booth and tried out Howard's new card. "You know what my code is?" Howard said as his fingers moved slowly over the keyboard. "Nah, I'd better wait until we know each other better." Alaiya shook her head and stood by the door, facing down several prospective customers while Howard concluded his business.

"We're rich!" he chortled, riffling a small stack of bills under Alaiya's nose as they returned down the side street. The night was beginning to cool off, and streetlights turned the trees into translucent green spheres. "I had my last few dollars in that savings account, and interest has turned it into a very tidy sum. Well, not really—but it's enough for a weekend of high living. Of course, if I were honorable, I'd pay all those past-due bills." He folded the crisp rectangles in half and stuffed them into his pocket. "Yeah, right!"

Someone was waiting for them in Mrs. Flowers' living room. "Helen, I'd like you to meet my nephew. You remember Howard, Morley."

The very large man nodded at Alaiya, then stuck out a hand and lightly whacked Howard's arm. "Yo, Howard," he said.

"Yo, Morley."

"I ought to bust you one, you know." Morley paced the braided rug, mammoth fists bobbing at his sides.

"Oh, yeah?" Howard watched him warily. Two years ago, Morley Flowers had been in the habit of wearing a motorcycle helmet with the words "Hulk Kills" hand-painted on the back. If anything, he had grown bigger since Howard had seen him last. "Why is that, Morley?"

"You know how long it was before we went up into your room? Four days." He held up a hand with fingers like sausages. "Four days those goldfish went without a meal. I don't think Shemp's ever really recovered."

Howard leaned back against the doorjamb. "The boys! Morley, you don't know how grateful I am. How're the little guys doing?"

"Not so little now—except Shemp, of course." He clapped Howard on the arm and pointed to the door. "C'mon up, you wanna see 'em? I just cleaned the tank yesterday."

"How about tomorrow morning?" Howard said. "We've had kind of a long day."

"Sure thing." He beckoned Howard to the doorway. "So, Aunt Bess was telling me about this government stuff—is this chick really with the Feds?"

Howard glanced at Alaiya, who had taken one end of the couch in her arms and was holding the entire thing several inches off the floor while Mrs. Flowers fussed with the concealed catch that turned it into a bed. "What do you think?"

"Yeah, I see what you mean. You're looking pretty good yourself, except for the fag haircut—you been lifting?"

"Not really. Hey, Morley, your Aunt said she kept some of my stuff for me up in the attic. You mind if I check it out before we turn in? We can stop in and say hi to the boys on the way up."

"Sure thing."

There was a round, shiny object sitting on the little table near the foot of the stairs. Faded green lettering caught the light.

"So, did you ever decide to actually get a bike to go with that helmet?" Howard asked as the two men started upstairs.

"Nah. Too dangerous," Morley said.

They got up early the next morning. Howard had a hard time limiting himself to twenty minutes in the shower, especially after Alaiya joined him for the final ten. He gave himself a wide smile in the mirror as he toweled dry. "Not too bad for seven months— or is it two years?—without a toothbrush. That foodstuff is pretty clever to take care of cleaning our teeth along with everything else it does."

"The Keyholders are an astounding race." Alaiya ran her hand along the cool tiles above the sink. "We must not rest until the last one lies dead."

"And with that cheerful thought, we're off to greet the morning. Come on, get dressed now." He handed her a pile of his summer clothing, which he had found neatly stored in the attic. Alaiya added a few extra holes to one of his old belts and used it to cinch a pair of loose white shorts about her waist. She replaced her black vest with a light blue tank top that had never fitted Howard properly and examined herself critically in the mirror. "Am I fit to walk your world now?"

Howard gave a soft whistle. "Dressed like that, you're fit to rule it."

They left a note for Mrs. Flowers propped against the napkin holder on the kitchen table and slipped quietly from the house. As they started down the street toward the Square, Howard clapped his hands together. "All right," he said, "let's go places and buy things!"

They stopped for breakfast at a tiny restaurant with more plants than tables and a twenty-six-page menu. Howard agonized over his choices, finally ordering enough for four people. Alaiya picked at her food, dutifully tasting everything, but leaving most of it on her plate. As Howard was finishing the last of the waffles, he glanced over to see her nibbling covertly on her wad of foodstuff.

He winced. "Jeez, what are you eating that junk for? Don't you like what I ordered?"

"It is hard to say. The flavors are strange and new, some appealing, some merely odd. But I do not think it would be wise for me to introduce my stomach to large quantities of unknown substances over such a short period of time." She slipped the gray-brown lump back into its pouch and dropped it into her pocket.

As they were leaving the restaurant, Alaiya stopped near the exit to tilt her head back before a large mirror.

"Is there some reason you're putting your fingers up your nose?" Howard required.

"The filterfluff is coming loose on one side," she replied. "There."

"Filterfluff! No wonder nothing tastes good. What have you got filterfluff in for?"

"I found it necessary to erect some barrier between myself and the environment shortly after our arrival," Alaiya confessed. "I am sorry, but I find the air quite noxious here." She touched his hand apologetically. "It is not so unpleasant as the Sinking Swamp World, however."

"Well, that's a huge consolation." Howard sniffed the air as a bus trundled past. "Yeah, it does sort of stink. Sorry—I guess I just expect it."

Alaiya smiled. "It is not your fault. I find your own odor quite agreeable."

"Give it up, buddy," Howard said to a man who was walking by, inspecting Alaiya's body as if it were something on a dessert cart. "She likes the way I smell."

They embarked on a shopping spree, Howard unfolding the bark-paper list he had brought with him from Field of Flowers. He led the way to bookstores, toy shops, hardware stores, and clothing emporiums. Alaiya found herself confronted by marvel after marvel as Howard demonstrated, explained, and extolled the virtues of selected aspects of human culture. They visited gourmet food shops and electronics boutiques, a store that sold only maps and another that dealt in athletic footgear, where Howard and his charge card were able to purchase a pair of top-of-the-line Reeboks, black with silver racing stripes.

"Shoot—the place where I got my last Timex has been taken

over by an upscale health-food co-op,'' he said, standing outside a window display that featured giant carrots in Spandex doing aerobics. "Remind me that I've got to get another watch before we head back, if only to cover this tan-line.''

They had a light lunch at the café they had sat in front of the previous night. They sat at an outside table in a small raised area, where they could watch the passing crowd. Nearby, men with serious faces tapped small timers with their palms as they faced each other across permanent chessboards set on concrete pillars. This early in the day, the black-clothed teenage contingent had been largely replaced by shoppers and tourists. "You can sit here and listen to people speaking languages from all over the world,'' Howard told Alaiya. "If you close your eyes, you can pretend you're in Paris or Cairo or Allentown. It makes for a cheap vacation.'' They drank coffee and ate almond croissants, which Alaiya insisted bore a striking resemblance to a large, sluglike creature from the World of Whirling Air that many Averoy considered a delicacy. Though she seemed a bit disappointed when she actually bit into the flaky confection, she was delighted by the tiny birds that dropped from overhead to squabble over the crumbs left on her napkin.

"Is this a custom, Ahwerd?'' she asked, tearing off a small piece of pastry and dropping it over the edge of the table. A dozen of the ravenous mites converged on the spot and began to dispute ownership of the morsel in shrill tones. In the end Howard bought another almond croissant and two chocolate ones, giving half of each to Alaiya to be parceled out to her new friends.

Soon he tapped the alligator postcard on the black metal tabletop. "I think I'm going to go try to call my sister,'' he told Alaiya. "Will you and your aviary be okay for a while?''

He went to the bank of phones by the newsstand and placed the call through an operator. After nine rings, a bleary voice answered the phone. Howard checked the big digital clock; it was 10 A.M. in San Francisco.

"I have a collect call from Howard Bell,'' the operator said, the tone of her voice hinting at her disapproval of anyone still sleeping at that hour of the morning. "Will you accept the charges?''

There was a long hesitation. "Oh, all right,'' the voice finally said.

"Claire? Is that you? This is Howard. I'm looking for Annie.''

There was a snort of derisive laughter at the other end. "What makes you think she'd be here?''

"Oh, she's moved out? I'm sorry, I didn't know."

"Why should you?" The voice assumed the sarcastic edge Howard remembered from years past. "It's only been two years."

"Yeah, well, I've been kind of out of touch. Listen, Claire, I don't suppose you'd have her new number or anything? I'd really like to get a hold of her while I'm here."

"You're in California?"

"No, Cambridge. Do you happen to know where I could reach her?"

"You're making about as much sense as ever, Howard. I haven't seen or heard from your sister since a few days after she left, okay? Try the Yellow Pages under 'Terminally Pigheaded.' "

"Yeah, well, thanks a lot, Claire. Have a life." Howard stuck his tongue out at the phone and returned it to its cradle. On an impulse he rang up information, first in San Francisco, then in Boston, and asked for Anne under the name she always gave to directories. There was no listing for an A. Gridley Bell in either city. He turned from the booth with a sigh.

"Hey, sailor." A short young woman in a floppy, wide-brimmed hat sat nearby on a broad concrete step. She was dressed in madras culottes and a pink halter top.

Howard saw silver gleam from several locations in the shadows under the hat. "Edith?"

"Give the man a vice-presidency." She knocked a flattened chocolate milk carton off the step with the back of her hand and patted the concrete. "Where's Wonder Woman?"

"Over at Au Bon Pain—or 'Oh Bone Pain' as my friends and I used to call it—sending a bunch of pygmy vultures into a feeding frenzy." He settled at her side. "You're looking different today."

"I take Fridays off. The regular crowd won't be out for hours, anyway. And speaking of different looks . . ." Edith surveyed Howard's clothing, wrinkling her face in puzzlement. "You're putting out radically mixed signals. The shiny new Reeboks scream yuppie, while the argyle socks say either ultra-hip or brain-dead. The Krazy Kat T-shirt is a total anomaly, but I think it saves the whole outfit."

"What can I say—I'm a fashion outlaw." He got to his feet. "Look, I've got to go rescue Alaiya from those feathered locusts. We'll probably be back tomorrow afternoon sometime, so maybe we'll catch you then. In the meantime, don't smoke, and try to resist the urge to put any more holes in your face."

Edith tilted the huge hat away from him with a sniff of disdain.

"Personal criticism from a space alien in argyles," she said. "I can *not* deal."

The table was empty when Howard returned to the café. He craned his neck to search the crowd, his heart beginning to pound in his chest. Alaiya waved to him from a small group that had gathered nearby to watch a pair of jugglers toss fluorescent Indian clubs at one another.

"You moved," he said.

"Yes, a man shaped like a Sarsi began to scold me for giving food to the birds. I told him that with a belly like his, it was rank dishonor to deny sustenance to another living creature. He began to speak very rapidly then, which made it hard for me to understand him, so I picked him up by his collar and the back of his pants and removed him from the vicinity of my table. He went inside—to complain to the proprietors, I assumed—but later I saw him leaving quite meekly from a different door." She shrugged. "I had no more crumbs for the little ones, so I decided to come watch these performers."

Howard shook his head. "You sure know how to get your money's worth out of fifteen minutes."

"Were you able to contact your sister?"

"No." He scratched the back of his neck. "She moved just about the time she sent me the card. Her roommate, the monstrous Claire, hasn't heard a thing from her since." He got the card out again and scanned it. "She mentions the house in here—which reminds me, our next project is to get out west long enough to make sure it's still standing." He looked around the Square. "I wonder if we could get a bus anywhere around here." He raised his eyebrows as a sleek black Mercedes glided by. "Or maybe we should just rent a car . . ."

CHAPTER XVI

Under Western Skies

HOWARD MANAGED TO SECURE A COMPACT CHEVY from a small rental company just outside the Square. Someone had overlapped two bumper stickers on the rear of the car to form the message:

> LIFE'S A BEACH
> . . . AND THEN YOU MARRY ONE

Before they left, they made a phone reservation for the following night at a moderately expensive hotel in Boston. Then they drove to Mrs. Flowers's to gather up their things and say good-bye. It was early evening by the time they finished their tea.

"I want you to leave me the number at that hotel, just in case I find something else that belongs to you." Mrs. Flowers stood on the porch as Howard and Alaiya carried boxes to the car. "And you know you're perfectly welcome to spend tomorrow night here and save yourself some money."

"Thanks, but we're leaving early Sunday, and I want to show Helen some of Boston before we go." Howard took the elderly woman's hand and pressed a narrow envelope into it. "You know I can't begin to thank you for saving all my stuff—and putting us up like this without any notice."

"What's this?" Mrs. Flowers peered into the envelope, then held it away from her face as if it smelled bad. "Howard Bell, how dare you offer me money! You take this back—Morley and I loved having you. Besides, those goldfish of yours have done him a world of good the past couple of years—his probation officer made a point of mentioning it to me." She gave them each a hug and took a handkerchief from her apron pocket. "Now, you children go on and have a lovely time, and if you ever get back this way again, be sure to come by and stay as long as you want."

They stopped to buy some sodas and a few groceries, then turned the car onto Route 2 and headed for the western part of the state.

Alaiya was impressed by the variety of the landscape; she asked Howard to pull off the road several times so that she could leave the car and examine the local flora. But she found the distance covered by the highway they traveled even more remarkable. When Howard gave her some idea of the size of the continent and told her that it was crisscrossed with such highways from one end to the other, she shook her head in disbelief. "Would my people have girdled Tai Inimbra with paths such as this if the Keyholders had never come to ravage them like a plague?" she wondered.

"People are people, I guess," Howard said with a shrug. "Though I'd rather have the flowers than the roads. Hmm, I bet there's a folk song to that effect."

"People are people," Alaiya repeated. "Ahwerd, how is it that there are two human races—the Averoy and the people of your world? For the past few months I have seen you as the Nonesuch—a unique being, yet still one of my own people. Now I walk on a world teeming with strange humans, and I must face the fact of their existence. The two races are not identical, it is true." She set her ivory arm against his own tanned one. "We have our range of colors and our different features, and they are not the same as yours. And yet it is undeniable that we are one people. Even the most disparate members of our two races resemble one another more than we Averoy resemble our closest cousins on the Fading Worlds, the Domenai or the Paspers." She leaned back in the seat and fingered an edge of torn upholstery. "Puzzle upon puzzle. Since I met you by that waterfall on the Black and Blue World, Ahwerdbel, the mysteries of my life have multiplied at an alarming rate."

"Tell me about it," Howard said.

He found their exit just as the sun was going down, and they left the highway for a winding road that took them through a series of small towns. Exactly two hours after they had said their farewells to Mrs. Flowers, they passed a small motel with a flickering red and green neon sign and pulled into a bumpy gravel driveway. Evergreens and maples lined the way to a two-story cottage, where a single pale light burned behind the curtains in an upstairs window.

"I wonder . . ." Howard turned off the engine and hurried across the dark lawn to the front door. Alaiya sat in the car and listened to the sounds of the night. The new moon had been visible at sunset as a narrow crescent; now it was nowhere to be seen.

A minute later Howard returned and stuck his head in the open window on the passenger side. "No answer. I had this crazy idea—well . . ." He opened the door. "C'mon, let's see if the Lenihans have left the key in its old hiding place."

"This world is filled with keys," Alaiya said, holding on to his hand as he led her around the house to where a bulkhead angled into a border of weeds.

"That's because it's also filled with locks," Howard replied. They both spoke softly in the warm darkness.

"There's a little rock garden Annie and I made over here, next to the cellar door," he told her, groping near the foundation. "We always kept the spare key under a particular rock. I hope they've continued the tradition—" There was a scraping sound, then Howard straightened up with a small cry of triumph. "Yes! And it's wrapped in its own little plastic baggie—that's Marge's touch."

They returned to the front of the house, where Howard held the heavy screen door aside with an elbow while he unwrapped the key and fitted it into the lock. "And we're in." He reached inside the doorway and flipped on a yellow porch light, then adjusted the outer door so that it would stay open while they unloaded their things from the car.

"This is the living room," he explained to Alaiya as they made a pile of boxes and clothing on the carpet just inside the door. "We almost never used this entrance. Everybody always came in over on the side there, by way of the kitchen door at the end of the porch." He fumbled at the switchplate, extinguishing the outdoor light and turning on a ceiling fixture in the living room a second later. "Yow—too bright!" He crossed the room and switched on a glass-globed table lamp painted with vines and flowers, then flicked off the overhead light. "That's better." He stood with his hands in his pockets and surveyed the comfortable room. "Funny how you get used to things. The light, the furniture, the way a place smells—it has to be just right, or it doesn't feel like home."

"This is your home?" Alaiya turned in a small circle. "Your true home?"

"Well, this is where I spent my life, starting from about age eight months till I was almost thirteen. My aunt let me go live with my friend Ryan's family in Cambridge when it was time for high school. I spent all my summers out here, helping her run the motel with Annie. Then, after I graduated high school, I came back to go to college, and I didn't leave again for any length of time till, oh, about half a year before I met you." He took her hand and collapsed into a nearby rocking chair, pulling her down onto his lap. "So, yeah, I guess it's my true home."

They climbed to the second floor to investigate the light they had seen from the driveway. "That's what I thought," Howard said when they entered the little bedroom with the partially slanted ceiling. "The Lenihans put it on a timer thingy."

In the kitchen they unloaded the groceries. The refrigerator hummed to life when Howard plugged it in, and the faucet sent a stream of clear water rushing into the sink after a cough of indecision. "I think they let their kids stay here when they visit," he told Alaiya. "Which is fine with me. Keeps some semblance of life in the old place." He filled the ice-cube trays and brought Alaiya out through the kitchen door onto the long side porch.

"Look, we couldn't see this from the city." He put his arm around her shoulders and pointed up at the Milky Way, stretched like a jeweled band above the black treetops. "A whole new sky, filled with stars you've never seen before."

"It is very lovely," she said, gazing upward with a child's wonder in her face. "Oh, Ahwerd, I am grateful that you have brought me to the world of your past life. Will you do another thing for me when we have returned? Will you come with me to the Holding of my birth—to Noss Averatu—so I may show you the stars of my own childhood skies?"

"Whenever you're ready," Howard replied.

The air was cooling quickly. By the time they came inside, the little thermometer in the kitchen window had dropped to below sixty.

"You want to build a fire in the living room? Just a small one, just for fun?" Howard went back out on the porch and returned with an armload of logs. Alaiya was standing in the center of the living room floor, looking doubtfully down at her feet. "Will not this cloth covering catch fire?"

"Not if we use the fireplace." He lifted a fat-cushioned chair and carried it awkwardly to the other side of the room. "See, we always kept this chair in front of it in the summertime." There was a stack of newspapers in the kitchen, and soon Howard had a cheerful blaze going. He ran upstairs to get a blanket from the linen closet to spread on the floor. When he returned, Alaiya handed him a folded paper bag.

"What's this?"

"For your fire," she said. "When you told me we were going out to a wooded place, I thought you might wish to start one. I used some of the currency you gave me in the grocery store."

Howard reached into the bag, and pulled out a plastic package full of puffy white objects. "Marshmallows! I don't believe it!" He laughed with delight. "You know, I picked up a couple Hershey bars at the checkout line, and there's a box of graham crackers out in the kitchen that doesn't look too old—we can make s'mores out of some and toast the rest!" He hugged her. "Oh, life is swell!"

"I had a difficult time remembering the pronunciation," Alaiya said next to his cheek. "At first the man tried to sell me something much larger—muskmelons, I think he called them—but when I told him they were for piercing with sharp sticks and burning over flames, he decided I must mean these. Are they indeed the correct items?"

"Yes, they're perfect."

"I am glad. I do not think we would have been able to fit as many of the muskmelons on a stick."

Much later they lay together on the blanket and watched the fire die. "I can go up and get another one of these if you want," Howard said, tracing Alaiya's profile with his forefinger in the flickering shadows. "We didn't pack our pajamas, and it's a lot cooler out here than in the city."

Alaiya moved her hand along his thigh. "After the last several hours, can you seriously believe that we will lack for heat?" she murmured, her tongue licking at his finger as it passed her lips.

"Ah, the hidden link between nostalgia and passion," Howard whispered, beginning to guide her hand with his own. "Who knew?"

He was awakened sometime later by a loud clicking noise and a blinding beam of white light. Before he could react, Alaiya gave him a hard shove, sending him rolling onto the carpet to one side of the blanket as she leapt to her feet on the other. She swept the blanket from the floor and flung it through the air at the dark shape behind the light, then dove across the room and whipped Silversting from her pack. A flashlight thumped heavily to the floor in the vicinity of Howard's head.

"Wait, wait—" Howard struggled to his feet and spread his arms out between Alaiya and the blanket-draped figure. "—I know those shoes." He reached for the flashlight, tugged at one end of the cloth, and shone the light into a pair of slightly skewed wire-rimmed glasses. "Bert! It's me—Howard!"

"Well, Howard, what a surprise!" The man pulled the rest of the blanket from his head and began to fold it automatically. "Maybe you and your lady friend would like to join Marge and me for some breakfast—say about ten o'clock? We can catch up on old times."

"That would be great. I'm sorry I didn't stop in down the road before coming out, Bert." Howard accepted the folded blanket and held it against his chest. "I guess I was just excited about seeing the old place."

"No trouble at all. Marge saw the lights a little while ago when she was up with the cat. Did I tell you we got ourselves a new one? Marge calls him Space—he's got kind of an absent-minded air about him—but he's a darned good mouser. Nothing like ol' Speedy, though. Well, I'll let you folks get your rest. Don't bother to show me out. Nice to meet you, miss." He leaned in toward Howard as they walked to the living-room door. "You did bring some clothes with you, didn't you, Howard? 'Cause if you need to borrow anything—"

"I think we've got some packed, Bert. Thanks." Howard patted the older man on the shoulder and pushed the door shut behind him.

"You know, it has gotten cooler out," he said, crossing the room to where Alaiya still stood staring at the door, dagger ready in her hand. He knelt on the hearth and poked at the embers with a stick. Patches of orange light flared among the ashes. "Are there any marshmallows left?"

"They are pleasant people," Alaiya said as they began their trip back to Boston the following noon.

"Yeah, they both worked for my aunt for a long time. She signed them on as partners shortly before she died, then left them her share of the motel in her will. Annie and I got the house, and Bert and Marge have been looking after it for us."

"What will happen now?"

"I gave Bert a little money for upkeep and told him to think of the place as his own, unless he hears otherwise from Annie or me.''

''You are right,'' Alaiya said after a while. ''The small animal—the cat—is very like a Pasper.''

''Isn't it? Y'know, I was thinking of picking up a small souvenir for my new pal, C'mu. Do you think I'd be insulting his culture or anything if I got him one of those little felt mice with catnip inside?''

It started to rain when they were about halfway to the city. Alaiya gave a little jump when the windshield wipers made their first sweep across the glass, then began to chuckle into her palm as they continued to squeak and thrum between her and the road.

''What?'' Howard said, looking over in amazement as his companion slowly collapsed into helpless laughter. Soon they were both laughing hysterically. Finally Howard pulled the car over onto the shoulder to wait out the brief storm. ''Oh,'' Alaiya said, wiping the tears from her cheeks as he turned off the wipers. ''Oh, oh, oh.''

They drove directly into Boston, stopping at Filene's Basement to buy two suitcases before proceeding on to the hotel. ''It'll look a little more respectable if we come in with matching luggage, rather than an armful of cardboard boxes,'' Howard explained as they parked the car in the hotel garage.

A message was waiting for them at the front desk.

'' 'Call Mrs. Fowler as soon as convenient,' '' Howard read from the yellow slip. ''They must mean Mrs. Flowers. Maybe she found my old Monkees albums . . . Nah, I'm sure Morley sold 'em on me.''

Their room was on the tenth floor. Howard showed Alaiya how to work the TV remote and she sat cross-legged at the foot of the bed, staring in fascination as she clicked slowly through the channels, while Howard placed a call to his former landlady.

''Mrs. Flowers? It's Howard. How are you doing?''

''Oh, off and on, Howard, off and on.'' Her voice sounded troubled. Some people came by today asking for you. Now, I don't know if I did the right thing, but I told them you'd left town for good as far as I knew. I did promise to pass on a message if I happened to hear from you. I thought it just might be important, so I called the hotel right after they left.''

''Asking for me?'' Howard leaned forward, resting his elbow on the nightstand. ''You're sure it was me they wanted, Mrs. Flowers?''

"Oh, yes, Howard, quite sure. Now, they didn't say your name right at first—they only started using it after I blurted it out, thinking they must be your friends because they described you so well. That was probably very foolish of me, I know."

"No, no, not at all. Can you tell me what these people looked like?"

"Well, they were tall—the one man and woman, anyway. They didn't come all at once, you understand. First there were two men. The tall one, like I said, and his friend. The other man was on the smallish side. He had a mustache. Now, they're the ones who left the message, and they weren't the politest individuals I've ever had on my porch, if you'll excuse my saying so. About half an hour later, the woman came by. She was tall, too, with blond hair in sort of a French cut. When I told her I'd already spoken with her friends she seemed upset. She left right after that. As for—"

Howard heard a low voice in the background, and then Mrs. Flowers said something away from the mouthpiece.

"What's going on? Mrs. Flowers? Are they there now? Are you all right?"

"Yo, Howard. It's me, Morley."

"Morley, what's going on?"

"Listen, Aunt Bess don't want to hurt your feelings or nothin', but I think there's some serious shit going down here. You know these bozos she's talking about?"

"No, I have no idea who they could be. Nobody knows I'm here, Morley—nobody."

"That's what I figured. Well, I think your cover might be blown, if you know what I mean. We prob'ly shouldn't go into it over the phone. Aunt Bess wants to read you the message they told her to give you. You take my advice, Howard, you'll get outta here pronto."

"Yeah, thanks. Look, I'm really sorry about this, Morley. I don't know what's going on, but I hope these people didn't frighten your aunt too much."

"Nah, she's doin' all right. Wish I'da been home when they were here, though. I woulda taken care of 'em." Howard winced at the sound of a fist slapping a palm.

Mrs. Flowers came back to the phone. "I'm sure there's nothing to worry yourself about, Howard, although I think Morley's advice is very sound. Now, here is what they asked me to tell you: They want to meet with you tonight at midnight. They said that it would be to your great benefit or some such words to show up. Do you have a pencil for the address?''

Howard scribbled for a few seconds on the pad next to the phone. ''Got it. Thanks a lot, Mrs. Flowers. I'm really sorry to have gotten you mixed up in whatever this is. Hopefully, they won't come by again.''

''Oh, don't you worry about it. Morley starts his vacation from the escort service day after tomorrow, so he'll be home much more often for the next two weeks. I'm sure we won't have any trouble.''

''I hope not. Well, thanks again for everything. I really appreciate it.''

''Not at all. My, you certainly live an interesting life these days, Howard!''

''I certainly do, Mrs. Flowers. Goodnight, now.'' He hung up the phone and sprawled back against the pillows.

''Look, Ahwerd.'' Without taking her eyes from the screen, Alaiya reached back and shook his leg. ''If this small woman correctly determines the concealed letters, she will win fabulous prizes!''

CHAPTER XVII

Rendezvous

"SORT OF PUTS A DAMPER ON OUR LAST EVENING, doesn't it?" Howard stood looking out of the hotel window, where the late-afternoon sky was framed with distant clouds. An airplane moved in the middle distance like a sliver of shiny metal being drawn across a turquoise.

"What had you planned for us to do during this time?" Alaiya watched him from the edge of the bed, where she had remained while he detailed his conversation with Mrs. Flowers and her nephew.

"Oh, I thought we'd take the car back to Cambridge and drop it off. Then get dinner at a really nice restaurant. Hang out in the Square for a while, maybe go to a movie and introduce you to Bogart and Bacall." He stretched the corners of his mouth in a shrug. "Now I don't know."

"You have decided to go to this place at midnight to meet with these individuals?"

"Wouldn't you? I mean, we could just turn the Key and get out of here, but I don't want them bugging my friends when I'm gone. And, anyway, I'm curious."

"Most certainly." She watched sunlight turn the windows of a nearby skyscraper into flashing copper mirrors. "Is there a chance we could accomplish all that you had planned for us and still return to Boston in time to make the rendezvous?"

"Well . . ." Howard glanced at the little square clock on the nightstand between the beds. "Yeah, if we left pretty soon—say, in an hour. Then I guess we could do it."

"And how far away is the meeting place?"

Howard picked up the note. "I'll ask at the desk to make sure.

148

I have a general idea of the area it's in. It shouldn't be more than fifteen minutes from here on foot."

"Then, if we acted with reasonable swiftness, it might even be possible for us to make a brief visit to this location before continuing on to Cambridge?"

"I suppose so," Howard said. "If we acted with reasonable swiftness. But—"

"Fine, then." She gave him a sunny smile. "The dampness is removed from the evening. If you wish to use the cleansing room first, I will be content to wait." She tapped her fingers idly on the remote control.

Howard clicked his tongue. "Battlechief or couch potato," he intoned solemnly. "You be the judge." He paused at the door to the bathroom. "So, what do you think—is this a trap we're walking into tonight?"

"Most certainly," Alaiya said again.

The address Mrs. Flowers had given them was in a rough section of town about ten minutes from the hotel. The area seemed mostly commercial, with no residences for several blocks. The only person they encountered as they walked the empty streets was an anxious-looking cyclist in bright green-and-yellow leotards who looked as if he had gotten separated from his road race.

The number they sought was on a battered metal door set flush with a brick wall at the far end of a broad alleyway. Weeds grew from deep cracks in a strip of buckled pavement that ran down the center of the alley. To either side, the packed earth was strewn with pieces of broken glass in clear, green, and brown, crumpled metal cans, and less identifiable refuse. A badly rusted fire escape clung like dead ivy to the three stories of crumbling concrete that bordered the alley on their right. On the other side, a featureless gray wall rose to at least twice that height, its bottom ten feet a riot of vine-covered graffiti. A weathered notice marked the building behind the wall as condemned.

The door was locked. Howard peered in through the filthy window to the right of it. "Looks like an old warehouse or something. No signs of life." He inspected the cul-de-sac. "Jeez, I'm surprised they don't have a big sign up on the wall here." He framed a section of the brickwork with his hands. " 'Welcome to the ambush. Please wipe your feet.' "

Alaiya walked back to the street and surveyed the area, hands on hips. "We must do something about these," she said, indicating the two nearest streetlights. "And there are a few other adjustments that should be made . . ." All told, Howard and Alaiya spent fifteen minutes at the site before the battlechief announced that they could leave.

They discussed their basic strategy on the drive into Cambridge, then agreed to keep the upcoming meeting out of their conversation for the rest of the evening. "To allow the enemy to invade one's thoughts too soon before the commencement of combat is to begin the battle at a disadvantage," Alaiya said gravely.

"Very wise," Howard replied. "You know, you'd have a great future in the fortune-cookie business, if you could just learn to be a little more concise."

They returned the car to the Kwik-Rent office and rode the bus to a stop near the Square, where they got off and walked the rest of the way. "This is the Cambridge Common," Howard told Alaiya as they strolled toward a statue down a grass-bordered path. "We used to play some serious Frisbee here, in the old days."

"Frisbee?" Alaiya stretched her arms out behind her. "A competition of some sort?"

"Competition?" Howard gave a disdainful laugh. "The pastime of emperors! And as a matter of fact . . ." He eased his pack onto the ground and extracted one of the new 150-gram disks he had purchased the previous day. "Wanna play?"

With reflexes honed by warrior training on the Fading Worlds, Alaiya was quick to master the basic art of throwing and catching a Frisbee. Soon they were sending each other racing back and forth across the small area they had claimed as their own. "I'd take you up to the Radcliffe quadrangle if we had time," Howard panted between catches. "Prime Frisbee country—we used to get chased out of there every other day when I was a kid."

He reluctantly called a halt to the game after half an hour of vigorous play, just before they passed what he termed "the sweatpoint of no return." By that time, they had acquired a small but attentive audience of eight- and nine-year-olds. The youngsters applauded enthusiastically when the pair took their final bows. "Yes, we *are* the champions," Howard said, stuffing the Frisbee back into his pack.

They could find no vintage movies playing within a reasonable radius of the Square. Finally, Howard brought Alaiya to see an early show of the latest fantasy thriller, a fast-paced adventure movie featuring clever dialogue and unrelenting gore. Alaiya was more impressed by the technology that produced the giant image, with its vivid colors and wraparound sound, than she was by the content of the film; she frowned through the repartee, and smiled scornfully during the blood-drenched fight scenes. "So false!" she whispered to Howard after one particularly messy triumph of stuntwork and special effects. "This is not even simulated combat—it is a clever dance, performed with loud noises and barrels of red pigment." She nodded at the hero, swaggering unscathed through a melee of swinging blades and whizzing projectiles. "Send him to me for a single day on the Fading Worlds—I will teach him a new dance!"

"Somehow, I don't think his agent will jump at the offer," Howard said around a mouthful of buttered popcorn.

They ate dinner in a high-ceilinged restaurant with a small artificial waterfall running down one wall.

"I have to tell you," Howard said, looking around at the soft-voiced serving staff in their black-and-white uniforms and the other patrons conversing under potted trees strung with tiny yellow lights. "right now, at this moment, the Fading Worlds seem like a dream to me—or at least the backdrop for a much better movie than the one we just saw. Hants and Trilbits, worlds with movable islands, cities that come and go . . . impossible."

"Is that what you are wishing right now?" Alaiya watched him without expression.

"I didn't say anything about wishing." Howard speared a piece of broccoli with his fork and shook it at her chidingly. "It's more like this tiny nervous voice inside that keeps saying: You never left, it's all a lie, you bopped your head on that washroom floor and never woke up." He set down the fork and slipped his fingers between the buttons of his shirt, pulling out a small loop of leather thong. He sighed with relief.

Some minutes later, a small bird that had apparently entered the restaurant earlier in the day began to fly back and forth above the diners. Alaiya tried without success to tempt it down to her plate.

"How about we go hang out at Bone Pain?" Howard suggested. "I'm sure you could persuade a few of the regulars there to share your dessert."

The Square was alive with sidewalk entertainment. As they made their way to the open air café, they passed musicians playing saxophones, accordions and hammer dulcimers; a fire-eater who claimed to have performed before the crowned heads of New York and Rhode Island; and a storyteller on roller skates. A juggler with a red nose did a clever stand-up comedy routine while keeping an assortment of kitchen utensils in constant motion above his head. Uncertain as to exactly what constituted public entertainment, Alaiya stopped once to stare expectantly at a couple necking quietly in a doorway. Howard had slipped into a nearby bank booth. He returned in time to lead her away with a promise of cotton candy just as the taller of the women began to get to her feet.

"She invited me to take a picture of them, Ahwerd," Alaiya told him, frowning back over her shoulder. "She said it would last longer. I wonder if she thought I was an artist." She took the paper cone from him and brushed the airy pink confection delicately with her fingertips. "I remember that you described this to me once," she said finally. She bit her lower lip. "What I have forgotten is whether it is food or a garment."

Soon Au Bon Pain glittered like a miniature carnival across the central intersection. In between, cars moved in fitful currents as pedestrians lined the sidewalks on either side of them. Feeling a sudden absence, Howard glanced around just as the WALK light came on and sent the crowd behind him surging toward the opposite curb. He spotted Alaiya several yards back, standing inches from a motionless, black-suited figure whose face was lost in the shadow of a partially folded green awning. His skin prickling with alarm, he fought the tide of bodies and came up behind her.

"What's going on?"

Alaiya's mouth was set in a snarl as she glowered at the frozen creature before her. With a face ghastly white beneath a cap of slicked-back black hair, it faithfully mirrored her menacing expression, head cocked to one side and thin body rigid.

"Oh, God," Howard said.

Alaiya looked at him from the corner of her eye. "I am about to kill someone, Ahwerd," she said softly, her hand lifting slowly toward her pack. "Do you have a reason why I should not?" Across from her, a stiff, white-gloved hand rose in a duplicate gesture.

"Boy, this is a tough one." Howard pushed his fingers back through his hair as he pondered the question. "I mean, it's not as though it would *really* be murder." He watched a bead of sweat trickle down the pancake makeup that coated the gaunt cheek. "Nah . . ." He shook his head in disgust. "Let it alone, Alaiya. It's pretty defenseless, as you can see—protective mimicry gone berserk. It's called a street mime, and while they're generally acknowledged to be a lower form of life, they're still technically a protected species."

"What if I promised to leave it alive—technically?" she asked.

"Hey," said the mime, unfreezing its face and taking a step backward toward the wall. "She's not kidding, is she?"

"You do any cute little bird imitations?" Howard asked. "That's about all I can think of that could save you now."

The mime turned and bolted out from beneath the awning, leaving behind a small white smear on the scalloped green edge.

They reached the café without further incident. While Alaiya searched for a table that would be easily visible to low-flying scavengers, Howard went inside for coffee. He spotted a familiar figure as he returned across the concrete patio.

"Hey, Edith!" He set down his tray and beckoned to the diminutive figure on the sidewalk, once more clothed in black. She was stopped by one of the café's employees on her way to their table, but after Howard responded to her pointing finger with a vigorous nod, the man reluctantly allowed her to pass into the eating area.

"They don't like us to hang around because we never buy anything," Edith explained as Alaiya brought her a chair from a nearby table. "I have this friend, Sal, he always gets a bunch of the little creamers from inside. Then he sits out here at a table, popping 'em open and slugging 'em down, just like he was doing shots."

"Well, our fortunes have improved considerably since the other day," Howard said, "so if you want anything . . ."

"No, I'm set. My mom took me out to dinner earlier. I think she figures if she feeds me a lot, I'll be too sleepy to make my way down here."

"You took your nose rings out," Howard observed. "How come?"

" 'Cause I feel like I'm starting to get a head cold." She raised her eyebrows. "Think about it."

Howard made a face. "I'd rather not."

"So enough—momentarily—about me." Edith got to her feet, rotated the black metal chair a hundred and eighty degrees, and sat down again, her chin resting on the top of the chair back. "Who are you guys running from, anyway?"

Alaiya looked up from the partially shredded croissant she was preparing to dole out to her eager flock.

"What makes you think we're running from somebody?" Howard asked.

Edith twisted her left arm to display a ring of ugly purplish bruises midway between the shoulder and elbow. "The guy who owns the hand that fits these prints was looking for you last night."

Howard felt the blood drain from his face. "Tell me," he said.

"Well. About eight-thirty I'm hanging with the skateboard set, when these two squamous jeeks show up and start circulating among the regulars. They're acting a little bit like cops, but not enough, you know? Plus, they both have these stupid-looking hats on that practically scream 'film crew.' So I'm thinking, aha, advance men for a major punkumentary, and big dollar signs pop into my eyes. I wander over to where they're giving Cubby and Blot the third degree and listen in. The little guy with the mustache is just saying something about 'tall, dressed in black vest and shorts with dark hair pulled back . . .' Hey, I'm thinking, it's 'Ah-werd,' my man from Mars. At this point the other guy, who's about three times my size, looks over and figures out I know something from the look on my face. 'Can you help us find our friend, little miss?' he says. 'We were s'posed to meet up with him here, but we got delayed.' Oh, I said, what happened—get stuck on the wrong world without a transfer? At this point he absolutely freezes, I swear he turns green, and the little guy snaps his head around like it's on a spring. 'Oh, you know our friend,' he says, recovering real quick, even though it's clear the two of them are totally blown away. He takes out his wallet—I can see he's got a couple old black-and-white pictures stuck in there and I think he's gonna show 'em to me, but he doesn't. Instead he whips out two lovely new fifties. 'Can we talk over here?' Meaning the little tunnel there that connects to the other street. Now, remember, I've still got these big dollar signs impairing my vision, only now they've each got 'fifty' written after them, so I take a small walk with the guys. The little one hands me a bill and says 'So?' So, I say, your friend's back on Pluto by now. I'm starting to notice the very bad auras these guys have got, and figure it's not the smartest thing in the world to tell 'em you'll be back here on Sunday. The little guy grabs my arm at that point, and the big guy sort of stands there like a roadblock in case anybody comes by. Out of the corner of my eye, I see a couple of the spiderheads on their boards, so I yell out 'Date rape!' in my best bullhorn voice, expecting a scene like from 'West Side Story,' where all the Jets come snapping their fingers to my rescue. What happens is, somebody else yells 'Get a cop!' The little guy lets go of my arm and he and the Terminator walk—not run—out the other end of the tunnel." Edith took a long sip from Howard's coffee cup and set it down dramatically on the tabletop. "Fade to black, roll credits." She tipped her chair back from the table. "So, tell me—who are you guys running from, anyway?"

Howard exchanged glances with Alaiya. "We don't know. Apparently it's a tall guy, a short guy with a mustache, and a woman."

"I didn't see any woman."

"No, but someone else did." He took her braceleted wrist and gently turned her arm, wincing at the bruises. "I'm really sorry about this, Edith."

"Hey, don't feel bad." She reached inside her shirt and pulled out a crisp fifty-dollar bill. "It wasn't a totally negative experience."

Edith bought a round of coffee to go and the three of them strolled through the warm evening streets.

"So who else saw these jeeks?" Edith asked.

"My former landlady. The guys left a message with her. Alaiya and I are supposed to get together with them in Boston later tonight."

"*Muy interesante*. And you have no idea—"

"—Who they are or why they're looking for us," Howard finished for her. "None at all."

"So, what're you going to do?"

"Play it by ear. We've been not-thinking about it all evening. Alaiya says that if you let an enemy intrude on your thoughts too soon before the battle, you've already given them a big advantage."

"In other words, you're clueless, so you might as well not depress yourselves worrying about it. Well, good luck. Pack some heat, and watch out for the little guy—he's got a grip like a gila monster."

"We can usually take care of ourselves," Howard said. "In fact, Alaiya—" He looked around. "What happened to her?"

"Don't get excited. She's back there a little ways." Edith glanced over her shoulder. "I think she stopped to talk to that street mime."

Their promenade eventually brought them back to the café. Howard looked up to check the time. "It's after ten," he told Alaiya. "We should be heading back. I'm allowing us some extra time, since it's a pretty safe bet there'll be at least one or two people on the subway you'll want to kill." He gave Edith a broad smile. "Just kidding."

"The hell you are." She folded her arms across her chest. "Well, if you guys ever plan a return trip to this part of the galaxy, and you need somebody to run interference for you . . ."

"We'll definitely come to you first." Howard reached out on impulse and gave her a quick hug. Her bracelets jangled against his back. "Keep a candle burning in the window for us."

"Yeah, yeah, sure. I'll torch the whole damn place." Edith and Alaiya hugged. "Send me a postcard, okay?" She started walking backward toward the small gathering by the newsstand. "Send it care of Rudi at 'Bone Pain'—he owes me a mammoth favor."

"Okay, Edith." Howard and Alaiya headed for the subway entrance. The small figure in black waved to them as they started down the stairs. "So, do we have a minimum age requirement for the Breakneck Boys," he asked Alaiya, "or can we send her an application?"

The subway brought them to within a block of the hotel. There were no messages for Howard at the desk. "You know," he said as the elevator carried them toward the tenth floor, "I never thought to find out if these guys have been asking for both of us, or just for me. I wonder if they'll be surprised when you show up, too— assuming, that is, that you're planning on accompanying me—which you certainly don't have to if—"

Alaiya cuffed him lightly on the shoulder. "No, Ahwerd, after all our preparations this afternoon, I believe I will spend the evening sitting at the television receiver box and watching that little woman win more money and vehicles."

"Okay, just checking." The doors slid open and they walked out into the corridor. "Hey, that was pretty funny," he said over his shoulder.

They changed into jeans and short-sleeved shirts from Howard's summer wardrobe, fastening their battle-gang belts about their waists. Alaiya organized her pack while Howard used the bathroom. When he came out, she was clipping Silversting to her belt. She tied the sleeves of a light jacket around her hips and adjusted it in the mirror. The dagger was hidden when she turned back to Howard. "Ready?"

They left the lobby at twenty minutes after eleven. When they had gone about half the distance to their destination, they stopped to unload a few items from their packs.

"Not the kind of neighborhood that improves with the onset of night," Howard said, looking around at the dark factories and abandoned warehouses. "But we're about half an hour early. That should give this stuff enough time to work, right?" They stepped into a recessed doorway. Howard tried not to flinch as Alaiya carefully applied a light coating of grayish paste to the surface of his eyes. Alaiya kept watch for the few minutes of tearful blinking before the nighteye began to work. Suddenly the darkened landscape took on an eerie clarity for Howard, while his color perception narrowed to shades of red and black. He duplicated the unpleasant procedure on Alaiya's eyes, and they left the doorway and continued on their way.

When they were still several blocks away from the door at the end of the alley, Alaiya gave Howard's hand a squeeze, then made an abrupt turn to the right and headed down a small side street. Howard continued on toward the rendezvous point.

The streetlights that framed the entrance to the cul-de-sac were both unlit, creating a zone of shadows that included the broad alleyway. His enhanced vision showing him that nothing larger than a rat was using the shadows for cover, Howard ventured into the alleyway. Pretending to feel his way along the brick wall, he peered through the dust-layered window. In lines of red on black, he saw a maze of crates and machinery covered in tarpaulins, but no sign of movement.

Forcing himself to move slowly, Howard opened a pouch on his pack and brought forth a long, narrow tube. He knelt on the filthy ground and deposited small amounts of translucent blue gel in several widely separated places, carefully measuring their distance from the wall with his outspread arms. He rose to his feet and dusted off his knees.

He pulled a Frisbee from his pack as he left the alley and headed down the street toward the closest light. Humming softly to himself, he stood in the middle of the street and tossed the disk up at an angle that sent it arcing back in his direction. He threw and caught it for several minutes, careful not to betray his new ability to see clearly beyond the circle of light. A clock began to chime midnight just as Howard leapt up to intercept a particularly high throw. As his Reeboks made contact with the pavement, a long black car turned the corner at the far end of the street. "Dum-da-*dum*-dum . . ." Howard said under his breath.

It was a large, expensive-looking vehicle. Howard stood waiting while it coasted to a stop just short of the entrance to the alley, its headlights bathing the area in brightness. He slipped the Frisbee into the side pocket of his pack and walked toward the silent car.

When he was about ten feet away, one of the back doors opened and a large man unfolded himself from the seat. His pale face was mostly hidden by his high collar and odd-looking hat. When he stood erect he looked to be over seven feet tall. He stepped away from the car, then eased the door shut as Howard approached. The headlights were suddenly extinguished. Howard immediately slowed his pace, as though unsure of his path in the darkness. The windows of the vehicle were smoked, but Howard had gotten the impression while the door was open that the car contained at least two more individuals.

"Evening," he said. The man motioned him toward the alleyway.

"After you." Howard gestured for the other to go ahead of him, but the big man shook his head sharply and pointed into the shadowed area. Howard shrugged. "Whatever you say."

He groped his way into the alley, taking obvious pains to avoid stepping on the careful patterns of blue gel he had laid out earlier. When they had almost reached the end of the alley, there was a loud complaint of rusted metal and the battered door in the far wall swung open. A second, much shorter man emerged. This one had a thin mustache and delicate features, and like the tall man, he wore a peculiar gray headpiece that hugged his skull like a sailor's cap at the bottom, then flared out and up to a round, flat top. The short man gave an abrupt, scornful laugh.

"Choosing a path with great care—afraid to soil your soles in the dark?" He had a high, thin voice, and spoke in an oddly monotonous singsong. "Or unwilling to step in the combustible we watched you lay out so carefully?" He laughed again, but his tall companion remained blank-faced behind the high collar.

"I have a better question," Howard said. "Who are you guys?"

"Carriers," the little man replied at once. He nodded to himself with a thin smile as if satisfied with the answer. "Yes, that's it: Carriers."

"What are you carrying? Is it something for me?"

"Knowledge. Thinking and talking." The little man spoke with a strangely distracted air, his eyes roaming the space between himself and Howard without ever quite focusing. "How easily such things are carried."

"I don't understand," Howard said.

"There is the difference," said the big man, speaking for the first time. "It is too warm here." He had the same flat intonation as the smaller man.

"Yeah, well, we could all be sitting in air-conditioned comfort, drinking Mai Tai's, but you guys wanted to hang out here." He took a breath. "So, listen, you've been going around looking for me, giving a hard time to friends of mine. You want to tell me what this is all about?"

"Yes, too warm," said the little man. "We require an exchange. Yes—*ahh*—an exchange." He had begun to twitch slightly as he spoke. "They—*ahh*—they—" One of his doll-like arms jumped into the air at his side and fell again. "*Ahh*—they—"

The tall man made a wheezing sound. He shambled past Howard, put his huge fingers under the band of his companion's hat, and tugged sharply downward. At once the shorter man fell silent and stood still, his eyes staring vacantly at Howard's knees.

"At rest," the big man said. "The heat has cumulative effects. Perhaps it will go better if we deal through the other one. Yes."

The hulking figure turned to Howard. "Give it to this one. To me."
He held out a hand the size of a bear's paw.

"You know," Howard said, "I'm really not following too much
of this. Give what to you? And what happened to that exchange
you were talking about?"

"Unnecessary, a trick of speech," the tall man said. "Your life
for the device." He tilted his head to one side. "Do you know the
source of what you possess? Worlds strung like beads on a string.
Do you understand extent, corollaries, ramifications?" The massive hand rose in the darkness. Howard's fingers went automatically
to his chest. "Maybe you should tell me," he said softly.

It was the giant's turn to laugh, an almost silent quaking of his
body. "Give it to us," he said, his voice gentle.

"So much for haggling." Howard edged backward toward the
silent car. "Look, if you want what I think you want, it's in my
pack."

The tall man shook his head. "Improbable." He reached out
and gave his tiny partner a shake. Instantly the small man lunged
forward, both hands raised, and ripped open the front of Howard's
shirt. Buttons clattered on the pavement. Howard's neck and chest
were bare.

"Way to go, pal," he said. "This was one of my favorite shirts."

The little man made a rapid clacking sound with his teeth, darted
behind Howard, and began to tug at the straps of his backpack.
Howard twisted away from him.

"Wait a minute! Look, friend—you'd better let me get it, if you
don't want to lose some potentially valuable body parts." He pulled
his palms apart, mimicking the sound of an explosion. "First,
though, you'll have to give me a good reason to turn this thing over
to you."

Perfectly synchronized, the two men reached inside their jackets
and pulled out intricate-looking silver objects. A flick of the thumb
activated the devices, which appeared to be some sort of hand
weapons; a wavering buzz began as the weapons' owners pointed
them at Howard's head.

"Nice choreography," Howard observed. "I think I've got my
reason." He noticed that his own hands were beginning to shake
as he hoisted the pack from his back and set it gently on the ground.
The two watched him impassively as he crouched and gingerly
inserted his hands into the main pocket.

He felt a wave of relief when his fingers closed on the hard length
of the Key. Shaking his head with regret, he looked up at the two
men. "You know, I was hoping to get something out of this little

meeting," he said, grasping the handle with his right hand as the fingers of his left moved on the shaft. In his mind he built a picture of the lavender plain on Field of Flowers. "But it looks like we're on different wavelengths entirely, and if I start loaning this Key out to just anybody, my folks'll never trust me with the Buick. Adios, guys—" He twisted the Key.

"You need to give it to us," the big man said several seconds later. "You need to do that now."

"Heh heh," Howard said. "I know the little devil's in here somewhere." He felt sweat run down his sides as his fingers spun the narrow bands of the Key inside the pack. He shut his eyes and tried again.

The small man's device buzzed and stuttered alarmingly as he moved it closer to Howard's head.

Whistling tunelessly, Howard released the Key and slid his hands from the main pocket. "Ha ha, I remember now," he said. "It's been in the side pocket all along. What a dope, huh? I only wish *Alaiya* were here to see what a fool I'm making of myself. Yes, sir," he said, raising his voice, "*Alaiya* would sure get a kick out of this one!"

"Decrease the noise," the little man said, nudging him with his shoe. The point of his weapon buzzed angrily near Howard's ear.

"Right, right, quiet as a little mouse in a trap . . ." Howard rummaged around in the side pocket. He began to pull items out at random, tossing them over his shoulder as he identified them. "Hairbrush—no, toothpaste—no, bag of M&M's from the movies—no . . . Aha!" He eased a black, disk-shaped object from the pack and hefted it thoughtfully. "Either of you ever toss around one of these babies?"

"No interest in the toy!" The giant moved a step closer, obliterating Howard's M&M's in the process.

"Aw, come on, it's a swell sport. You mean to tell me you've never answered the siren call of the original flying disk?" His left hand rested on his belt for a few seconds. "My friend—*Alaiya*, in case you didn't hear me before—she got the hang of it just like that. Shall we flip a few?"

"Get rid of it!" the small man howled, starting to twitch again as his weapon jerked a few inches from Howard's nose. "Get rid of—*ahh*—it!"

"Okay," Howard said with a shrug. "If you say so." He turned nonchalantly and sent the disk sailing the length of the dark alleyway toward the street.

The small man made a strangled sound.

The big man spun in his tracks, aimed his weapon, and fired. The device chattered like a squirrel and a thin pulse of red light shot out, striking the gliding Frisbee just as it was about to settle on the roof of the car.

"Hey," Howard said.

There was a hushed explosion; trails of sparkling liquid fountained from the vaporized disk and splattered onto the roof and windshield of the car. Howard heard the sound of steam escaping under tremendous pressure. Then metal groaned and creaked as the car began to rock ponderously back and forth on its tires. Columns of vapor shot up from it, and something ate rapidly through its outer surface and began to work on what lay inside. The big man stared, frozen, while the little one gave a horrible warbling wail and raced toward the dissolving vehicle.

The front passenger door opened with an ugly sound, and something tumbled out onto the pavement beyond the car. Howard's view was blocked by the slumping vehicle. He twisted his head downward and saw a gray-robed figure writhing through the curtains of vapor. A hollow voice cried out a string of words in a guttural language, and something brushed at Howard's memory. The figure held a small object that caught the light: a ring of silver, about four inches in diameter. The hairs stood up on the nape of Howard's neck. The frame of the car collapsed.

The big man stood watching the scene with a look of mild puzzlement on his broad face. Howard almost felt sorry for him.

"It's this stuff called 'eater,' " he explained. "They distill it from these fronds that grow around the bases of bed-mounds on the Red Desert World. I had a packet of it in my belt, and I stuck it up under the rim of the Frisbee before I threw it. I don't think it would have been nearly as effective if you hadn't zapped it when you did." He looked at the remnants of the car. "Dissolves just about everything."

The giant made no response. At the end of the alley, the little man was dancing in a frenzy by the driver's side of the car. Suddenly, he reached forth and clutched at something that protruded from the twisted metal. A wrenching sound came from the center of the melted vehicle and a long gray tentacle shot straight up into the air, its end snapping and coiling like a whip. The sinuous length fell back onto the little man, who grasped it again and began to pull. Another tentacle sprang up near the first, wrapping itself around his waist. Howard's jaw dropped as something huge struggled upward from the wreckage. It seemed to grow, as with the little man's help, it pulled itself free of the steaming mass. Where is it coming from? Howard wondered. Could it be pushing up from under the pavement? Horror gripped him as great sinuous limbs lashed forth, wrapping themselves heedlessly around the little man still attempting to free it.

"Jeez . . ." Howard found his voice. "Alaiya!" He cupped his hands around his mouth and turned his face upward. *"Alaiya!"*

"Ahwerd!" She waved to him over the edge of the lower roof. She held two globular objects in the crook of her elbow, one blue and one yellow.

"Now! Before it gets all the way out!" He pointed to the thing that was heaving its bulk out of the wreckage in great spasms, its many arms snaking into the alleyway in search of something to grasp.

Alaiya took aim and lobbed the yellow globe at the center of the wreckage. The sphere fell short by several yards and disappeared in a mound of refuse.

Howard ran to the base of the wall. He jumped to the first level of the fire escape and reached out his arms. "Drop the other one. Gently!" He grimaced as the delicate sphere fell into his palms, dropping his hands several inches as it landed to lessen the impact. He ran past the big man and tossed the blue globe onto the pavement at the base of the wreckage. There was a small, wet splash.

"Water?" the little man said, seemingly oblivious to the tentacles that crushed him. The big man, who had stood silently watching the spectacle, shook his head and turned to Howard with an expression of perplexity. "Water?" he echoed.

"Wait for it," Howard said. The asphalt surrounding the ruined automobile made a whooshing sound as it erupted into flame. "Surprise! That's where we put the real firejelly this afternoon. This stuff in here is just toothpaste gel." He turned and scooped the narrow tube up from the ground. "See? Minty fresh. We were trying to fool you."

Flames engulfed the car and whatever was attempting to pull free of it. Tentacles beat the air as a keening wail that hurt Howard's ears rose above the blaze's crackle. The little man was lifted and held above the blaze for a few seconds before the whiplike arms flung his body in a high arc to land far up the street.

The giant seemed to waken from a trance. With a bellow of fury, he turned and lumbered toward Howard, his weapon upraised. There was a flash from the nearby rooftop and a bright pellet arced through the air behind the big man. Howard looked away as it made contact with the back of the great head. A bright light flared and the unusual hat flew past him to land near the wall. He glanced at it and felt ill.

There was something moving inside the gray headgear, a mad writhing as if a nest of newborn snakes had been suddenly uncovered.

Howard stepped back, looking up to where Alaiya stood silhouetted against the pale light of the city with the firebug projector under one arm.

"Dead?" she called.

He bent toward the big man, then jerked back. The top of his shoulders and the stump of the thick neck were charred and bloody. "That'd be my guess," he said.

Alaiya descended the rickety fire escape. "I thought you said there were no slakes in Massachusetts." She embraced Howard.

He turned back toward the smoldering wreckage. "I don't understand it . . ."

"Somehow a doorway was opened between this world and another one. The creature was being sent through to destroy us. Did you feel the presence of a Traveler?"

"Not this time." Howard described the robed figure he had seen, and the silver ring it held. Alaiya nodded. "Keyholder," she said quietly.

Howard pointed at the strange hat lying on its side across the alleyway. "It got knocked off his head when you shot him. I looked inside. It's full of wormlike things." Something rose in his throat at the memory.

Alaiya raised the projector. Another bright bee flew across the darkness, and the headpiece exploded in a burst of searing light. She lowered the weapon. "I must apologize for my tardiness. It was difficult to scale the other side of the building while holding the—what did you call them?"

"Water balloons," Howard said.

"Yes. Then I encountered a woman—at first I thought it was the tall woman your landlady mentioned—as I was crossing the rooftop to come to your assistance."

Howard blinked. "You're kidding. Who was it?"

"She was small in stature, and had hair of a dark reddish color."

Howard whistled soundlessly. "It's a whole army." He glanced at the roof. "Where is she now?"

"What is left of her body remains on the rooftop." Alaiya shrugged. "She was a Carrier, like the males."

"You know that word, then. What does it mean?"

"They are personal agents of the Keyholders, controlled somehow through the headgear. Occasionally, one appears at the taletell, though they are seldom seen outside of Stillpoint."

"Son of a gun," Howard said.

"Well." Alaiya surveyed the scene of destruction. "A few un-expected events came to pass, but basically it all went quite well."

"Not all of it. I'm afraid we've got a problem," Howard said.

Alaiya raised her eyebrows.

"I tried to use the Key a little while ago. It seemed like the only way out. I was going to head for Field of Flowers, then come back to the roof and pick you up." He paused. "It didn't work."

"Which part did not work?"

"The whole thing—the Key. I turned it and nothing happened."

"Perhaps you were under stress." Alaiya watched him intently. "It must work."

Howard bent and lifted the golden object from his pack. Closing his eyes, he concentrated on the rose moss and soaring mountains of the Black and Blue World. His fingers moved on the Key and he turned the handle.

He opened his eyes. Alaiya was staring at him expectantly. "Nothing," he said. He clicked his tongue. "You know, I'm not entirely surprised by this."

"What do you mean?"

"Well, the whole thing's been a little fishy. You know—me popping back here now and then, but always to the same place, always finding myself standing in front of that damn washroom door, with the Key sticking in the lock."

"And you believe—"

"That the only place this Key's going to work on the whole planet is right back there in that hallway." He gave a slow nod. "That's what I'm starting to believe, all right."

They heard sirens beginning to wail in the distance as they left the alley. They found the body of the little man lying next to a fire hydrant, his limbs arrayed at impossible angles. Howard bent and gingerly removed the dead man's wallet from his back pants pocket before Alaiya used a final firebug to obliterate the gray headpiece.

When she came to join him, he was standing still in the middle of the street, staring down at two small rectangles. The same young man and woman were featured in both of the black-and-white photographs. In one they were dancing, and in the other the man was boosting the woman onto a low stone wall while they both grinned at the camera.

"He was carrying these in his wallet," Howard said, looking up at her with a strange expression on his face.

"What is wrong? Do you know these people?"

"No, but I've seen other pictures of them." He cleared his throat. "These are my parents."

CHAPTER XVIII

The Big Bash

AN HOUR LATER THEY WERE SITTING IN THE HOTEL bar, Alaiya wrinkling her nose at each sip of her sparkling water while Howard nursed a diet root beer.

"Ahwerd?" She raised her eyebrows at him.

He shrugged. "Okay, one more time." He opened a button on his shirt and stuck his hands partway inside. He closed his eyes while his fingers moved on the Key. "Nothing."

"You got an itch, buddy?" The bartender was watching him dubiously.

"I'm okay," Howard said, buttoning his shirt. He pushed his empty glass to the edge of the counter. "Hit me, Joe."

"The name's Raymond," the bartender said. He picked up the glass and moved away.

"Shall we leave for the washroom building soon to try the Key?" Alaiya asked.

Howard looked up at the clock set inside a ship's steering wheel on the wall. "It's almost two A.M. And it's Sunday now—the day of rest. That means the building will be closed all day."

"I thought you said people were resting yesterday."

"They were. It's called a two-day weekend. Obscenely lazy, aren't they?" He yawned. "I'm too beat to go now. And to tell you the truth, I don't relish the thought of sneaking back in through the garage and climbing sixty-odd floors tomorrow, either. How about if we get a good night's sleep, then hang out for one more day? That way we could go back there like normal folks, bright and early Monday morning when the building opens up."

"That would be fine." Alaiya nodded. "Perhaps you will be able to introduce me to Go-cart and Cabal after all."

"Go-cart?" Howard wrinkled his forehead. "Oh, I see." He chuckled. "Yeah, as a matter of fact, I think 'To Have and Have Not' starts tomorrow."

"Here you go." The bartender returned Howard's glass filled with fizzing brown liquid.

"Thanks—oh, Ray? Can I have a new lime wedge?"

The bartender sighed, reached under the counter, brought out a small white dish lined with dessicated green slices, and banged it down in front of Howard. "Last call in fifteen minutes," he growled, and walked away.

Howard shook his head. "Ray, here, is gambling big time with his tip," he said to Alaiya. He squeezed two of the wrinkled wedges over his drink and downed it in three long swallows. "Ready to go up?"

They stayed in bed until noon. When Howard got out of the shower, Alaiya was standing outside on the tiny balcony, braiding her hair. She was barefoot, dressed in one of his oversize sweatshirts.

"Nice out," he observed, squeezing through the sliding door to stand at her side.

She nodded. "No one was competing for anything on the television receiver. I came out to listen to all the bells."

"Mm. Church."

"I am reminded. Yesterday we passed a large stone building. You told me it was a house of worship. When I asked you what was written in such tall letters on the sign out front, you said 'Bingo.' This made perfect sense to me, but you drew your hand down your face, like this, and said we would have to discuss it further sometime." She pursed her lips with a questioning look.

Howard dropped his head so his chin rested on his chest. "Can we eat first?" he asked.

They walked to Newbury Street for brunch. Alaiya found her Belgian waffles delicious, but refused to touch Howard's Eggs Benedict, warning him that he did not really want her to tell him what they reminded her of. The sidewalks were filling with shoppers as they left the restaurant.

"I thought all workplaces were abandoned on this day," Alaiya said.

"Most of them are. A lot of the retail stores open at noon and close at five."

They were standing outside a shop that sold Tibetan rugs.

Alaiya pointed across the street to the window of a swank clothing store, where sophisticated mannequins in evening dress snubbed one another. "You do not own any garments of this type. Do they denote a particular profession?"

"Yeah, lounge lizard. No, actually, I haven't had a really good suit since my high-school days. I've never gone to many fancy parties. Hey—" He lifted his head, staring at the window. "Hey-hey-hey," he said.

"Hey?" Alaiya looked back and forth between Howard and the elegant dummies.

"You want to go to a party tonight—a 'big bash'?" He bounced his eyebrows at her. "You and I have an evening to kill. Shall we crash my high-school reunion?"

They visited three different stores before Howard was satisfied with their wardrobes.

"I think it starts at eight," he said as they returned to their room. "So we've got plenty of time to see Slim and Steve in a matinee. They're holding the reunion at another hotel down near the Charles. I threw my invitation away, but it shouldn't make any difference. I graduated same as everybody else, right?"

"Right," Alaiya said solemnly.

They went to the theater. Alaiya found the film, enthralling, and told Howard that she particularly liked the relationship between the two main characters. "I enjoyed the humor, as well," she added as they made their way back to the hotel.

"Yeah, I noticed you were laughing at most of the right places," Howard said.

They dressed in their new clothes. Looking at the two of them in the mirror, Howard decided to splurge and take a taxi. "We look too good to be seen on the streets," he told Alaiya. "Men would weep and strong women faint. There could be riots."

The cabdriver complimented them on their appearance, and Howard tipped him lavishly as they got out in front of a soaring concrete-and-glass edifice. A schedule board in the lobby told them that the reunion was being held in the fifth-floor ballroom. Alaiya put her hand on Howard's arm as they were walking down the corridor from the elevator. "I have decided to go into the female restroom for a few minutes to attempt to apply a thin coating of this to my lips." She raised a slim golden tube. "All of the inanimate women in the clothing store seemed to be decorated in this fashion."

"Okay. I'll wait over here."

"No, you should go in now—it may be a lengthy procedure. Also, it will be better for you to greet your old companions without distractions. I will come into the room shortly and join you."

"Oh. Okay." Howard puffed out his cheeks in a long breath and adjusted his tie. "How do I look?"

Alaiya surveyed him critically. "Not so good as when you are unencumbered with garments, but still extremely presentable."

"Thanks—you, too. Well." He squared his shoulders and turned to go. Alaiya touched his elbow.

"Ahwerd, you seem so ill at ease. You were not this anxious when we fought our way through the chamber of tentacles beneath the dead city."

"I guess not." He rubbed his chin. "But this is different—I went to school with these people!"

There was a small table set up outside the door to the ballroom. Two women in evening dress were copying check marks from one long list to another beneath a sagging banner made from computer printouts. They broke off their conversation and beamed up at Howard as he approached.

"Don't tell me, don't tell me!" The small blonde closed her eyes and brought a plastic cup filled with something pink to her forehead. "I know exactly who you are." She opened one eye and stared up at Howard. "God, you look good, whoever you are," she said under her breath. "You sure you were in our class?"

"Millie!" Her companion nudged her with her elbow. "The punch is heavily spiked," she said to Howard. "I remember you. Your name is Harold, isn't it? Football team?"

"It's Howard, Althea. Howard Bell. Literature Club."

"Howard Bell? You're kidding." She put a hand to her brown cheek. "You sat behind me in homeroom."

"That's right. Senior year."

"My, my." Althea gave Millie another nudge. "Close your mouth, girl, and look up Howard Bell."

"I am," said Millie, staring at Howard with her chin on her fist. She shook her head. "I mean—we don't seem to have your name on the list, Howard. Did you send in your money?"

"No, I'm sorry, Millie. I've been out of town for a while. Any way I can pay at the door?"

"Oh, here." Althea reached for a name tag. "You can go right in. Admission's always free to the—" She glanced down the list of typed names. "—seventy-sixth person to show up. Old high-school tradition—right, Millie?"

"Oh, definitely." Millie pried open a plastic holder while Althea printed Howard's name in careful block letters.

"That's really nice of you," Howard said. "But actually, there's two of us."

"Doesn't that just figure," Millie muttered.

"I'll be glad to pay for my friend."

"No, no." Althea plucked another tag from the box. "We ended up with a small surplus of funds when Ralph Osterman volunteered to play DJ. Just tell us her name and we'll send her right in when she arrives."

"Alaiya," Howard said with a small nod. "A-l-a-i-y-a. That'll do it."

The ballroom was softly lit. Howard smiled to himself, remembering the line on the invitation about counting wrinkles. Taped music from two decades past came from overhead speakers festooned with balloons in the school colors. Two cash bars were staffed by hotel personnel, and several long buffet tables were laden with food. Smaller circular tables were set in clusters around the outside of the room.

Howard pinned his name tag to his jacket and headed for the bar. He nodded to the heavyset couple standing next to him and ordered a gin and tonic. Then he turned and watched the doorway, willing Alaiya to appear.

"It is! I don't believe it!" Somebody tapped him on the left shoulder, then punched his right as he swung around. "It's Bell!"

The stocky, red-haired man who had hit him directed his two companions' attention to Howard's name tag. "What'd I tell ya?" he said.

"Hi, Artie." Howard nodded at each of the men. "Len, Tony. How's it going?"

"How you doing, Howie? Christ, you look different!" A thin man with a fluorescent tie and wisps of white-blond hair combed crosswise over his scalp stuck out his hand. "We were just wondering if our fourth Stooge was gonna show up."

"Musketeer!" The third man, plump and bearded, made a face of mock exasperation. "We were the Four Musketeers, you moron. Sheesh, Howie, these guys are even dumber than they were back in school."

"Oh, right." Artie shook his head. "Like we could get any dumber."

''So whaddya been up to for the past seventeen years, Howie?'' The thin man rubbed his fingers on his forehead. ''Interesting haircut.''

''Oh, you know, Len. A little bit of this, a little bit of that.''

''I think his hair looks terrific.'' A tall woman with earrings the size of wind chimes came from behind to link her arm with Howard's. ''You guys should be so daring.'' She leaned away from Howard to inspect his head. ''You remind me a little of Mel Gibson, in this light—he wore a ponytail in one of his films, didn't he?''

''Hi, Suzanne. I don't know.'' Howard shook his head self-consciously and hugged the tall woman. ''It's good to see you. Anybody else here I know?''

''Oh, Billy Nowell's around somewhere—probably at the nearest bar. You know we got married pretty much right after high school, don't you?''

''Yeah, I think Midge told me. She wrote to me for a while after graduation.''

''That's right. I always thought the two of you were going to end up together. Didn't they put your pictures inside a heart in the yearbook?'' She craned her neck above the crowd. ''She's supposed to be here tonight, and I hear she's still unattached. You might get a second chance.'' She poked him in the ribs with an exaggerated wink. ''Oh, there's Billy waving at me like a windmill. Probably needs drink money. I'm going to leave you here with these delinquents for a little while, Howie. Don't let them talk you into anything crazy.''

''I won't, Suzanne.''

''So, just like old times, huh, Howie?'' Artie looked at a group of women clustered in conversation near one of the buffet tables. ''Course, the girls've put on a few pounds here and there—mostly there.'' He shook his head. ''I was gonna say it was mighty slim pickins here tonight, but then I got a look at those keisters.''

''You here stag, like the rest of us?'' Tony asked, scratching under his beard with a fingernail.

''Hey, I coulda brought somebody,'' Len said. ''But it's a reunion, you know? She just woulda felt out of place.''

''Right.'' Tony rolled his eyes.

''Well, actually . . .'' Howard began.

''Jesus H. Christ!'' Artie said, reaching out to grab the wrists of the other two. ''Do you men see what I see?''

Tony gave a soft whistle.

"Holy shit!" Len tugged at his glowing tie. "She's *got* to be in the wrong room."

Howard looked over his shoulder to see Alaiya standing in the doorway. He waved at her and she smiled, waving back. He watched heads turn in the crowd to follow her as she slowly crossed the room.

Alaiya was dressed in a simple pale blue shift, belted at the waist with a clasp of gold. When Howard had told her how good she looked in that shade of blue, she had remarked that it reminded her of the uniform she had worn with the Ferocious Rulebenders. She had on sandals and a single gold bracelet set with a turquoise. Her long hair hung down her back in a shimmer of red-gold.

"No way," Artie said as Alaiya slipped her arm through Howard's and pressed against his side. "She's with *you*?"

"Alaiya, I'd like you to meet Tony, Len, and Artie. We were very tight in the lunchroom back in high school. Artie here used to pour his milk onto my homework to amuse his pals."

"Interesting." Alaiya inclined her head to the wide-eyed threesome. "Ahwerd, is it possible for you to accompany me to the food display? I am famished and in need of your advice."

"Sure," Howard said. "Catch you later, guys." He squeezed her hand and chortled as they walked away. "Thanks, Alaiya. Those three faces just made up for four years' worth of sour-smelling homework!"

"They were not truly your friends then, were they?" Alaiya said as they picked up plates and began to inspect the buffet table.

Howard shook his head. "I didn't have a lot of friends in high school. Sometimes you just hung out with people because they were misfits, too. Unfortunately, that was no guarantee that you'd all be nice to each other. There were a few kids I was close to, but they were all pretty much loners like myself, so we probably won't be running into them here." He lifted a silver server and deposited something with brown and yellow layers on Alaiya's plate, then covered it with a thick red sauce. "Here. I have no idea what this is, but it smells like it's got a Velveeta base, so it can't be too bad."

They loaded their plates and left the buffet. "When we finish this stuff, we can tackle the desserts," Howard said, pointing to a second long table, where a variety of colorful pastries were presided over by a sweating ice sculpture in the shape of a rather thick-necked swan. "Let's find a place to sit down."

Most of the round tables were already taken. Howard spotted one over in a shadowed corner of the room that seemed to have only a single occupant. As he and Alaiya moved through the crowd, their way was blocked by two women who stood speaking in hushed tones while glancing over their shoulders at the lone figure.

"I can't believe he had the nerve to show up," the shorter woman was saying. "There really ought to be some sort of law."

"Did you see him hug Marilyn What's-her-name when he came in?" replied her companion with a theatrical shudder. "Law or no law, if he tries to touch me I'm telling Jimmy to throw him out of here. I'm on the Committee, after all, so I think I have that right."

"Excuse us." Howard tapped the second woman on the shoulder. "Can we slip by here? Oh—hi, Midge."

"Howie? Oh, my Gawd!" Howard struggled to hold onto his plate as the dark-haired woman wrapped herself around him, her outthrust cigarette sending up a thin blue line of smoke several inches below Alaiya's face. "I can't believe it! I thought you weren't coming, you rotten boy." She pushed him to arm's length, then pulled him in again. "Oh, you look good enough to eat!"

"Yeah, it was kind of a spur-of-the-moment thing. Listen, I'd like you to meet somebody." Howard pried himself from Midge's embrace. "Alaiya, this is Midge Packard and Phyllis Babirusa."

"Babirusa-hyphen-Horschein," the small woman corrected him, patting her frosted hair. "I'm one of those modern girls, you know. Besides, Leo thinks it's cute, as long as I don't put it on the checks or anything." She extended a plump hand to Alaiya. "Nice to meet you. Can't you get Howie to cut his hair?"

"Ahwerd has beautiful hair," Alaiya said. "He chooses to honor the warriors of my people by wearing it in this fashion."

"I know what you mean. My Leo would let his grow down to his knees if I didn't make the appointment. Not that he has that much left to grow anywhere but his eyebrows."

"We're trying to find a place to set these down," Howard said, hefting his plate. "Would you like to join us?"

The man at the far table had gotten to his feet. He peered under his hand in Howard's direction, then started to walk toward them.

"Whoops—we'll have to catch up later, Howie." Midge clutched at her friend's shoulder and began guiding the other woman toward the center of the room. "Phyllis is supposed to be getting her Leo a Wallbanger, and she's already been gone half an hour."

Howard watched them go. "I kissed Midge Packard once in a moment of confusion, under the bleachers in the gym during my senior year," he said. "A week later, she asked the Yearbook Committee to print an engagement announcement for us." He shivered. "I had to take out a disclaimer in the school newspaper."

"Pardon me." Howard felt someone tap his shoulder. "I'm looking for Howie Bell. You seem to have gotten hold of his body somewhere, but it's been renovated in such an incredibly hip fashion that I know you must've misplaced his mind."

Howard stared at the man who had been sitting at the far table. "Ryan? *Rip?*" He flung his arms around the smaller man. "Yaah!"

"Likewise." The two men patted each other's backs for a few seconds before stepping apart. "Wearing the Reeboks with the suit to an affair like this was an inspiration, Howie. And the ponytail—" Ryan shook his head. "You sure you haven't been sleeping near space pods?"

"Alaiya, I want you to meet that statistical rarity, an actual friend of mine, somebody I used to read comics with under the porch at my aunt's motel. Ryan Innes Paxton—known as 'Rip' to his friends."

"Which pretty much means to Howie, in this crowd." Ryan shook hands with Alaiya. "Nice to meet you. You're an incredibly stunning-looking person, as I hope Howie's already told you many times. Shall we go over to my table before you two start decorating the rug with the contents of those plates?" He sniffed as Alaiya walked by. "Oh, you're going to like that stuff—I had three helpings. I think they put Cheez Whiz in the sauce."

When they had settled at the table, Ryan rose and tapped his wineglass lightly with a fork. "Ladies and gentlemen," he announced, "I hereby call to order this slightly overdue Executive Session of the Breakneck Boys!"

Alaiya looked up from her plate in astonishment. "What did you say?"

"Breakneck Boys." Ryan gave a small bow. "A little-known but very elite group. I'm a charter member. You mean Howie's never mentioned it?"

Alaiya sat staring at him as understanding slowly came into her face. She smiled. "Actually, I believe he has. You are speaking of a very long time ago, correct?"

"Only if you consider almost thirty years a long time." He seated himself and took a sip of white wine. "Some bonds never weaken. I'd show you the secret handshake if we'd ever gotten around to making one up."

Alaiya looked at Howard, who was grinning back and forth between the two of them. "I haven't seen Ryan in a million years," he said to her. "This is great!"

"So, are you responsible for the new and improved Howard Bell?" Ryan asked Alaiya. "He sure didn't look like this in high school."

"Look at you," Howard said. "You look like you've been working out—though you could probably stand to gain a few pounds."

"Quite a change from my younger days, isn't it? Yeah, I joined an exercise place about five years ago and started pouring my money into the black hole of personal fitness." He opened his suit jacket and tapped the left side of his chest. "I figure this pec alone cost me eighty-seven dollars and change." He frowned down at the silk shirt. "Or is that a lat?"

"You were children together in Ahwerd's home village?" Alaiya asked Ryan.

"Yeah, till my family moved to Cambridge when I was about sixteen. Then Howie's aunt let him come live with us during high school. She thought the local schools were too rigid and provincial." He lifted his brows at Howard. "Speaking of which, how's Annie doing?"

Howard shook his head. "We've been out of touch for a while. As a matter of fact, I've just been trying to track her down and I haven't been able to find her. You've probably seen her more recently than I have."

"Nah, the last time we got together was before I left Frisco, and that was almost three years ago. She and Claire had us over to dinner."

"I talked to Claire day before yesterday. I guess Annie moved out over a year ago."

"Thank God." Ryan raised his glass. "To the absence of Claire!"

Howard took a sip of his gin and tonic. "So, how's Lewis these days?"

"Mm." Ryan gave a small nod, studying one of the elaborate

chandeliers clustered in the center of the room. "Lewis isn't with us anymore."

"Oh." Howard pursed his lips. "That's too bad—I guess. I mean, he seemed like an okay guy, but then I never really got to know him, so it sort of depends on whether *you* think—"

"I mean he died, Howie."

"What?" Howard set down his glass. "When?"

"Oh . . ." Ryan rubbed the tip of his nose. "About eight and a half months ago."

"Jeez," Howard said. "I'm sorry."

"Ahwerd." Alaiya touched his arm. "I notice that there is a balcony structure beyond those doors. I believe I will escape the artificial air and breathe the city fumes for a few moments."

"Oh. Sure." Howard got to his feet and followed Alaiya for a few paces. "Thanks. This can't be easy for him to talk about. I had no idea . . . Look—if anybody asks you where you're from, just tell them Liechtenstein, okay?"

He reseated himself at the table. Ryan was making an origami animal out of his cocktail napkin.

"I'm really sorry, Rip," he said. "What happened?"

"*Pneumocystis* pneumonia, among other things." The other man held the folded paper up to the light. "What do you think? It started out as a lemur, but I think it looks more like an okapi." He crumpled the napkin in his palm. "He lasted a year and a half after the diagnosis. He was in and out of the hospital, in and out, weaker each time. They put him on one of these experimental drug programs, and it seemed to help for a while, but the side effects were worse than some of the symptoms, y'know? He shook all the time like he was freezing, and he started to drool—can you imagine Mr. Immaculate drooling?" He gave a short laugh. "Then it got into his head, so at least he didn't have to watch himself fall apart. That was left up to me. Near the end, I think he was willing himself to go. He had gotten to the point where he just winced all the time, like there was nothing that didn't hurt anymore. Eating, breathing, blinking his eyes. So one night he just stopped."

"Whoa," Howard said softly.

"Yeah, whoa." Ryan took a shaky breath and straightened up in his seat. "Haven't talked about this for quite a while, Howie. You caught me off guard." He looked around. "I don't know what made me show up here tonight. I sure didn't expect to see you."

"Yeah, me either."

"The funny thing is—we were just about to call it quits when Lewis got the word that he'd tested positive. After that . . ." He shrugged, narrowing his eyes. "There was nobody else to stay with him. Some of our friends, I think they misunderstood. Y'know, it became like this big tragic tale of devotion and eternal commitment. But it wasn't that at all." He gave another weary shrug. "In the end, it was just that there was nobody else to stay with him . . ."

Neither of them said anything for several moments. Then Ryan smiled and drained his glass. He tipped his chin toward the large double doors. "She's fantastic, Howie. Where did you meet her—some agency that specializes in wish fulfillment, High School Reunion Division?"

Howard nodded. "Wait'll you get to talk to her. She's a Breakneck Boy, too."

"Ah, simpatico, huh? That's great. So what are you up to, workwise?"

"Oh, pretty much the same old thing. Going around to different places and trying to fix stuff that needs fixing." He picked up the wadded napkin and bounced it in his palm. "I've been doing a bit more traveling lately than I used to. How 'bout you—you famous yet?"

"Nah, I don't have the drive for it. I've still got my review columns, though. Did I tell you I've been talking with a publisher about maybe doing a collection? Speaking of publishers—how's The Book coming, or shouldn't I ask?"

Howard gave a rueful smile. "To tell you the truth, I haven't even looked at it for several months, though I did pick it up again the other day."

"You lazy lout. You oughta finish the thing. I bet it's great!"

"Yeah, like you ever finished a damn thing in your life." Howard tossed the napkin at Ryan's tie clasp. "Whoa, I like that tie. Those are little tyrannosauruses, aren't they? 'Tyrannosauri'? Hey, whatever happened to that movie thing you were working on with that funny Southern guy? Remember, we all went out years ago and he brought out this dinosaur puppet in the restaurant and got us kicked out? You were gonna do a screenplay together. What was his name—Matt?"

"Mack." Ryan picked the napkin up off the floor and set it on the table. "Mack Dwyer. He died about a year and a half ago. His family had the papers call it 'a lengthy illness.' Talk about funny—you should've seen the funeral. He'd been telling everybody he was gonna have himself stuffed, right, so after the eulogies, these two buddies of his come wheeling a clothes dummy in through the back door with this old moose head stuck on top, and it's got Mack's best suit on it—God! Lewis and I almost died.'' He looked up at Howard with a crooked smile. "Bad choice of words, actually."

"Aw, Rip." Howard reached across the table and put his hand awkwardly on Ryan's. "I'm sorry."

"Yeah. Me, too." Ryan let out a long breath. "Y'know, that bastard Lewis left me his record collection, which nobody—me included—was ever allowed to touch, and when I finally went through it I found that half the albums were mine. *Ow*—God, Howie, you want to break my knuckles? Let go." He retrieved his hand, rubbing it with an exaggerated grimace. "Besides, this crowd might get ugly at any minute." He squinted at the other tables. "Oops, too late—make that uglier . . . They didn't want to let me in, y'know. Millie at the door said it was 'cause I hadn't answered the invitation. Then Marilyn Sidloski came by and told them that was bullshit—she hadn't either, and they let her in." He laughed. "Course, I think they charged me double in the end. Then good old Phyllis Hyphen-what's-her-face, her cousin went to school with Ralph Beckan, who was a good friend of Lewis, so of course, she's suddenly got the scoop of the century. I sat here for a while just watching the news rebound from one end of the room to the other. Amazing."

"Yeah, if only we could harness that energy for world peace," Howard said.

A new tape started and couples drifted onto the floor, slow dancing in the soft light.

Howard picked up their glasses. "Look, I'm gonna get another one of these—you want something?"

"Yeah, a seltzer. Thanks, Howie."

A crewcut man with a sizable paunch squeezed in next to Howard at the bar. "Hey, Bell," he said. "You were always a smart guy."

Howard glanced at the man's name tag. "Hey, Victor. Thanks for noticing."

"So what're you doin' holdin' hands in the corner with Paxton?" The big man smelled like a brewery. "Don't you know the decent people in here have been tryin' to get that fag to take a hike for the past half hour?"

"Oh, the decent people." Howard frowned and surveyed the room. "I wonder which ones those are? Is it on their name tags?"

"That's his glass, isn't it? Jesus!" Victor screwed his face up in disbelief as people nearby turned to watch them. "You got a death wish? Thomasetti says you can catch it that way."

"I shared a lab table with Thomasetti in Biology," Howard said thoughtfully. "He used to think plankton was something pirates made you walk." There was scattered laughter among the listeners. Howard paid for the drinks and moved away from the bar.

When he got back to the table, Alaiya and Ryan were laughing together. "Your friend is very amusing, Ahwerd," she said as he resumed his seat. "He claims to have taught you all that you now know."

"What can I say? Old Rip's got more brains in his little finger than I've got in my whole hand." Howard set the glasses down. "So, how was the balcony?"

"Very pleasant, at first." Alaiya took a sip of Howard's drink, set it down quickly with a grimace, and spat into a napkin. "Then a man came out and stood very close to me. He seemed to be having some trouble walking, and his breath had a noxious odor." She pointed to the gin and tonic. "He said a few things that made no sense, then he put one of his arms around my shoulders."

"God." Ryan shook his head. "Alaiya, please let me apologize for my class, which obviously has none. If that happens again, get Howie to—"

"Wait a second." Howard raised his hand. "So what happened next?"

"Well, I removed the man's hand from my body and moved about three steps to the left. He came after me and tried to touch me a second time, so I grasped his wrist and told him that he must go back inside or I would hang him over the edge of the balcony." She gave Howard a guarded look. "I was attempting to be polite."

He grinned and nodded. "And?"

"And he reached for me yet again, so I lifted him out over the little railing and held him there by his wrists for a short time. He made quite a lot of noise." She glanced around the room. "You know, I am very impressed by the ability of these walls to screen out sound. Perhaps they contain a layer of filter-fluff . . . There was a metal hook with a plant hanging under it, stuck high in the wall between the two doors. I tested it for strength, then lifted the man back onto the balcony and suspended him from it by his belt. Unfortunately, I soon found that

I could not enjoy the evening with his constant cries in my ears, so I decided to come back in." She indicated a small plate arranged with intricately frosted pastries. "I finished the first portion of my meal and have made an initial trip to the dessert table. Is the large transparent bird intended for consumption, or is it only decorative?"

"Just for show," Howard said.

Ryan was chucking across the table. "I like this woman's imagination a lot," he said to Howard. "I can see why you two get along. She's a bit twisted—like us."

A small commotion began on the other side of the room. As they watched, a tall, thin man in a maroon tuxedo was escorted in from the balcony by two of the hotel staff. One of them was carrying a belt. The man held his pants up with one hand and staggered across the dance floor, shouting incoherently and flailing wildly with his free arm. The employees looked bored as they half led, half dragged him out through the main doors.

"Isn't that Wally 'How Can a Man with No Brain Live?' Thomasetti?" Ryan turned to frown speculatively at Alaiya.

"This one is my favorite," Alaiya said to Howard, popping a forkful of coffee-colored cake into her mouth. "I will share it if you get us more."

Howard was looking around the room at his former classmates. He saw few faces he recognized. "Tell you what," he said. "Why don't the three of us blow this clambake and find a better place to talk? We can swipe some dessert on the way out and take it with us."

They brought a small stack of napkins with them to the dessert table for wrapping purposes. As Alaiya was reaching for the only remaining piece of mocha-frosted hazelnut torte, another woman darted in front of her and scooped it onto her plate, keeping her eyes averted as she moved quickly down the table.

Alaiya's eyes were wide. "She knew I was about to claim that item," she said to Howard.

"Hey," Ryan said. "Allow me." Strolling up behind the woman, he smacked his lips and pointed to her plate. "Excellent choice, Belinda," he said. "I've been literally drooling over that very piece for the past half hour. You'll have to let me know how it tastes."

The woman looked from Ryan to the dessert. "No—here!" she said, thrusting the plate hastily into his hands and backing away from the table with a stricken smile.

Ryan returned to Alaiya and presented her ceremoniously with the slice of cake. "See? Magic."

They found an all-night doughnut shop where the waitress brought them coffee and then agreed to let them devour their smuggled desserts in return for a bite of the torte. Howard and Ryan amused Alaiya with tales of their childhood until she began to yawn, covering her mouth with her palm as she had sometimes seen Howard do. "I am not used to so much sweetness," she apologized. "I think it is making me sleepy."

"Yeah, I sometimes have that effect on people," Ryan said. He laced his fingers together and stretched out his arms. "Well, kids . . ."

"It is getting pretty late," Howard said, automatically checking his wrist. "Damn, I never did buy a new watch." He looked at Ryan. "Where are you staying these days—with your folks?"

"Nah. They made it pretty clear a couple of years ago that they'd derive extreme pleasure out of my conquering the urge to darken their doorstep again. Turns out I wasn't the son they thought they'd raised, or words to that effect—in which case, I wish the real Ryan Paxton had shown up to get bitten by that pony at my ninth birthday party." He drank the last of his decaf. "No, I'm sort of between residences these days. Currently I'm hanging out at the Y."

"You're kidding. Look—" Howard raised his eyebrows at Alaiya, who nodded. "We've got this spacious room with two beds in it for another night. Why don't we head over there and continue the merriment? You can leave when you feel like it, and crash with us in the meantime."

Ryan pondered the offer. "You sure this is okay? Can we stop and pick up a few of my things on the way?"

They took a cab to the YMCA. "I'll just be a second," he promised, and dashed up the broad steps.

Alaiya looked after the retreating figure. "Your friend has been ill for quite some time, I believe."

Howard turned to her in the shadows of the backseat. "What makes you say that?" His tone was sharp. "Why do you think there's something wrong with him?"

"Many small indications. Most recently, when you were out trying to summon this vehicle, he started to cough and could not stop for a few minutes. It left him quite debilitated, and he seems too thin for his size and build."

"Aw, c'mon," Howard said. "I was hoping—"

Ryan came clattering down the steps, an old suitcase in one

hand. "This is it," he said, sliding back into the cab as the driver stowed the suitcase in the trunk. "All the worldly possessions of Ryan Paxton in the handy concentrated size!"

When they reached the room, Alaiya excused herself and went into the bathroom to get ready for bed. Ryan went out onto the narrow balcony while Howard waited to say goodnight.

"Will we keep you up if we sit out there and talk for a while? It doesn't seem like there'll be another chance."

"Talk with him for as long as you want." She smoothed his cheek with her palm. "Tonight I sleep weighted down with sugar."

"Thanks. I figure we can all have breakfast tomorrow, then you and I can make it to the Matrix Building around noon, when people are leaving for their lunch break."

Ryan was kicked back on one of the balcony's spidery metal chairs when Howard sidled out through the sliding doors. "Look," he said. "I think I see a star."

Howard adjusted his own chair and sat down. Something clinked by his foot. "What's this?"

"Oh, just a little something I was saving for a special occasion." Ryan reached down with a flourish and pulled a tall, dark bottle from a paper bag. "Want to get looped?"

Howard went inside for glasses. They sipped their drinks in silence for a while.

"So how long have you been sick?" Howard finally asked.

"Ah. The Question." Ryan stretched out his legs between the bars of the railing. "I officially sero-converted seven months ago last Tuesday. Got the word while I was in the middle of cleaning the last of Lewis's things out of the apartment. Seven months. What anniversary is that—Lucite? Polystyrene? I bet Hallmark's got a card for it." He smiled in the light from the room. "And if you wanna buy a card, you better do it soon, Howie."

"Are you—is there any medicine or . . ."

"Yeah, they've tried a few things, just delaying tactics, really. But it's expensive. And the side effects are a bitch. I recently made the decision to remove myself from treatment, so to speak. I'm doing okay right now." He shrugged. "Things start to get bad, I'll remove myself from everything."

"Whoa," Howard said.

"Drooling, shaking, sixty-eight-pound weakling? Not for me, Howie. It's a question of who makes the decisions, y'know—

me or it. I'll fight this thing until it's clear that I've lost, and then . . .'' He waved his hand at the city. ''Later, dudes.'' He turned to look at Howard's shadowed face. ''Maybe it sounds cowardly, but then, you haven't been in all the little white rooms I've seen in the past couple of years. I don't want anybody to remember me as the guy who barfed all over their shirt before he croaked.'' He refilled their glasses. ''A toast—a toast to the power of decisions.'' Howard touched glasses with him in silence.

''You know what I used to like?'' Ryan said. ''I used to like it when we were about nine or ten, and we'd sit out on the porch behind the motel and make up adventures. Ol' Speedy purring away between us and a couple of Hostess fruit pies at our sides. God, it was easy to believe stuff back then. You were always so good at coming up with stories that took me right out of there.''

''Hey, Rip.'' Howard cleared his throat. ''You want to hear a story?''

''Yeah.'' Ryan reached for the bottle and leaned back. ''A good one, Howie.''

''All right, then. Once there was this guy, a very ordinary person, like you or me—until one day he finds this golden key . . .''

Half an hour later, Ryan divided the last inch in the bottle between their glasses. ''You should be writing this stuff down, Howie,'' he said drowsily. ''It's the best story I've ever heard. Except for the slakes. Don't write that part down, I don't like 'em.''

''Yeah, me either.'' Howard swirled the liquid in his glass. ''So, what was I saying?''

''Yam.'' Ryan settled back into the darkness. ''I like Yam.''

''Oh, yeah. Well, Yam and me are in the dead city, checking things out, and he—or maybe it was she at that point. Yam changes back and forth every once in a while.''

''Yeah, I've had a few friends like that.''

Howard continued talking, Ryan sitting quietly by his side, as the lights began to flicker off around the city.

In the morning he woke to find himself still out on the balcony, curled up stiffly in the tiny chair. Someone had draped a jacket over him. Ryan was gone.

CHAPTER XIX

Heading Back

"IT WAS GOOD THAT YOU SPENT THE TIME TO-
gether." Alaiya folded a T-shirt with the words SAVE THE
MANATEES printed in blue and green on the front and slipped
it into her pack.

"But he didn't even say good-bye." Howard sat on the edge
of the bed, cradling his forehead in his hands. "At least I don't
think he did. I don't remember too much after I told him about
the Sinking Swamp World. I think he found that part a little hard
to take. Ryan's always loved hot-air balloons, but he hates spiders." He fell back onto the sheets with a groan. "Oh, never
let me drink again."

Alaiya came to sit next to him. "Never let me eat so many
sweet things." She massaged his temples. "I feel as though
small Trulls had been running in and out of my head all night."

"Mmm." Howard closed his eyes. "I wonder if all Averoy
get chocolate hangovers . . ."

They left the hotel room an hour later, Howard stopping in
the lobby to buy a stamp at the front desk. "Look." He help up
a postcard for Alaiya to see. On the front was a surreal black-
and-white photograph of a woman who seemed to be levitating
several inches above a crowded city street.

" 'Dear Edith,' " he read from the back. " 'We enjoyed
meeting you a lot and hope to get together again someday. We
were able to straighten out a few things with the jeeks who
roughed you up, so they won't be bugging you again. Promise
you won't talk to any more strangers until you're about thirty-
five—you can't always be as lucky as you were with us. Take
care of yourself and keep your nose clean, ha-ha. Love and

Kisses, Howard and Alaiya.' '' He tapped the pen on his chin. ''You want to add anything? There's room on the side here.''

''Ask her to make sure the little birds are getting enough to eat.''

Howard rotated the card and added the sentence, his tongue sticking between his lips as he carefully printed the tiny letters. ''Okay.'' He dropped it into the mail slot on the desk. They hoisted their packs and their luggage and left the lobby.

They rode the subway, then walked for several blocks, arriving at the Matrix Building a few minutes after noon. Howard peered in through the glass doors. A security guard was chatting with a young female executive while he ate his lunch. They waited until a large crowd had emptied from the elevators, then slipped inside, using the departing throng as moving cover to slip by the guard. Howard lunged into the elevator as the door was closing, and Alaiya squeezed in next to him. He watched nervously as winking red lights showed their ascent. He took a deep breath when 60 appeared framed in light above him.

Mirror-bright doors slid open to reveal a long beige corridor. Two gray-clad security guards were conversing near a far bend in the hall. One of them looked up.

''Damn.'' Howard punched CLOSE DOOR. He bit his lip indecisively, then leaned forward and hit 61. When the doors opened again, it was to a similar, but deserted, corridor. They stepped from the elevator.

''That's lousy timing. I wonder why those guys are hanging around down there.'' Howard sat down carefully on one of the suitcases. ''They might find it a little peculiar if we both went to use the men's room, especially with all this luggage.''

''Is there another way to access the washroom?''

Howard thought. ''If we follow this to the end, we could go down the stairs and come back in beyond the guards. They're standing right where the hall bends, though, so they'd still see us come in. I suppose we could wait in the stairwell awhile.''

''What if they do not leave?'' Alaiya said. ''Let me go first. I will distract them toward the other end of the corridor. You bring our carrying packs and prepare yourself to use the Key when I come back.''

''Distract them how?'' Howard was dubious.

''Perhaps I will discuss the tabulated results of recent athletic competitions with them.'' Alaiya knelt to slip her dagger from her pack. ''We do not have many choices in this matter, Ahwerd.''

Howard stayed out of sight on the concrete landing as Alaiya opened the heavy door and slipped out. He held the door handle to prevent it from closing completely. Hearing sounds of conversation gradually receding down the hall, he cautiously pried the door open. The corridor was empty. He held the door with his foot while he silently transferred their baggage to the thick beige carpet, then eased it shut behind him. He tiptoed to the door of the Executive Washroom and removed the Key from beneath his shirt.

Howard heard the sound of running water and jerked back as the door swung inward. A gray-haired man in a business suit emerged, rubbing his hands on a paper towel. He sidestepped Howard with a disapproving glance. Howard smiled broadly. "Hi."

The man turned on his heel and headed down the corridor in the direction of the stairwell. When the heavy door had closed behind him, Howard gave a sigh of relief. He moved back to the washroom door and inserted the Key into the small opening just below the faceted knob. "Okay, Alaiya, come on," he breathed.

Rapid footsteps approached from the other end of the corridor. Howard grimaced in surprise as a man dressed in shorts and T-shirt came around the bend.

"Yo, Howie! Is it lift-off time?"

Howard stared. "Rip? What are you doing here?"

"What do you think?" The other man swung a huge backpack onto the floor and leaned against the wall. "God, this thing weighs a ton. Could've been worse, though—I could've tried to bring my stereo." He flashed a wide grin. "So, I ran into Alaiya back down the corridor there. She was busy tying up a couple of cops in the janitor's closet. Should be here any second."

Howard closed his mouth. "You believed me. You believed the story."

"Well, you did kind of forget halfway through that it was supposed to be about somebody else. And there's Alaiya, who's definitely not your average Boston career woman. I got to talk to her for a few minutes at the reunion, y'know. C'mon, Howie—Liechtenstein? So when you said you were coming back here today at noon . . ." He made some adjustments to the straps, then hefted the backpack with a grunt. "Not as spry as I used to be. So where do I stand? Is there any kind of a launching pad, or do we just sparkle and disappear?"

"Rip, I can't—" Howard looked pained. "This is a really dangerous place most of the time. People keep trying to kill us, and there's slakes and Dratzuls, not to mention the kind of bizarre germs that must be floating around. I mean, I don't want to be responsible for—"

"Howie, remember what we were talking about before you started your story last night? About making decisions? I already have something that's trying to kill me, and it's a lot more certain than getting chowed on by a spider-balloon. Dying's one thing, letting something control the way you live is another." He made a few passes in the air with his hand. "If it makes you feel any better, I hereby absolve you of all responsibility for my wellbeing. I just want you to promise me one thing—that you'll honor my decisions about my own life, okay?" His face was pale and beaded with sweat in the air-conditioned corridor. "Please? For old times' sake."

"Stand over here," Howard said. "When Alaiya shows up, you have to grab my arm and not let go. She'll be on the other side." He shook his head. "Where'd you take off to this morning, anyway? I was afraid you were out doing something stupid."

"Nah. I went shopping on my last charge card." Ryan tapped the small cassette player clipped to his belt. "This magic kingdom of yours sounds like it could use some tunes. You like movie themes?"

There was a soft footstep at the bend in the corridor.

"All right," Howard said. "Get ready."

A slender, dark-skinned man stepped around the bend. He had his right hand inside his jacket pocket, and on his head was an oddly shaped gray hat.

"Whoa," Ryan said.

"Get behind me!" Howard released the Key and took a step forward.

The dark man drew a silvery object from his jacket. He was grinning, his eyes on the Key. "Not so difficult," he said, thumbing a switch. The device began to buzz and crackle rhythmically. Howard reached down slowly for the handle of one of the suitcases.

"No," the man said calmly. The weapon chattered and a streak of red light struck the suitcase. Howard yanked his hand back with a cry. His fingertips felt as if they had been slammed in a car door. A lazy curl of gray smoke climbed from the small outline of ashes where the suitcase had been sitting.

"Now," the man said, and advanced toward the washroom door with his hand stiffly outstretched, the crackling weapon swaying back and forth between Howard and Ryan.

Suddenly Alaiya was standing behind him, her face stark with determination. She raised Silversting above her head with both hands and brought it down directly in the center of the gray headpiece. Stabbing through the yielding material, the dagger disappeared almost to the hilt. The man made a gurgling sound as small wormlike things dripped from the sides of the headpiece and fell to the carpeted floor. As he crumpled, Alaiya snatched the weapon from his fingers and began firing methodically at his body and the writhing creatures. A horrible odor filled the hallway.

"God," said Ryan. His face was white.

"Quickly, now!" She leaped the smoldering remains and took Howard's arm. "There may be more."

Howard took a shuddering breath and grasped the Key again, gasping at the pain in his injured fingers. He closed his eyes, struggling to clear his mind. Slowly he formed a picture of the encampment on the lavender plain, behind it an endless field of flowers stretching out under a lilac sky. He heard noises coming from somewhere down the corridor, and the image wavered like a dream. He forced himself to rebuild it, investing it with life and color, remembering the scent of the forest and the cool touch of the breeze.

"Okay," he murmured, and turned the Key.

Alaiya's fingers bit into his arm. He opened his eyes and blinked in bewilderment at the scene before him, then glanced quickly over his shoulder as he fought to get his bearings. They still stood in the corridor of the Matrix Building, but the door to the Executive Washroom had vanished. In its place, a tunnel of smooth gray stone stretched out endlessly in front of them. The Key was pointing directly ahead of them into the passageway; to Howard it still felt as if it were firmly seated in the absent door. The gray walls were moving. His body swayed slightly back and forth as he watched the tunnel expand toward them, the diameter of the opening gradually widening until they seemed to plunge down the passageway at dizzying speed. "Where . . ." He looked down at his feet, half-convinced that he would find them in frantic motion along a smooth stone pathway. His sneakers were firmly planted on the beige carpet. He looked up again. The scene in front of them sped on.

"Like the movie film," Alaiya murmured at his side.

They reached an intersection in the passageway and the perspective changed with stomach-turning swiftness as their point of view shot down a branch corridor to the right. Howard noticed for the first time a strip of wan light that ran along the roof of the tunnel. A series of chambers appeared on both sides of this section, but they whizzed by too quickly for him to make sense of their contents.

This branch of the tunnel was shorter than the first. A figure in a gray robe sat with its back toward them some distance away, hunched forward beneath a wall covered by elaborate machinery. Howard narrowed his eyes as the wall and the figure grew, wondering what would happen if they did not come to a halt before they were flung into that solid-looking barrier. While they were still several hundred feet away they took another abrupt turn, this time to the left. At the last instant, the robed figure lifted its head from the console. Howard could not tell if it was aware of their presence. He saw a flash of dark hair above pale, human-looking skin as they whipped out of sight.

With each turn their speed increased dramatically. Now they traveled along a thoroughfare that seemed to be gradually descending. Howard watched in fascination as they passed through an extended dark section, bursting forth into the light again in a matter of seconds.

"Ahwerd!" Alaiya cried at his side. "We are being drawn into it!"

He gave his head a shake and looked around. To either side of the opening, the walls of the Matrix Building were being slowly replaced by the racing tunnel. Above their heads, the strip of pale lighting ate steadily into the ceiling tiles. He looked down again. Now there were only a few inches of beige carpet remaining between their feet and the rushing stone. He wondered what would happen when there was no more carpet and no more Matrix Building beneath them. Fear tingled through his body like a jolt of electricity.

"Wait!" Howard tugged frantically at the Key, still locked in the empty air in front of him. He spun the bands and twisted the shaft in desperation. Around them, the beige corridor darkened and fell out of sight as gray walls twisted forward like the inside of a serpent. They began to pass small knots of dark objects, moving so swiftly now that Howard could not tell if they were living creatures. They shifted tunnels again. A howling noise grew in their ears and fierce winds buffeted them.

"I don't know what to do!" he shouted.

Out of nowhere an image appeared and hung suspended in the space before them. A tall human in a long cloak stood calmly in their path. She drew a hood back from her head, and her short golden hair remained untouched by the wind. Seeming to look through the travelers rather than at them, she moved her lips briefly. If there were words, the noise of the wind stole them before they could reach Howard's ears. Then she held out her hand and touched it to the tip of the Key, her fingers slipping through the golden metal as if it were made of smoke. The howl grew to a shriek. Everything went black.

Howard pitched forward, raising his hands at the last instant to protect his face. He landed with a jarring impact, then bumped against something soft. Alaiya moved on his left with a groan and lay still. Howard listened to her breathe for a long moment. Then he pushed himself carefully up to a sitting position, blinking in the bright sunlight. There was a suitcase on the ground next to him. Ryan lay to the right, sprawled with his cheek against the smooth lavender stone. His eyes fluttered open.

"God, Howie," he said weakly, struggling to prop himself up on one shoulder. "Call your stops, will you?"

CHAPTER XX

Settling In

HOWARD LAY AGAINST THE SUN-WARMED STONE AND
waited for his heart to stop pounding against his rib cage. He
was just getting to his feet, muscles aching, his right hand feeling as though it had been dipped in fire, when he heard a cry of
discovery from the direction of the encampment. He bent to
help Alaiya pull herself erect, then shuffled over to where Ryan
still lay on his side.

"Well, we made it." He held his left hand out to the other
man. "Welcome to Field of Flowers. The reception committee's
on its way. Are you ready to meet your fellow Breakneck Boys?"

Ryan blinked up at him solemnly. "We really went somewhere, didn't we?" He swallowed. "I mean, we really . . .
went somewhere." His eyes darted to the lilac sky, then returned to the plain of stone.

"Can't put one over on you, can we?" Howard went down
on one knee and shook him gently. "You think you can get up,
Rip? If not, it's no problem. We'll just bring you into camp and
have Awp look you over. He'll give you a little finger-tea and
have you feeling right as rain in no time."

"Awp. Awp was the little scrawny guy who turned into a great
big guy with a mouth like a clamshell." Ryan slowly extended
his hand and, wincing, let Howard pull him to his feet. He stared
out at the vastness of the flower sea, where colors changed in
great tides as the constant wind moved through the blossoms.
"Field of . . . It's really . . ." He turned to Howard, brown
eyes wide. "We're really . . ."

"Well, I can see you're still working on your statement for
the press." Howard supported the smaller man with one arm,

190

lifting his other to wave cheerfully at the approaching warriors. "Maybe for right now you should leave any substantive comments to Alaiya and me." A small, gray-white figure detached itself from the crowd and raced toward them on short legs. "Yo, Yam!" Howard cried. As the Trilbit bounded up, he leaned down to catch her in his free arm and hoisted her into the air.

"Ow-er-bel, you come lately—and with stranger!"

"Yep," Howard said, supporting Yam on his right hip. "And they don't come much stranger. This is my old buddy Rip!"

Ryan stared into shining black eyes inches from his own set above a blunt, velveteen sheep's muzzle. "Yo, Yam," he said weakly. Then his eyes rolled back into his head and he sagged against Howard's shoulder. The Nonesuch scratched the base of Yam's ear and sighed as Alaiya came from behind to put her arms around the three of them.

"Do you believe this scene?" he said as the Hant strode forward and bent to add its massive arms to the huddle. "Dad's home!"

At Howard's request, Awp gave Ryan a cursory examination and pronounced the newcomer completely exhausted and more than a little traumatized. "But beneath that, Hawa . . ." The Hant took its ropy fingers from the unconscious man's cheek and turned to Howard with an expression of concern.

"I know, Awp. He's infected with a very strong virus. I need to talk to you about it later." He lifted his shoulders helplessly. "It's killing him."

With Awp carrying Ryan, and various other warriors helping with the luggage, the Breakneck Boys returned to the camp. First the Hant produced an infusion of brownish liquid that stopped the throb in Howard's right hand. Then the Nonesuch requested some recuperation time for the three travelers, promising an informational get-together later that evening. As Howard was turning to carry his surviving suitcase to his tent, the black-furred Pasper broke through the ring of warriors and fell to his knees in front of them. "Nuh'suh!" he cried, spreading his arms.

Howard dropped immediately to his knees and flung his own arms wide. "C'mu!" The startled Pasper looked around, then rose slowly to his feet. Scratching his bewhiskered cheek, he walked off toward his tent, deep in thought.

That night they held a tale-tell. Howard and Alaiya recounted their adventures in Massachusetts while Ryan slumbered in the small hospital tent that had been established near the center of the camp. As Howard listened to Alaiya's descriptions of his world, their weekend getaway began to take on an aura of unreality. He looked into the orange fire crackling on the stone in front of him, and then raised his eyes to the ring of tents and buildings beyond. Had he really sat in a doughnut shop the previous night, seen a movie, and taken a cab to his high-school reunion?

"And then," Alaiya was saying, "after we blew the clambake, we returned to our bed-nest many hundreds of feet above the ground, where I was so taken by fatigue from the recreational food I had consumed that I did not activate the television receiver box. Not," she added with a shrug, "that one is able to locate decent game shows on Sunday anyway."

News of their encounter with the Carriers caused some excitement, as did Howard's account of their excursion through the gray tunnels on their way back to Field of Flowers.

"This Averoy woman." Kimmence leaned into the circle, her purple face glistening in the firelight. "She say something?"

"If she did, I couldn't make it out," Howard said. He glanced at Alaiya, who sniffed in negation. "Too much noise."

"Think Stillpoint," a Ga'Prenny wheezed from the other side of the gathering. "Hear gray tunnel downdeep, maybe Stillpoint."

Heads nodded.

"It was my thought as well," Alaiya said. "In the low regions of the city where the warriors never go, there are said to be warrens of interconnecting tunnels. And we did see a gray-robe at the end of one passageway."

"Yeah," Howard said. "A human gray-robe. Well, whatever it was, we got out of it alive." As the tale-tell dissolved into small knots of conversation, he rose to his feet and clapped his hands. "Meeting adjourned. Thanks for your attention. Everybody do whatever you feel like doing. If we have any more insights, we'll let you know." He strolled over to where the Hant stood and patted the massive back. "Can I look in on my buddy, Awp?"

"Certainly. I was about to check his status myself." The Hant looked thoughtful as they walked toward the hospital tent. "Hawa, when I examined your friend . . . This illness runs through his blood."

"Right." Howard stopped short. "You didn't ingest any of his blood during the examination, did you? God, I should have said something."

"Your concern is appreciated, but my physiology is quite alien to your own. In addition, my analytical faculties include very strong barriers against such contamination. It is not necessary for me to take a substance into my own system in order to perceive its makeup.''

"Did you get an idea what this disease is doing to him?'' Howard chewed at his lower lip. "Awp, I might as well ask this now. I've seen you work miracles with those fingers of yours. Any chance you can help him out?''

"Sadly, no. Your friend has lost most of his natural immunity to outside infection. My small adjustments may ease his temporary discomforts, but they can do nothing to protect him from those invading elements that will seek to capitalize upon his lack of defenses.''

Ryan was awake when they arrived at the tent. One side of his face was badly bruised. His eyes grew wide when Awp followed Howard into the cramped space. "Hi, Howie.'' He swallowed. "This must be the wise old Hant, right?''

"You got it. Ryan Paxton of Earth, I'd like you to meet my buddy Awp.''

Awp lowered itself to a crouch and extended a moplike hand. "It is a true pleasure to make the acquaintance of Hawa's childhood friend.''

"Yeah, likewise.'' Ryan lifted his arm from the bed of soft needles and allowed a score of white, boneless fingers to partially enclose his hand. "Neat,'' he said.

Alaiya found Howard sitting in front of her tent later that evening with a thoughtful expression on his face.

"Where have you been?'' she asked him. "I have been trying to describe cotton candy to Ya-mosh and needed your assistance.''

He gave a pensive smile. "I was testing a theory of mine,'' he said. "More a feeling, really, but it turned out to be true.'' He scratched his jaw. "It's not there anymore. Like it's been closed off or moved away, like I just can't reach it.'' He shrugged under her questioning gaze and lifted the Key. "Earth. I visualized every place I could think of, from the Executive Washroom to a pet store in Baltimore. Whatever happened during that last trip, it seems to have shut the door for good. I can't go back.''

Ryan recovered rapidly from the trauma of his journey. Thanks to the Hant's ministrations, he soon pronounced himself feeling better than he had in weeks.

Two days after their arrival, Howard dropped by the hospital tent and found his friend no longer in residence. "Go-go out! Go-go that way!" squeaked a passing Po'Ellika, rising in a half turn to extend some of its whiplike arms in the direction of the flower sea.

Howard climbed the broad ledge of lavender stone that bordered the mass of flowers. Ryan was stretched out on his back on a multicolored beach towel several yards from the shore, wearing a pair of striped knee-length shorts and mirrored sunglasses. On the towel at his side sat a small tube of suntan lotion, a crossword-puzzle magazine, and several cassettes. A black wire led from the narrow box at his waist to a pair of tiny earphones. Howard shook his head and tapped the sole of the other man's foot with his sandal.

"Hey!" Ryan lifted his glasses and peeled back the headset. "I thought this was a private beach."

"Looks like you've found your element pretty quickly." Howard sat crosslegged on the smooth stone. "How you feeling?"

"Not too bad." Ryan shrugged with his face. "I was tired of lying around—well, indoors, anyway. I figured it was time to catch some rays and start working on my reputation." He spread his hands out above him. "Exclusive to the *Midnight Star*: 'I Was a Beach Bum on the Fading Worlds.' " He looked down at his gaunt body with distaste. "Not that I'm too proud of the famous Paxton bod at the moment. I wish I could put some weight on. All these expensive muscles and nothing but bones to hang 'em on."

Howard tipped his head to the flower sea. "When you're feeling up to it, I'll take you out there for a little exercise."

Ryan twisted on the blanket. "Yeah, that's the low-gee area, right? Unbelievable."

Howard smiled. "You think that's strange, wait'll you see the Sinking Swamp World, or Thousand Islands."

"A whole planet named after a salad dressing." Ryan turned onto his stomach and propped his chin on his arms. "I can't wait."

That afternoon, Alaiya asked Howard to join her in a meeting with a few of the other Breakneck Boy strategists to determine their next move in the campaign against the Keyholders.

They decided to resume their recruitment raids with the next world scheduled to be brought into play. Arpenwole formally requested permission to express herself briefly in Averant, then spoke vigorously in opposition to the plan. "After the None-such's recent ill-advised trip to his homeworld, it must be clear that the Keyholders now regard us as a threat. We should strike directly at their heart if we wish to catch them without warning. I say we must go to Stillpoint."

"The raids remain useful so long as they bring us new members with a minimum of casualties," Alaiya responded. "When they lose their effectiveness, that is the time to consider an attack on Stillpoint."

"She really hates me," Howard said as they headed for Alaiya's tent after the meeting. "Don't you think we need a permanent envoy to, say, the Sinking Swamp World?"

Alaiya smiled. "Arpenwole is a clever and relentless warrior. If she becomes uncontrollable we may have to kill or otherwise deal with her, but until such action becomes necessary, we cannot afford to lose her services. Besides, you should not feel that you are the personal target of her sourness. Kormender knew her many years ago. He says she has always acted in this manner toward those in authority."

"I don't know," Howard responded glumly. "She strikes me as the type to put rat poison in the Jell-O."

Alaiya organized a small celebration to officially welcome Ryan to the Breakneck Boys. Howard sat to one side speaking quietly to his friend as the team members drifted together at the center of the camp.

"Ready?" Howard asked.

Ryan flipped open his small notebook and touched the point of his pencil to his tongue. "Fire away."

"Okay, you already know Awp and Yam."

Ryan nodded. "Yam calls me Rai-ya-pac. Sounds like a vitamin supplement, doesn't it? We get along great." He shook his head. "It's hard to imagine her as a male, though."

"Ha," Howard said. "Just wait." He looked out over the crowd. "Let's see. The big, flat ones are the Ga'Prenny. They come from a world of high winds that I've never been to. See those slits on their chests? They talk through those. I can't pronounce any of their names." He shifted on the fiber mat. "You used to bowl, didn't you? Well, the Po'Ellika are the little guys shaped kind of like candlepins. You'd never guess it to look at them, but they've got this habit of flipping the top of their heads back just like an old Zippo lighter. They're from the same windy world as the Ga'Prenny, but the two races don't get along all that well."

"I should make a note of that," Ryan said. "Never seat Ga'Prenny and Po'Ellika next to each other at dinner parties."

"Right. The Paspers are the ones that look like furry people with cat masks. That dark one with the bib is C'mu, my very own groupie.

"Those rotund individuals with the big feet are called Sarsi. They have pouches like kangaroos.

"The Beranoi are the ones with the ropy stuff on their faces—they all look like they've swallowed half an octopus. From the way they shuffle around, you might think it hurts for them to walk, but Alaiya says it doesn't. I think they used to spend a lot of time floating in shallow pools on their homeworld. That one she's talking to right now makes maps.

"The tall lizards with the extra set of arms are called Attercacks. They dye their quills.

"The other more or less human-looking ones with the white manes are the Domenai. See how they move? They remind me of something from a Ray Harryhausen movie.

"That singular-looking gentleman with the pink elastic skin and all the protuberances, just arriving at the rear of the crowd, is known in these parts as a Goshwao."

Ryan gave him a sidelong glance. "No way."

"I kid you not. When I first met him, he was racing toward me like an animated bag of bones with several claws extended. I haven't spent much time with him since that unfortunate incident, but Alaiya assures me that he is a creature of high refinement."

"Huh." Ryan tried not to stare at the ungainly figure, which indeed resembled an elastic sack filled with randomly placed bony structures. "I bet he has to get all his clothes custom made."

"Let's see, who's left? Oh, the Intzwam. Don't go near the Intzwam."

Ryan studied the sticklike creatures. "How come?"

"It's complicated. Just trust me." Howard blew out a deep breath. "Anybody else you need to know about?"

"Yeah, what about the *people* people?"

"Oh, right, the Averoy. Well, in addition to Alaiya we've got Kimmence over there. She has only one arm as the result of some industrial espionage. The brown-skinned guy next to her is Omber Oss, a good friend of Alaiya's. Kormender, with the reddish skin and golden-brown hair, is a recent recruit. He seems like a good guy. I haven't had much chance to talk to the little silver-haired man. He used to fight for the Dreadful Noise, and he's the newest Averoy to join the team."

Ryan chuckled. "Dreadful Noise—I love it. Who's the short-haired woman with all the attitude?"

"Ah! That, my friend, is Arpenwole. I'd keep my interactions with Arpenwole to a minimum if I were you. Chances are she already hates you because she knows you're my friend, and she definitely doesn't like me . . ."

Alaiya approached with a bowl full of white objects. "If you two are through whispering," she said, "I thought we might toast some muskmelons."

Over the next few days, Ryan felt well enough to do some exploring with Awp in the purple-gray forest, as well as accompany Yam on a few slow-paced strolls through the flower sea. Alaiya helped him erect a tent for himself and gathered sweet-smelling evergray boughs for its floor.

On the newcomer's fifth evening on Field of Flowers, Howard found him sitting with his cassette player on the ledge overlooking the blossoms. The first moon was a shimmer of silver behind a bank of low clouds on the far horizon.

"So." Howard sat next to him, dangling his legs over a jut of purple rock. "Are you settling in okay?"

Ryan nodded, removing the earphones. "I think I'm finally getting to know everybody. Of course, yesterday Yam caught me talking to an outcropping, but that was just because my contacts were fogged up."

"Oh, yeah," Howard said. "Talk to Alaiya. I bet they have some sort of magic eyedrops that'll take the place of those."

Ryan shrugged. "I've got the kind you can keep in for quite a while. They'll probably last me."

"Ah." Howard got slowly to his feet. "Well, I'm bushed. Big pep rally tomorrow for the upcoming raid. Are you coming in?"

"In a minute. You and Alaiya each have your own place, don't you?"

"Yeah. She built herself a swell hut with a door and everything. I scrounged an old tent off of somebody."

Ryan clicked his tongue. "Separate residences. You modern couples."

Howard laughed. "We just sort of make everything up as we go along," he said. "See you in the morning."

"Hey, Howie," Ryan turned and called after him. "I like it here. Thanks."

CHAPTER XXI

The Traitor

RYAN SAT IN ON THE PEP RALLY TRADITIONALLY HELD by the battlechief and the Nonesuch the day before a recruiting raid. "Not bad at all," he said after Alaiya and Howard had finished doling out assignments and encouragement to the warriors chosen for the raid on the world called Cloud. "You guys make a very charismatic team. Now, if we can just figure out a place in your administration for a rising young glory-seeker."

"You just relax for a while," Howard said. "We have this longstanding rule that nobody in the Breakneck Boys has to do anything she, he, or it doesn't want to."

An hour later Ryan came to Howard with a request.

"Find me something to do in this upcoming enterprise, Howie. Seriously. I want to be more than just Jimmy Olsen, the Nonesuch's pal. It does a number on my self-esteem not to be a fully contributing member of society."

With some misgivings, Howard agreed to allow Ryan to join Kimmence's quarantine team at the interim camp. They had decided to return to the Black and Blue World, this time choosing a campsite several hundred miles west of the one where the Brindled Intzwam had met its demise.

Howard brought Ryan with him on a brief scouting run the day before the raid. They stood on the wrinkled lip of a gigantic black crater and gazed down at a great circular waterfall, miles away, that was formed by the confluence of dozens of powerful rivers rushing in from all sides of the basin. It made a continuous rumble like distant thunder. "Alaiya calls it a riverfall," Howard said as they watched the plunging spectacle through curtains

198

of spray. "Most of the larger craters have one. They're supposed to lead to vast underground seas."

"Neat," Ryan said.

Kimmence and Arpenwole asked to trade places at the last minute, the former joining the team of warriors on Cloud while the latter took over as head of the quarantine camp. "Oh, swell," Ryan said when he heard the news. "I was just getting tight with Kim, and now I'm stuck with the Bitch of Buchenwald."

"Fortunes of war." Howard spread his hands. "You can always stay home and wait for the next raid."

"No, no." Ryan raised his palm. "Civic duty, teamwork, moral fiber, and all that stuff. I'll be there."

"He didn't look all that hot today," Howard told Alaiya that night. "You know . . ." He slumped down in a corner of her hut. "This isn't going to be a lot of fun, when he goes." He broke off a sprig of evergray and tossed it aside. "Damn."

The world known as Cloud turned out to be another in a series of locations Howard was beginning to think of as Theme Park Worlds.

The projected battle site was in the midst of an unusual mountain range that stretched in all directions as far as the eye could see. Every inch of the mountains' brownish rock was taken up by wide, shallow steps, some of which extended fifty feet to either side. The horizontal surfaces rose from three to twelve inches in height and averaged a foot in depth. "This bottom part's kind of Escher-esque," Howard observed, as he stood with the other Breakneck Boys midway up a flight that extended some five hundred feet into the air. Only the lower halves of the intersecting staircases were visible to the combatants; the upper portions were permanently shrouded in billows of thick white cloud.

Groups of stairways were lit with different colors. Howard could not figure out where the light was coming from, and finally decided that the rock itself must be translucent and glowing softly from within. Nearby cloud masses reflected antique gold, rose, and shades of cool purple. "Beautiful job on the clouds. Reminds me of N. C. Wyeth," Howard commented to Alaiya. "And the lighting's definitely Maxfield Parrish."

The angled tiers of steps met at different points, forming a landscape that resembled thousands of Mayan pyramids jammed helter-skelter on top of one another. There was no maneuverable stretch of flat ground to be found anywhere—battles were fought in the constricted, V-shaped areas where neighboring staircases came together.

"So who's responsible for all this zaniness?" Howard asked. "It's certainly not natural. But did they find the world in this condition, or is this some bright young Keyholder architect's idea of an award winner?" He looked around, shaking his head. "Can you imagine trying to go about your business here in a wheelchair? I hope they get lots of flak from the equal-access people."

"Ahwerd," Alaiya said finally, holding up a finger to the Ga'Prenny with whom she was conferring, "would you mind walking to the far end of this step to continue your commentary? I am having some difficulty communicating with the other warriors."

"Hmm." Howard rubbed his chin. "I bet that was intended as some kind of hint, wasn't it?" He sat down on the step and whistled softly to himself while Alaiya concluded her instructions. When the last of the warriors had been briefed, she came to sit by his side. "Now I will be happy to listen to your musings upon the origin of this awkward world."

Howard pursed his lips and looked off into the clouds. "Yeah, well, now I don't feel like saying anything."

"Imposter!" Alaiya's eyes widened. "The real Ahwerdbel would be incapable of such an assertion. I demand to see proof that you are indeed the Nonesuch, before I am forced to toss you from this step."

"Ah, the Carol Burnett of the Breakneck Boys. Didn't you lecture me once about the dangers of excessive humor during battle?"

Alaiya indicated the quiet steps around them. "As you can see, we are not engaged in battle at the moment, and so need have no fear of such peril."

"Yeah, I noticed it's pretty low key here." Howard watched as the other members of the team slowly climbed the nearest stairs. "When are they scheduled to face off?"

"According to the Hant's calculations, the Disturbing Vision and the Mortal Thrust should be appearing within the hour." She got to her feet. "Come, let us ascend."

Three hours later, Alaiya called the warriors down from their places of concealment just above the cloud level.

"Something has changed," she said. "Either the Hant miscalculated—a highly unlikely possibility—or the Keyholders have altered the schedule of battle.'' She looked around with a sigh. ''We knew that this was bound to occur at some point. It would have been beneficial to gather a few more members, but we must read the map as it is drawn.''

Howard brought out the Key and the warriors formed their traveling ring.

''Poor Rip,'' he said when they had delivered the Cloud contingent to Field of Flowers. ''He doesn't get a chance to participate this time, after all.'' He offered Alaiya his arm. ''Want to go pick up the interim staff with me?''

When they appeared on the Black and Blue World, Howard thought at first that he had brought them to the wrong location. The rim of the black crater showed no signs of recent habitation. He lowered his hands. ''What'd I do, overshoot?''

Alaiya moved away from his side, her head tilting slightly as she scanned the landscape. ''This is the correct place,'' she said to him, her hand moving to her belt. ''I remember that rock there with the double fangs.''

''Oh, jeez.'' Howard shaded his eyes and turned his head in a wide arc. ''Where are they?''

The level area extended for almost a mile to either side of them on the crater's rim; it was strewn with mammoth boulders and pocked with hundreds of holes large enough to contain the bodies of warriors.

''We'd better split up,'' Howard said. ''How many of them came over—who was here?'' He closed his eyes and counted on his fingers. ''Arpenwole, Kormender, one of the new Ga'Prenny—''

''Dokkalin of the Attercack,'' Alaiya continued, ''Huliper Apperdoy—''

''And Ryan,'' Howard finished. His hands were shaking. He and Alaiya began to comb the area, moving off in opposite directions over the black rock. Fifteen minutes later he saw her waving to him from the far end of the level strip.

He broke into a stumbling run, forcing himself to concentrate on the pattern of the jagged upthrusts and shadowed crevices he had recently negotiated. It took him almost five minutes to reach Alaiya. He arrived out of breath, his legs aching from having twisted them in numerous hidden potholes. Alaiya was standing by a jumble of freshly broken rock. She led him behind a large flat chunk, seven feet tall, that reared up from the tortured surface at a forty-five-degree angle. A deep, narrow pit with inward-slanting sides lay beneath the angled rock. In the pit were several bodies. There was a horrible freezing feeling in Howard's stomach as he knelt to look down at them. Dokkalin and Apperdoy lay about five feet down, their bodies twisted like old rags. Partially visible below them were other black-suited warriors.

"Ahwerd." Alaiya touched his arm gently. He lifted his face and realized that tears were streaming down his cheeks. "I could not reach them by myself. You must help me get down there so that we may remove them."

He anchored himself on the edge of a small crack that led away from the pit, and leaned over the edge. Alaiya held on to his free hand and carefully lowered herself into the narrow crevice until she could touch the nearest body. She pulled the Attercack to the side with one arm, then used the corpse as an uncertain platform from which to grasp the Sarsi. Howard shuddered and looked away. "Ahwerd," she said a moment later, loosening her grip on his fingers. "I am able to stand now." He released her hand. She bent and began to pull slowly at the enormous Sarsi, grunting as she lifted the body to waist height. She changed her grip and pushed the bulky corpse up past her head, then wedged it into a small niche in the side of the crevice. She turned back to the pit. "The Ga'Prenny is alive," she reported in a minute. "She has stiffened her backbones to form a shield for the softer ventral part and relinquished consciousness to conserve energy." Alaiya bent over the broad, still form and began to stroke it lightly just below the mound of the head. A quiver of movement came from skin stretched taut as a drumhead and the Ga'Prenny made a sound like a great wheezing sigh. Alaiya lowered her head so that her ear rested on the skin of the creature's back and murmured a brief question. There was a faint response. Alaiya lifted her head, her face expressionless. "She says there are others below her. She does not know if they are alive or dead." She surveyed the body wedged like a giant platter into the narrow opening. "It will be difficult for her to release the tension. The stiffening is a reflex reaction when death is imminent."

Sounds came from the Ga'Prenny, a faint urgent chord repeated over and over. "Can you understand her? What is she saying?" Howard asked.

"Traitor," Alaiya said. "The traitor."

She lowered her head again, humming softly with her cheek pressed against the canvaslike skin. Vibrations passed in rippling waves along the distended dorsal surface. Finally the

Ga'Prenny emitted a long, low wail as the center of her back tented suddenly upward. Alaiya continued to hum, stroking the broad back as it folded like an umbrella toward the surface.

Alaiya braced herself with one foot on the wall of the crevice and another on the body of the Attercack and pulled with the Ga'Prenny. "Ahwerd, help us." He reached down and slipped his hand under the edge of the Ga'Prenny's body, helping Alaiya raise it past Huliper Apperdoy and up over the edge of the crevice. The creature was surprisingly light. He dragged the feebly moving body several inches from the opening, then turned back to peer down into the pit. Alaiya stood over two black-clad humans, their bodies jammed together in almost standing positions near the bottom of the crevice. She looked up at him. "Arpenwole and Kormender." She pressed her own body to the side to give him a better view. "Look."

Arpenwole stood with her back against the stone of the pit. Kormender was in front of her, his back pressed against her belly, and her right arm encircled his chest. In Arpenwole's hand was a slender sword, its point entering Kormender's body at the juncture of throat and collarbone.

"The traitor," Howard breathed. "That's why she switched assignments. She killed him and then died herself."

Alaiya shook her head. "She is unconscious, but alive." She covered Arpenwole's hand with her own and yanked the sword from Kormender's throat. Caked blood fell away. Prying the two Averoy apart, she pulled the man's body upward, then held it with one crooked arm while she reached back for Arpenwole.

"Alaiya, where's Ryan?" Howard kneeled at the edge of the crevice. The bottom of the pit was now visible some fifteen feet below. "There's no more room down there. Where is he?"

"Arpenwole is still alive. I must bring her to the surface." Alaiya puffed with exertion, sweat streaking her ivory face. "Then we will see."

"I don't care about her." Howard stared numbly as Alaiya allowed Kormender's lifeless body to tumble back into the tiny space and pushed herself and Arpenwole up the side of the pit. "We have to find him."

He held out his hand and grasped Alaiya's wrist, straining to hold the combined weight of the two women as they rose toward the rim.

"There—" Alaiya pushed the unconscious woman over the edge ahead of her, gripped the rim with both hands, and levered herself onto the rock. She lay panting for several moments before rising slowly to her knees. Leaning over the Ga'Prenny, she murmured a question next to its faintly pulsing hide. The response seemed infinitesimal, a moan that Howard could barely identify as a sound.

Alaiya leaned back. "They took him," she said, turning her face toward the spot where the level ground fell off gradually into jagged peaks. "That way—"

"Rest," Howard said. "I'll be back."

He heard the pounding noises when he was about fifty feet from the edge of the plateau. Ryan was lying on a small outthrust of rock, a tangle of shattered metal and plastic clutched in his bloody hand. "Heard you shouting before," he said in a badly slurred voice, lifting the remnants of his cassette player to smash it once more on the rough surface. "I thought if I made enough noise . . ." He closed his eyes and dropped the ruined box as Howard knelt by his side. But his eyes flew open again when Howard gently lifted his head from the rock. "No! Get away, you idiot!"

"Ryan, it's me, Howie."

"I know who it is. Don't you see I'm bleeding? You can't touch me!"

Howard sat back for a moment, then raised his hands. "Look: no cuts, no scratches. No problem. I let Alaiya do all the dirty work back there." He reached down and slid his arms under Ryan's body. "I'll be careful."

Howard carried Ryan back to where Alaiya sat between Arpenwole and the Ga'Prenny and laid him down. He removed his vest, folding it into a thin pillow for his friend's head. Alaiya watched silently.

"We've got to take them back," he said, getting to his feet. "We've got to get them to Awp."

"I do not think they should be moved at all now, Ahwerd, not even for such a journey. Go get the Hant. I will stay with them."

Howard looked down at Arpenwole, who lay with eyelids fluttering weakly, her head propped up on Alaiya's lap. He clenched his fingers tightly around the Key. "Did you get anything out of her?" he grated.

"No, she has not yet regained consciousness. But the Ga'Prenny was able to speak some more." She reached out her palm and absently smoothed the pale flat skin. "It was an attack by a group of Stillpoint warriors. They had a mountain gun. The interim team took refuge below the lip of the crevice just before the gun was fired. Because of that they were not all killed instantly, though the force of the concussion widened the pit. They fell in and were spared the full devastation of the second attack." She paused to moisten her lips and brushed lank strands of hair from her face. Then she lifted a small disk of reddish material from the black rock. "It was a signaling device of some sort. The attackers must have already been on the planet, waiting to be contacted by their agent. Arpenwole came upon Kormender as he was beginning to speak into the device. She stopped him before he was able to give more than their general location."

"Kormender." Howard stood swaying, unable to make sense of the information. "The traitor?"

"Because of this, they were able to strike the camp and begin their retreat. It gained them precious time in which to locate this refuge." She looked down at the three battered bodies. "Bring the Hant now, Ahwerd, or I fear it will be too late."

CHAPTER XXII

Home

"IT'S SO GODDAMN STUPID!" HOWARD *PACED* IN front of the tattered tent. "People dying like this for no reason—I hate it!" He sat down on a supply box and began to crack the knuckles of his right hand sharply, one by one. "How could you live so long with this—this stupidity?"

"How did you live so long breathing the noxious air of your home world?" Alaiya stood next to the crate, her eyes on the open tent flap and the Hant moving inside. "Until you found the Key," she added quietly, "the choice was the same for both of us: to live with it or to die."

"I know, I know, I'm sorry." He began on the left hand: *crack, crack.* "I have no right to judge you—I'm *not* judging you. I'm just angry at myself."

"At yourself?" She turned to stare down at his bowed head. "What do you have to do with what happened here today?"

"Right, that's a good one." Howard nodded. "I brought them all to this world—I brought Ryan here from Earth. What do I have to do with it? Everything!"

"Bullbit!" Alaiya said. "Think of yourself as an instrument, if it makes you feel better. Think how all of us have used you to accomplish our own goals, as if you were nothing but an extension of the Key." She shook her head in frustration and looked away. "Think whatever you need to in order to get on with things."

Howard looked up, incredulous. "Is it really that easy for you to get over something like this?"

"No, of course not!" She took his chin in her fingers and gave his head a sudden shake. "You do not, you cannot ever get over the death of friends or battlemates. But you do get on with things, and try to see that it does not happen again. I am sorry for what happened to those warriors. I am thankful it did not happen to the entire battle-gang—to my friends Ya-mosh or the Hant. With my entire being I rejoice that it did not happen to you. These are victories, no matter how small, and they are to be savored, despite the blow that crushes.'' She released him and took a step toward the tent. "The Hant beckons."

Howard sat for a second, rubbing his jaw. "Did you say 'bull-bit'?" he asked with a weary laugh. He got to his feet.

A broad slinglike affair had been erected at one end of the tent to support the flounderlike Ga'Prenny. She lay supine with her small limbs drooping off the sides of the sling, her upper and lower eyes blinking in slow semaphore as Howard paused by her side. He rubbed the warm skin with his palm. "How are you feeling?" The Ga'Prenny responded with a prolonged chord, in which Howard thought he could detect some variation for the first time. He raised an eyebrow at Alaiya.

"As if someone had skimmed me across the jagged rocks like a flat stone on water," the battlechief translated, pausing to catch a final fillip of sound. "But that is much better than dark, folded death."

"We're lucky you were there," Howard said. "If you hadn't gone all stiff in that crevice, Arpenwole would most likely have died with the others. Thank you for saving her." He moved away from the sling and followed Alaiya to the next patient. "Where'd you learn to speak Ga'Prenny?"

"Once, many years ago, I was separated from my team on one of your Theme Park Worlds, and could not make it back to Stillpoint before the Fade. I found myself transported to the Sunless/Moonless World, where I soon discovered a Ga'Prenny from the opposing battle-gang—also alone and obviously in a ship identical to mine."

"Ship? Oh—in the same boat," Howard corrected with a nod. "Right."

"We were both inexperienced and new to combat. We decided to flout custom and form a temporary alliance, giving both a chance for survival where each alone might have had none. As we made our way to Stillpoint, we taught each other the rudiments of our tongues. Later we became teammates when I ascended to the Dreadful Noise and continued the practice. Another tiny victory."

"Sounds like it would make a great miniseries," Howard said. "So, is she asleep, do you think?

They stood near a raised pallet cushioned with masses of rosy

moss. Arpenwole lay with one arm flung back awkwardly behind her close-shaven skull, the other resting on her flat stomach. Howard reached out his hand, drew it back with a grimace,
hesitated. "Oh, what the hell," he said. Gently grasping the ivory
arm, he brought it down and folded it on top of the other one.
When he stepped back, Arpenwole's gray eyes were on him.

"Oh, you're awake," he said. "You know, you can cut off
the circulation sleeping like that." He took a breath. "So, I'm
glad to see you looking so much better." She made no response.
He exhaled in a rush. "Look, Arpenwole, I know we haven't
always gotten along so well. I want to thank you for what you
did. The Breakneck Boys owe you a debt of gratitude."

"Kormender weak mind, love Keyholders." The warrior curled
her lip. "Knew before, same team. Always smile, smile, never
dispute, friend to all." She sniffed. "Tell myself: Watch that one."

"That simple, huh?" Howard stuck out his hand. "You think
maybe we can be friends now?"

Arpenwole eyed the proffered hand. "Not necessary warriors
have affection for one another to function efficiently in battle-
gang," she said matter-of-factly. "Besides, you not true warrior—though I pretend so for good of teammates."

Howard pulled his hand back with a sigh. "Hey, get well
soon, Arpenwole." He turned away from the pallet, rolling his
eyes at Alaiya. "I'm sure the cards and flowers are going to be
pouring into this room," he said softly.

"Ahwerdbel." The warrior lifted her chin at him from the
pallet. "Thank you for moving the arm."

"I know," Howard said to Alaiya as they moved toward the
end of the long tent. "Another small victory."

The third patient also seemed to be asleep. The Hant was
bending over his body as the two approached the pallet. It
straightened up and came to meet them.

"How is he?" Howard asked.

"Some blood has been lost. He was beaten quite savagely. I
have controlled as much of the pain as I could." Awp looked
over its shoulder at the quiet figure. "Hawa, there is a compli-
cation."

Howard's heart sank. He tilted his head back to look at the
Hant's broad face. "What is it?"

"Hey, Howie." Ryan raised himself weakly onto one elbow
and attempted a wave. They walked to the side of his pallet.

"How you doin', sport?" Howard surveyed the gaunt form.
"You're looking good."

"Liar," Ryan said, slumping back onto the moss. "Hey, Alaiya."

"Hello, Ryan. I am pleased to see you conscious."

"I'm pleased to be conscious. I feel like I've been out for a long time."

"Most of one day." Alaiya leaned forward and smoothed damp hair back from his brow. "Do you remember what happened?"

"Yeah." His face darkened. "The bastards." He swallowed with difficulty, wincing. "I was out wandering around, listening to my tunes, quite a ways from the camp. I heard a ruckus and looked back to see them taking down the tent and tearing out in my direction. I started running back to meet them, but they waved me off. Then I saw a bunch of gray uniforms coming up onto the rock behind them, dragging some kind of doomsday cannon, so I turned and took off. There was a big explosion. It knocked me down." Ryan started to cough and held up his hand. When he finished, he was trembling. "I didn't know if anybody was still alive. Then they caught up with me. They knocked me around for a while, screaming at me. Then they did it, the bastards." He pointed to the inside of his left elbow, where the Hant had applied a bandage. "One of them—this white-haired guy with fangs?—he comes over and tells the others something that makes them stop killing me. He has them hold me so I can't move at all. Then he takes out his knife. While I'm watching him, he just sets it on his palm and saws it back and forth a couple times like it's perfectly normal behavior." Ryan closed his eyes. "I could see what was coming, and I started yelling like crazy at that point, but they're all just standing there, mimicking me and laughing." His eyes were rimmed with moisture. "Then they held me down and he cut me, Howie. I was screaming at them, trying to get them to understand, but they *cut* me and then the white-haired guy reaches down and presses his palm into my arm and grinds them together, and won't let go, and he's *laughing*." He shook, his breath coming in spasms. "I conked out pretty soon after. It felt like a bad fever. I think it was much later when they slapped me awake, and then they started asking me all these questions and after a while I realized some of them were beginning to make sense."

"Parleybugs," Howard said, glancing at the Hant. "They were mixing the team's blood with yours in order to give you their parleybugs so they could question you. Strange as it may seem, they weren't really trying to kill you."

"Kill me?" Ryan gave his head a small shake. "I know that.

They thought I was you. Y'know how it is with these alien types—one human looks pretty much like another. But I guess they figured it out pretty soon, because they got real pissed at my answers. They lit into me again for a while, and then they just left me there.'' He changed position carefully on the pallet, his face haggard with pain and fatigue.

"It's all over now, Rip. Try to get some sleep, okay, and don't think about it.'' Howard gestured toward Awp, who lifted a small cup of steaming liquid.

"Don't think about it? Howie, don't you get it?''

The Hant brought the cup to Ryan's lips, and he took a small reflexive sip. His eyelids fluttered and he lay back into the moss.

"Thanks, Awp. I hope he can—'' Howard stopped abruptly. "Oh,'' he said. "His blood.''

Alaiya's dark gray eyes were wide. "The virus.'' She looked at the Hant. "Will the infection be transferred?''

"It was a Domeny who mixed blood with Ryan,'' the Hant replied. "Domenai physiology is very like your own. We cannot say what will happen.''

"God,'' Howard said. "He could pass it on. Oh, God.''

"I had wished the Keyholders defeated.'' Alaiya stared numbly at the sleeping man. "But this is a cowardly way.''

"It won't stop with just the bad guys,'' Howard said. "It's a virus—it doesn't care who it's killing.''

They stood in silence.

"There is another matter,'' the Hant said. "Ryan's own blood now contains active parleybugs.''

Howard nodded. "We can take care of that quickly enough.'' He turned to Alaiya. "Are there any purge pods left?''

"Enough for one or two individuals. We can bring them back from Field of Flowers whenever you wish.''

The Hant raised a rippling hand. "Unfortunately, Ryan's system has suffered multiple shocks. He must have several days to recover before we attempt to cleanse his blood. Introducing the purge pods at this stage could prove highly dangerous.''

Howard shrugged. "Then we'll wait till he's ready.'' He let out a long breath. "Except—while he's got the parleyblood in him, he's like a beacon to the Keyholders, isn't he? We can't take him back to Field of Flowers until he's been purged. But if we leave him here, we run the risk of another attack.''

"Or of having him taken from us,'' Alaiya said. "If indeed the parleyblood is what makes one susceptible to the Fade, then the Keyholders need only activate it on this world and transport him to wherever they wish.''

"This is a mess.'' Howard looked at Awp. ''Are there any alternatives you can think of?''

The Hant hesitated. ''There is a long-held theory that the Keyholders' reach extends only to the surface of most worlds. There are tales of warriors hiding themselves within mountains or in deep caverns and emerging days later, having been left behind by the Fade.''

"They are only tales,'' Alaiya said.

The Hant nodded. ''At any rate, he is far too weak to be moved to such concealment at this moment.''

"So we can't hide him and we can't get rid of the bugs for another few days. In the meantime, he's at the mercy of the Fade.'' Howard looked grim. ''I guess we just hope they prefer to get all of us at the same time. At least if they attack again, we'll have something tangible to protect him from.''

"It seems the only solution,'' Alaiya agreed.

They decided to move three-quarters of the team to the Black and Blue World until Ryan was well enough to accept the purge pods. A nervous night passed. When Howard went to the hospital tent the following morning, he found Ryan sitting up on the pallet, sipping broth from an earthenware bowl. Omber Oss stood at the end of the pallet.

The warrior bowed his head slightly to Howard. ''Ahwerdbel. I allow you private speech with your friend.'' He nodded to Ryan. ''I will visit later again.''

"In a while, crocodile. Thanks for stopping by. Next time, bring candy.'' Ryan set down the soup bowl and stretched cautiously. ''And another morning begins,'' he announced, ''filled with an endless round of social obligations.''

Howard laughed. ''Somebody's looking chipper.''

Ryan glanced over his shoulder. ''Well, this is the last bed on the left,'' he said, ''and there's no way it could be Madame Iron Butterfly over there.''

Howard sat carefully on the edge of the pallet. ''I guess that leaves you.''

"Yeah, aside from all the bruises, I don't feel so terrible. Awp keeps feeding me his liquid cure, of course, so I'm spending half my life in the bathroom.'' He looked around the dilapidated tent. ''Or I would be, if we had one.''

"This is great!'' Howard said. ''At this rate, we'll be able to get you purged and out of here in no time.''

"Purged," Ryan said. "That has a pleasant ring to it, doesn't it?"

"Good morning." The Hant ducked under a central pole and joined them at the pallet. It glanced at Ryan. "Hawa, may I speak with you a moment?"

Howard started to get to his feet when Ryan held out his arm. "Wait a minute here. Nobody leaves the room." He looked up at Awp. "I've heard enough doctors say 'May I speak with you a moment' to know I want to be included in this little powwow." He turned to Howard with a pleading look. "C'mon, Howie. All he needs is a clipboard to remind me of my last twelve physicians. I want to be in on this if it's about me."

Howard raised his brows at the Hant. "Awp?"

"You are quite correct, Ryan. The matter concerns you as well as the rest of the Breakneck Boys. I merely wished to allow Hawa the opportunity to receive it first in his position as Nonesuch."

"Oh, I know I'm going to enjoy this." Ryan propped his chin in his hand.

Howard felt a cold tightening in the pit of his stomach. "What is it, Awp?"

"An unusual phenomenon that I must admit I had failed to anticipate. I have examined Ryan this morning and found his condition much improved. Improved beyond our hopes, as a matter of fact." It paused, choosing its words. "It appears that the parleybugs in his system have organized against the virus."

"Huh?" Ryan raised his head. He looked at Howard. "Huh?"

"The parleyblood has long been known to possess very strong healants. Aside from its translation function, it is responsible along with the foodstuff for maintaining the warriors of the various battlegangs in peak condition. At the moment, it seems that a sizable portion of the parleybugs have adapted themselves in such a fashion as to provide your body with a secondary immune system. While it is too early to speak with any certainty concerning duration or extent, my analysis indicates that the destructive progress of the disease has been completely halted."

"Please." Ryan raised a trembling arm. "Don't anybody say anything else, just for a minute or two. I need to replay those last few words in my head a few thousand times."

The Hant excused itself, and Howard remained with Ryan for a while, then ran to find Alaiya. He found her talking to Awp.

"Did you hear?" He came up and put his arms around her. "Did Dr. Casey give you a peek at the patient's chart?"

"I hope you are not upset, Hawa. I understood that Ryan did not object to the dissemination of this information."

"Not at all, Awp." Howard leaned back, smiling. " 'Let the joyous news be spread,' to quote him exactly."

"It is joyous news indeed, Ahwerd, but . . ." Alaiya was watching him uncertainly.

"But what? How can you add a 'but' to news like this?"

"The Hant and I have been discussing the further implications of its findings. It is due to the parleybugs' presence that Ryan's illness has ceased to worsen."

"Yeah, but we can forgive and forget in this case. The little monsters are actually doing some good for once. Surely you're not going to hold a grudge."

"Ahwerd, the Hant believes there is a strong chance the virus will resurface if the parleyblood is purged from Ryan's body."

Howard looked at her blankly for a moment, then turned to Awp. "You mean he'll always have to—"

"I would not say always. But I believe that until a true cure can be found for this disease, we would be ill-advised to remove any of the micro-organisms from your friend's body. Perhaps the virus will be utterly defeated and his own immune system will regenerate at some point. We must wait and see."

"I understand." The cold feeling had returned to Howard's stomach. "Ryan can't live without the parleybugs, and we can't live with them."

"The answer's simple, Howie." Ryan spoke calmly. "I just have to go away for a while." He lifted his shoulders. "Maybe kind of a long while."

"Go away where?"

"Well, I've been thinking that Boston might not be so bad to start with, if you wouldn't mind dropping me off. I mean, all I've gotta watch out for are those guys in the funny hats, right? And they've got no reason to come after me. I know a few researchers who might be able to get somewhere with a sample of my blood. It could help a lot of folks. And now that we're in touch again, you could visit me every once in a while, maybe even bring me back for a short . . ." Ryan's voice trailed off. "Why am I not getting the response I expected here?"

"I can't take you back to Earth, Rip. The Key won't bring me there anymore—I tried just after we arrived." Howard lifted his hands and let them drop. "It's like they've changed the locks on me."

"Oh." Ryan pursed his lips. "I see. Then I guess we'd better find some place that none of you guys are going to mind avoiding for the next few years, huh?" He looked at the ground, scuffing his sandals in the moss. "Who would've figured, Howie? All dressed up again and no damn place to go." He lifted his head with a wan smile. "Just promise me you won't make it that Stinking Swamp World, okay?"

"See, this is why I shouldn't have this job." Howard was sitting on a fiber mat outside his tent, which had been temporarily relocated to the Black and Blue World, methodically snapping twigs into ever-smaller pieces.

Alaiya sat at his side, cleaning her dagger. "What are you talking about?"

"I get sidetracked too easily, I let stuff like this upset me and I obsess about it and I can't look past it. I mean, who cares what happens to humanity? I'm worried about my friends." He sighed. "I just can't see the big picture."

Alaiya laughed. "There is no movie film here," she said. "What is important, if it is not friendship and true caring?" She reached to scoop up a handful of tiny sticks. "Ahwerd, I watch you agonize over every scrape and bruise suffered by your teammates. It may not be a thoroughly enjoyable occupation for you, but it is because of that unrelenting compassion that you are best suited to lead the Breakneck Boys."

"Ahwerdbel, may I speak with you?"

Howard looked up to see Omber Oss standing outside his tent. "Sure, come on in. What's on your mind?"

The dark-skinned warrior ducked into the tent and seated himself across from Howard on the flooring of soft needles. He ran his hand self-consciously through his loose black curls. "Concerning current dilemma . . ." he began in his accented English.

Half an hour later, Howard summoned Ryan to the tent.

"Yo, Howie. I was just doing some packing. Y'know, I brought a few things back from Earth that I've been planning to give you. I was waiting for your birthday, but that doesn't look like a good plan right now." He seated himself on the ground, blinking in the dimness. "Hi, Oss. How's it goin'?"

"Omber Oss has a proposition you may find interesting," Howard said. He nodded to the Averoy warrior.

Oss cleared his throat. "Recently I start to plan expedition. First I think to go alone, but now I think again. Maybe need another pair of legs, hands—another clever brain to help me.'' He leaned back against a tent pole. ''You remember riverfall on Black and Blue World? Some warrior say can go down, far down.'' He walked his fingers in a descending spiral. ''Find great seas, hidden caverns, far from touch of Keyholder. I decide to go, try find this place.''

''You just happened to get the urge to visit the center of the Black and Blue World now? Come on.'' Ryan scowled from Oss to Howard. ''What's going on?''

Oss straightened. ''Going on truth,'' he said. ''Last raid, I hear rumor—maybe right, maybe wrong. Say my friend name Shing escape down riverfall, one, two Round past. I start think to follow, try find. Now I ask you to come along.'' He got slowly to his feet. ''You talk to Ahwerdbel, listen to wisdom of Nonesuch. I go to plan. You not frightened, you think idea fine, we both go to find this hidden sea.'' The warrior lifted the tent flap and stepped outside.

Ryan looked at Howard, who shrugged with his eyebrows. ''Hey, up to you.''

''It could be fun, I guess. I signed up for one of those shoot-the-rapids trips once, but they started rerunning 'Green Acres' that week, so I ended up not going.'' He squinted toward the tent flap. ''I sure wish I hadn't smashed my Walkman, though. This guy's not exactly personality plus. If it's just me and him, I think I'm gonna need some tunes.''

''Oh, I don't know. Alaïya says he's got a great singing voice,'' Howard said. ''Maybe you can talk him into belting out a few Averoy battle chants.''

Ryan snorted. ''Gimme a break.''

Omber Oss planned to depart the following morning. That night they held an impromptu farewell party. After the others had dispersed, Ryan sat in front of the hospital tent and presented Howard with an astonishing collection of items he had purchased before their return from Boston.

''It's like Christmas morning,'' Howard said to Alaïya as Ryan pulled the gifts from his backpack. ''Look, Cheez Whiz!''

''Yeah, you better save that till you're hungry enough to kill the jar. See, it says 'Refrigerate after opening,' and that might be a bit of a problem around here.'' He dug in the pack for a small pile of garments. ''Don't unfold these till you're alone, 'cause I only bought three of them—two for you guys and one for little Yam. I hope she takes Large Child.''

Howard lifted the edge of the first T-shirt. "Yah!" he said. "Mr. Bubble!"

"Oh, here—this is the last thing." Ryan pulled out a small, gift-wrapped package. "Think of me when you use it."

Howard began to carefully remove the bows and colored paper. Finally Ryan took the box out of his hands and ripped off the remaining wrapping in one quick motion. "Don't you hate people who unwrap stuff like that?" he said to Alaiya.

"Aw." Howard looked up from the little box. "A new Timex!" He strapped the watch onto his wrist, then reached behind him. "And now I've got something for you." He brought forth a small rectangle wrapped in black cloth and removed the covering with a flourish.

Ryan gaped at the assemblage of metal and plastic. "My Walkman! You fixed it!"

"I'd be careful with it, it's just sort of cobbled together—but it does play." Howard held one of the earphones to his head and hummed the theme from the 1959 production of *Journey to the Center of the Earth*. "Good luck finding batteries, of course . . ."

Howard sat by himself on the ledge overlooking the flower sea. High in the sky a crescent of silver hung surrounded by stars. On the rock at his side were two small, flat rectangles. A smiling woman and man looked out at the world from the black-and-white images. He heard a noise at his back.

"May I disturb you?" Alaiya asked softly.

"You couldn't possibly," he said, scooping up the photographs and moving slightly to allow her room to sit.

"I meant, do you mind if I join you?"

Howard lifted the stick he was holding and pointed it into the blue-black heavens. "For you, kid, the moon."

Alaiya pursed her lips and nodded to the far horizon, where a silver glimmer was just becoming visible. "Do you forget that there are two of them on this world?"

Howard cocked an eyebrow and turned to her. "I'll work on it."

"In truth, you feel there is much to work on." Her tone had become more serious. "Many mysteries bedevil your problem-solving mind."

"You got it. I went back to Earth to get a few things settled, and stirred everything up instead. Where'd these pictures come from? I've never seen them before. And how did the Keyholders get ahold of them? My sister's misplaced, the Matrix Building's infested with wormheads, and somebody told the bad guys about my Key." He hefted the stick like a weapon. "So I guess it's time we knocked on a few pertinent doors."

"I have informed the others of your plan to raid Stillpoint," she said. "There is much enthusiasm."

"Yeah, but first you and I have another trip to take." He tapped the stick lightly on the purple rock. "This time we go to Noss Averatu and check out *your* hometown."

Alaiya looked at the stars for a while. Then she slipped her hand into his. "Ahwerd, I am sorry that you can no longer return to your Earth. Now with Ryan's departure it will be lonely for you."

Howard turned to her. "Lonely?" he said.

"For a short time, you had something to remind you of your former life. I know how important this concept of home is for you. I watched the joy in your face when you showed me your old residence, the delight when we walked through the streets of the city. Now the way is closed and you have lost your home."

"Hmm. I think you may have been misinterpreting the source of that joy," Howard said thoughtfully. "I haven't lost my home at all." He looked around him in the darkness. "Why, it's right over there."

Alaiya frowned. "Over where?"

"Here, I'll show you." Howard took her hand and rose to his feet, stepping a few paces back from the ledge.

Alaiya peered out over the restless blossoms and shook her head. "I don't understand."

"Look—" He drew the Key from beneath his vest and transferred Alaiya's hand to the crook of his arm. He closed his eyes. When he opened them again, they were standing in a vast desert of orange-red sand. The sun was rising behind them and the sky was clear, pale green.

"Kansas?" Alaiya dropped her hand from his arm and looked around in perplexity. "The Red Desert World is your home?"

"Nah, I just needed the sand." Reaching out with the stick, he drew a small circle directly in front of them, then stepped into it. "Where am I now?"

Alaiya was watching him warily. "Standing inside a circle on the Red Desert World?"

"Right!" He nodded emphatically. Then he held out his hand and drew her into the circle next to him. He looked into her eyes with a lopsided grin and put his arms around her. "But now I'm home."

About the Author

As a globe-trotting vagabond, earning his living in a variety of exotic undertakings while probing the hidden recesses of a myriad of fascinating cultures, Geary Gravel would be much too distracted to get any writing done.

Instead, he has wisely chosen to spend his time sitting in a small room with good lighting in western Massachusetts, typing quietly as the world goes about its business.

The mystery of the Fading Worlds
continues in Book Three,

WORLD OF THE NIGHT WIND

In which a cook's girl—who may or may not be a goddess—befriends a creature that travels between dimensions, snatches half a million people from the jaws of certain death, and learns the ancient art of world-making . . .